THE STARS GROW PALE

Karl Bjarnhof tells the story of a clever sensitive boy marked out from his fellows: he is gradually going blind. Brilliantly, he creates the whole picture of a childhood in a small provincial town in Denmark, with a gallery of unforgettable characters, some pathetic, some comic, but all drawn from life.

Karl Bjarnhof

THE STARS GROW PALE

TRANSLATED BY NAOMI WALFORD

METHUEN & CO LTD
36 ESSEX STREET · STRAND WC2

First published by
Gyldendal Ltd. Copenhagen
in 1956
Copyright in all countries signatory to the
Berne Convention
English translation © 1958 by
Methuen & Co. Ltd
Printed in Great Britain by
Butler & Tanner Ltd · Frome & London

72270

CATALOGUE NUMBER 6037/U

I

AT the corner, the first of the chestnut trees was already waving a green leaf-hand. The chestnuts went with us all the way to school. One took over from the other. In the spring they shone; later they soughed with summer wind until it was autumn and they let their foliage fall. Their leaves came sailing through the air in tilted flight like yellow birds or brown-speckled birds, and settled on the road and on the paving-stones.

First you went through the gate and across the railway-line. Then came the churchyard and after that 'L. Pode's Home for Blind Women'. There was something arresting about all this; not always equally so, but you could never pass by unnoticing. For instance, the Home for the Blind had a stringed instrument over the front door. It sounded whenever the door was opened or shut, and the sound lingered, vibrating in the air. Strange. You could almost believe that that door led into a world quite different from the one you knew.

Behind the wide, tall window-panes facing towards Lange-linje there were usually two or three pale ovals. These were the faces of the blind girls who sat knitting in the window. They were always knitting. I can't remember a time when they were not knitting, and their knitting was always grey. It was grey and long. They were knitting infinity.

There were no flowers on the window-sills. Only a knitting-basket or two with balls of wool in them. And behind the faces a big, dark space, a room that looked quite empty. Yawningly empty and dark.

You could stand outside and look at the girls knitting in there. You could look at them just as if they were photographs. People often did; I wasn't the only one. It was like staring into the face of a portrait. Nothing happened.

Now and again you met the blind girls in the street. They were never alone. They walked in twos. Sometimes there were three of them: one in the middle who could lead the two others. They were going to the woods or coming back from the woods. Just making the time pass. The older ones walked in the churchyard. Nørre Woods weren't far from L. Pode's Home for the Blind, but the churchyard was nearer. In a way it was the blind girls' garden. They often went there, and there was always a sort of faded smile round their mouths; a smile that someone had forgotten to brush off and bury.

I was preoccupied by L. Pode's Home for Blind Women. I was obsessed by it – by the faces behind the big, dark panes. By the door with the stringed instrument. I used to stand at the corner, hearing it ring and vibrate in the air.

The little street ended in nothing. It ran to grass, as they said, and continued in a winding path over the meadows to the lime-kiln. In summer it was a dust-grey path through green grass flowered with daisies and cowslips. In winter the grass was withered and the path brown, with water shining on it here and there.

A fiery tongue licked out of the tall, thin chimney of the lime-kiln, flame-yellow at the bottom, then sulphur-yellow, then red. It turned into a pennon of black smoke which drifted away towards the harbour and disappeared between the masts of ships and the roof of a warehouse. There might be a smell of fresh wood from the ships that were being unloaded, or from the timber-yard. But almost always there was a smell of mud, from the ditches in the meadow and from the fjord.

I stood at the corner looking out over the meadow and the fjord and hearing the strings sound in the air. But I never dreamt that I might pass through that door myself. I never imagined for a moment that one day something might take

6

me into those big, dark rooms. And if anyone had told me that I myself would one day become a photograph behind other window-panes, it wouldn't have frightened me in the least. I should have been interested. But nobody did tell me. Nobody even thought of it. And I didn't, either.

2

In the beginning my mother was a night-nurse. Every evening at seven o'clock she tied a kerchief round her head, took her chip basket on her arm and set off to the hospital. She always went 'in Jesus' name'. She tied on the kerchief, put darning-wool, old socks and knitting in her basket and said,

'Well, in Jesus' name . . . I'm off.'

She really meant it. It wasn't just something she said. If she was going into the town – to the shop, for instance, or for cream – she simply went. But if she was going far enough or for long enough to lock the door first and slip the key under the mat, she always went in Jesus' name. Also at nightfall when she lit the lamp; or when we went to bed and she put it out. There were rules about it; not always simple or easy to understand, yet as the years went by one picked them up. In the evenings, at any rate, when she was starting for the hospital, she always went in Jesus' name.

In the mornings when she came home her chip basket had bread in it which the sick people had been unable to eat. It lay well hidden under the socks and knitting and sometimes an old newspaper. Nobody must know that the night-nurses took bread home from the hospital; it was supposed to go into the pig-bucket. But we often lived on it. There were days when we had little else. And if we didn't need it, there were others who did. At any rate the pigs never had it. Bread was holy and one didn't throw it to pigs. It was eaten in Jesus' name. Those who wasted bread were sure to repent; one might need

8

it one day, and badly. It had to be so, and was no more than justice. That was the curse of bread, and it could and should be averted.

Not many words were used at home. As with everything else, we saved them, and avoided wearing them out. One of us asked a question, and the answer was yes or no; seldom more. Silence could be oppressive, but not always. It might be quite natural. One didn't notice it the whole time, or one noticed it only when it was broken by somebody coming: by a woman, perhaps, who wanted to borrow something – a box of matches, a drop of paraffin or some coffee. Or by somebody who just wanted to talk; but no one went at it steadily. Not at first. And when she left nobody spoke. Stillness returned. It crept forth from every corner. It seeped out of the walls.

'Is the Hamburg boat unloaded?' my mother might ask.

'Yes,' said my father.

'So you got nothing more this week?'

'No,' he said.

'Other men can find work all right,' said my mother.

Silence.

Wind against the attic window. Cold wind perhaps, and rain slashing down the pane. The wind came from the hills round the town, from the woods and from the fjord. It soughed in through the gateway and up the stairs, whistled in the key-hole or between the door and the worn threshold, and swept across the floor. Stillness.

Mother was idle only when she slept. She never knew what it was to sit with her hands in her lap. She had always to be doing something, busy with something, active. When she had rested for a few hours in the morning she got up and began her pasting. We made paper bags for the paper-mill. A man brought great stacks of paper cut by machine – a little pink-faced man without a hair on his head. He had eyebrows but no lashes. And everything he said was frayed in a funny way, because he hadn't any teeth; just bare baby gums.

The trains were our clock. We knew when they were due,

9

either from the north or from the station. We heard the signal-bell at the level-crossing, and we heard them come. Sometimes they stopped some way up the line and hooted. The signals were against them. One could sit and watch them from the attic window as they went by: goods trains a mile long with rows of horses' heads in them, some with a blaze on their foreheads and some without. But they all looked just as sad. There might be cows, too. The trains ran by and disappeared round the bend into the station.

Sometimes a trolley appeared, with men on it pumping themselves along. Or a single man on a hand-car. He sat rocking back and forth, back and forth, and was very busy.

'Was that the express coming in?' my mother might ask. 'As late as that, is it?'

When we worked my mother talked to me. She talked to me as if I were a grown-up person. People said it would make me precocious, but she had nobody else, and it only happened when she and I were alone making paper bags. Mostly in the daytime.

In the evenings when my father was at home he sat at the table too. He would sit staring in front of him, twiddling a matchbox between his fingers and smoking his pipe. He stared and saw nothing, and heard nothing but the stillness, which rang in one's ears. He was both absent and present. He sat remembering everything and forgetting everything. Then all at once he would get up, fetch the Bible and sit down again to read it. He read the Book of Job and the Book of Judges and Ecclesiastes and Revelations. And having read for a time he folded his hands on the book and stared in front of him, hearing nothing. We could talk to him and he wouldn't answer, or only after a long time when we had almost forgotten what we had said. But for the most part he remained quite silent, with a deep, invincible distaste for the least little word, the faintest utterance.

Stillness except for the noise of the paper bags: the paste-brush and the paste-spreader and the paper under smoothing fingers. Perhaps a cart passed along the street, or footsteps sounded on the paving-stones.

Some evenings my mother didn't have to go to the hospital. She wasn't needed there. She could stay at home. On those days we were ordinary. We were like other people, and as a rule we weren't. My father spoke Swedish. People couldn't always understand him, and there were some who even made fun of him. It was embarrassing to have a father who spoke Swedish . . . And then he was often out of work. And then my mother . . . She was on duty all night and had to sleep in the daytime. Nobody else lived like this.

Every now and then she was able to stay at home, but most evenings she had to have her basket on her arm and her ker-chief on her head by seven o'clock, and set off in Jesus' name. And if my father hadn't been at the docks and the weather was fine we would go with her. In Wood Street people were sitting out on their steps. Some had brought out chairs. The women knitted and chatted and the men smoked and chatted. There were children too, but none that I knew. We walked with mother as far as the hospital gate. There we halted and watched her go until she disappeared up some wooden steps, across an open veranda and in through a door that shut behind her. Then we turned and walked home again. We almost always went by Lovers' Lane along the foot of Pilke Hill and the rest of the wood. The trees leaned over the path, and sometimes they would stick out a gnarled and twisted root-finger. One had to take care not to trip and fall.

When we got home my father sat down to read his book. It was a book in a red cloth cover. 'A Novel' it was called, and my mother said it in such a way that one knew it was some-thing bad. That must have been why my father only took it out when he and I were alone. But he read it many times. He read it over and over again and never really finished with it. Perhaps he thought that the people in it would do something different between one time of reading and the next. He couldn't quite get it into his head that the action stopped when he shut the book and hid it at the bottom of a yellow wooden chest where it belonged.

'Yes, but is it true what it says in it?' I asked.

'M'well, true –' said my father; he too was less taciturn when we were alone together. 'True – the man who sold me the book said it was.'

We reached home and my father went back to his red book, hoping perhaps that things would work out better for the people now – better than the last time he'd had it out. For it was a sad book. Before him stood the lamp, the little kitchen lamp with the green glass container and the brass shade, as shiny as a golden plate. It shed its light down upon the book. He read, and read so intently that one got no answer whatever if one spoke to him. He really didn't exist at all in the place where he was sitting. He was in another world.

Awake all night, asleep for a few hours in the morning, sticking paper bags in the afternoon, and then away again. But it was to end one day. It was to end sooner than anyone expected.

One morning when the night-nurses were leaving for home, the new inspector was standing by the hospital gate. He wanted to look into their baskets, just to check that all was as it should be. My mother was nearest, so she was first. Beneath her knitting and an old newspaper he found some bread.

'What's this?' he asked.

'Bread,' my mother answered.

'Did you bring it in with you last night?'

'No,' she said.

('I didn't try to lie myself out of it,' she explained when she got home. 'I don't steal or lie,' she said.)

'Then I must take it away from you,' said the new inspector. 'And I must tell you we shan't be needing you any more.'

He took the bread and tossed it under a hedge. The birds could have it.

'The birds have got to live too,' he said. 'Well, that was just a sample, and we'll let it go at that. But I'm warning the rest of you; you never know when I might do it again.'

My mother had to go with him into the office and get the money that was owing to her. When she came out the other women were waiting for her.

'You haven't dragged us into this, have you?' they said. 'We'll have nothing to do with it.'

'No,' she answered. 'I let him think I was the only one.'

'Oh,' said they, 'you let him think that, did you? Well, maybe you're not always the only one, but today you were. He could have looked in my basket and welcome,' said one. 'And in mine,' said another. 'That's why we don't want to be mixed up in anything. You'll have to manage this on your own.'

My mother left them. She turned her back on them and went on her way without another word. But at home she cried. She knelt at the green ottoman in the bedroom and prayed to God and cried. She said it was a stain which He must help her to wash away.

'At this rate folk will think we're collecting stains,' she said.

I thought it made us more like other people.

3

THEY wouldn't let me play with them. They said I was too stupid.

'If you're so stupid you can't see a ball when it's under your nose,' they said, 'we don't want you.'

I tried to explain that I could see a red ball very well. Of course I could see it, once I'd got my eye on it.

'Buzz off,' said Rudolf the beer-merchant's son. 'We don't want somebody who's too stupid to spot a red ball.'

It was a Saturday evening in the middle of May. I know it was a Saturday because there were so many people in the yard. Almost all the people who lived in the house were there; they stood about in groups, talking and laughing. There was a smell of ammonia from the dungheap in the corner and from the stables. Inside the stables in the twilight you could see the golden-brown flank of a horse and its thigh, a black tail and two fetlocks. It kicked at the stone floor, and sometimes sparks flew out in the darkness, smelling of sulphur and iron. And there were thick cobwebs over all the window-panes and in the roof.

In the coach-house stood Klyver's wagonette and landau. The landau had the hood down; it was lined with blue cloth. Above was an empty dovecot, and through an open shutter you could look into the loft and see the long bar of the chaff-cutter. The cartshed had been swept and so had the lean-to, where the wagon and the cart were standing because it was Saturday.

The girls were playing hopscotch. They had drawn lines in

14

the earth where there was no paving. Lydia and Gertrud and Else.

Lydia called to me to come over to them. She said they needed one more. She had blue eyes and bare arms. She caught hold of my blouse and pulled me.

'Come on,' she said, 'we're one short.'

There was no girl I liked more. Not in the whole world.

I hit her over the fingers so that she let go. I said,

'Leave me alone, can't you! I don't play with girls.'

Lydia's eyes went dark. Her mouth quivered. She had such a pretty little mouth.

'Leave him alone,' shouted Gertrud. 'He's no good. He's so stupid he steps on the lines and treads on your toes and bumps into you. Let him go and play with Silly Anders.'

Anders had come into the yard too. He was standing with his red knitted reins in his hands, staring at the girls and silly in the head.

'Will you play horses with me?' he asked. Anders was four-teen – or fifteen. He didn't know which. We used to amuse ourselves by asking him how old he was, but he didn't know.

'I haven't learnt it yet,' he said.

'Go away, Anders,' said Marie, who was Else's sister. 'Go away and be silly somewhere else.'

They always said the same thing.

'Go on, buzz off,' they said. 'It makes us sick to look at you.'

'Does it?' said Anders.

'Yes,' they said.

The red reins trailed on the ground. He held them in a full-grown hand, a hand which was big and soft and gristly. And everything hung upon him. His blouse hung and his trousers. All his clothes were too big.

'I'll go, then,' said Anders, but he lingered as if expecting someone to ask him to stay. But nobody did.

'I'll go, then,' he said again, and went. He went slowly out through the gateway, and his backside was like the backside of an elephant.

On the other side of the shopkeeper's garden wall there was a cherry-tree: a dome of white blossom. In between the branches and above them you saw the sky, the lilac-coloured evening sky in the west. In a house further away, at an open kitchen-window on the first floor, Lydia's mother was shouting and waving her arms. But nobody listened to her, for we all knew that when Lydia's mother shouted like that and waved her arms it was because she was drunk. Lydia pretended not to hear her, and for Lydia's sake we didn't hear her either, nor did we look up at the window; we just peered sideways. Christensen the moulder laughed in his black beard and went out through the gateway with Klyver the carrier and Ravn.

'Go on, now,' said Else to me.

'Yes, buzz off,' said Marie. 'Go and play horses with Anders.'

There was a Saturday light in the general store. In the baker's too, and in the dairy. Yellow light in all the big shop-windows, though it was not yet dark. From the yard gate one could smell meat from the butcher's – the dead bodies of animals. There was a smell of smoked food, of forcemeat and sausage. And from the baker's a smell of hot Viennese bread; hot bread with a crisp crust and cream filling. And there was a smell of coffee and spices and paraffin and dried cod from the shop. A smell of dust too, because people were sweeping the street. They swept the pavements and they swept the gutters, which were full of dry horse-dung and cigar-butts and bits of paper.

Some people were standing at their doors. Some were leaning from open windows, chatting. A landau drove by with a lady in it. A commercial traveller. A mill-girl.

'What are you loitering about here for?' Christensen the moulder asked me. 'Cut along into the yard with the others. And if you can't be friends with 'em then you better go in to your mum and ask her to put you to bed.'

I stayed where I was in the gateway. I wasn't loitering, and I didn't want to go in yet.

'What are you hanging about here for?' he asked again.

'I'm just looking,' I said. 'That's all.'

'Just looking, eh,' he repeated, with a little laugh.

When I went in my mother asked me why I hadn't been playing with the others. She had seen me from the window.

'I didn't want to,' I said.

'You mustn't be awkward,' she told me.

'I'm not awkward.'

'Try to be like other people,' she said. 'Why can't you play with Rudolf and Aage? Or with Lydia?' she asked.

I didn't answer. It had something to do with a red ball that I couldn't get my eye on, but it was too difficult to explain.

'Well, sit on the platform with your toys,' she said.

I had a cigar-box and in it a button and a bit of rare wood with a knot in it, and part of a horseshoe and a piece of string. These were my toys. My father had found them for me – he had found them all. I must like them because my father had found them.

'And you can help me count some bags,' said my mother.

From the window one could see the backs of the houses in Freden Street. And the yards with their dustbins and privies and rusty iron and old junk. There was the railway too. And the signals up by the station. And furthest away on a hill-top the windmill. The sails were turning this evening.

'I said you could help me count some bags,' said my mother again. 'Until your father comes back and you go to bed.'

The sails of the windmill went round, and the sky behind them was red or mauve. And the signal lights by the station changed from red to white, whatever that might mean . . .

'What a tiresome thing it is,' said my mother, 'that what you can do you won't do, and what you want to do you can't.'

Little by little the yard became quiet. They weren't playing ball any longer. The girls weren't playing hopscotch. They were being called indoors.

'Why, it's time to light the lamp,' said my mother. 'What's become of your father?'

17

'Well, in Jesus' name, then,' she said, and went to light the lamp. 'Glad I haven't got to go to the hospital and sit up all night. Must be thankful for that. My mother always found something to be thankful for.'

Soon afterwards we heard the tramp of clogs coming from far away. Only one pair of clogs. One man. All the other footsteps were shoes, leather shoes. But a man was coming from a long way off wearing clogs: my father. He walked slowly and heavily. He always sounded tired. Even in the mornings when he started out. I recognized the clumping of my father's clogs; it was different from everybody else's. Even when he was one among many – one in a whole army of men in wooden shoes. We could hear him coming nearer. Now he was passing the shop. Now he was turning in at the gate. Now up the steps and into the passage. He was taking off his clogs. All the people in the house left their clogs under the stairs. They jostled there together, little ones and big ones side by side and in between each other. New and old, shiny and dusty. And sometimes you couldn't find your own because they'd been kicked apart. But you always found them in the end because they were all so different. It wasn't just that they were big and small, new and old; they became like the person who wore them.

My father put away his clogs and began to come upstairs. The stairs creaked, first the five leading to the first floor, and then the next ones. But he didn't come up quickly like other people. He paused on the landings, for a long time. But he reached the top at last, and came right up to our door. We could hear him out there, but he didn't come in. He stood listening. He had a way of standing and listening outside the door. It was something that came over him, or up inside him, at times.

My mother had raised her head.

'You'd better get to bed,' she said, and she stopped brushing on the paste. 'Hurry now; you can hear what your father's like tonight, can't you?'

18

My father entered the kitchen. He didn't say anything – just stood still out there in the darkness.

'Is that you? You're late tonight.'

'Who else should it be?' he said, not moving. 'Expecting somebody else, were you?'

I went into the bedroom and began undressing. But the door was ajar and I could hear all they said.

'Why were you standing and listening out there?' my mother asked.

'I wasn't listening,' my father said. 'I was wondering . . . I was wondering whose hat that was on the peg.'

'Hat? I don't know about any hat.'

A long silence.

'Oh, no – of course not,' said my father. 'Have you had any visitors?' he asked.

'Crowds of 'em. What d'you think?'

My mother stood up and pushed her chair aside.

'What's this hat you're talking about? Let's see it.'

She went and opened the door. On the wall outside were three or four pegs where we used to hang our outer clothes in the winter.

'Why, that's Ravn's hat,' she said from the stairs.

'So *he's* been here, has he?'

The Ravns were our neighbours; they lived on the attic floor too, but opposite.

'If Jens Ravn wanted to call on me,' said my mother from the passage, 'do you think he'd put his hat on to do it? You put it there yourself to have something to be cross about. That's what you were doing before you came in.'

The kitchen door was slammed from inside. Plaster fell from the wall.

For a time everything was quiet. My mother stayed out in the passage. My father stood in the kitchen. He didn't stir. It was only a step or two from the bedroom door to the kitchen, and I could hear him breathing. I could hear him puffing as if he were out of breath, and I dared not move. I dared not speak. I was afraid that he might notice I was in the bedroom and that the door wasn't shut. I was afraid of my father when he was like this. I was afraid because when he was like this he didn't want to see me. He couldn't bear me.

Then somebody spoke to my mother out in the passage. It was Mrs Ravn.

She was smiling. One could hear by her voice and by what she was saying that she was smiling.

Soon afterwards my mother came in again and tidied away her things: the bowl of paste, the finished bags, the lamp. She began wiping down the oil-cloth with a wet rag.

'Now I'll see about supper,' she said. 'I didn't know when you'd be in.'

I lay in bed. I heard my mother cutting bread in the kitchen and boiling water. I heard my father sit down with the newspaper. Mother brought in the cups. Then he began to eat. Neither of them spoke. I heard him munching, and now and then I heard his teeth grind together. He rustled the paper. He shifted the lamp. He munched. But they didn't say anything. They remained silent. Sometimes they didn't talk for a whole evening.

The door was still ajar. A bar of yellow light fell across the wash-stand and along the floor. It bent and ran up the wall. Through the skylight I could see the sky. And when I woke in the middle of the night and it was pitch dark I could see where the window was. Sometimes there would be a star in one of the four panes, and sometimes, mostly in the mornings, one could see clouds sailing by.

My mother brought her things out again and began working. I could hear her spreading paste on the bags. I could hear her making the folds and her fingers smoothing the paper from the middle outwards. There was a definite rhythm to it.

Once she said,

'Don't you think we should have another word with the doctor?'

My father made no answer. Long afterwards he put down the

paper and picked up the Bible. I could hear it was the Bible when he laid it on the table. He opened it and began to read as usual; I knew he was sitting with the kitchen lamp with its brass shade in front of him, and with his heavy, clay-grey hands resting on the table, one on each side of the big book.

'If you want to go running to the doctor again,' he said, when a long time had passed, 'if you must gossip to somebody about all your affairs, all right. But if you bring back any medicine I'll pour it down the sink, mind. Just like I did before.'

People were passing in the street below. One could hear their footsteps before they turned the corner. Then came a cart. Out in the fjord a steamer hooted for the pilot. And far away the church clock struck.

My mother pasted her paper bags in her steady rhythm. My father must have been reading the Bible or staring into the lamp-light. Neither of them spoke. Neither of them would say any more tonight, and perhaps not tomorrow night either. Perhaps there would be silence, absolute silence, for days.

Was it like this with other people, I wondered? Anyhow, I didn't want anybody to know what it was like with us.

But perhaps they did know, all the same. Just as we knew that Lydia's mother sometimes got drunk.

My father came in. He thought I was asleep and he undressed in the dark. His clothes had a sour smell of sweat. He stood under the window in the roof and looked up at the sky; it was to see what the weather would be like tomorrow morning early, when he went to work. In the living-room my mother went on with her pasting at exactly the same tempo. Father was over by his clothes now; he found his pipe in a pocket and a cigar-butt which he crumbled; I heard the dry tobacco crunching between his fingers. In the flame of the match I could see his face; there was nothing special about it. He looked as my father did look when he lit his pipe. Then the flame went out and he sat down on the edge of the bed. There he stayed with his head propped on his hands. From time to time he sighed.

There was a pause before he drew his breath again and began smoking. His pipe squeaked when he sucked it, and snored a little too.

'Ye – es,' he said tonelessly, and after a long pause. 'Ye – es,' and sighed.

I dozed a little. And woke. And saw him still sitting on the bed. His bowed shoulders. The back of his neck. His elbows on his knees and his hands supporting his head. I woke during the night too, and saw him lying beside me, staring with wide-open eyes at the skylight.

It was not quite day when he had to get up. That summer he had a job at a brickworks, and had two miles and more to walk. He had to start early and he came home late. He got the jobs nobody else would take, my mother said. He wasn't fit for steady work.

Out in the kitchen my mother was cutting bread and pouring milk. There again was the strip of yellow light round the door, which stood ajar. Just as it had been when I fell asleep. Then my father put on his clothes and crept out, moving quietly so as not to wake me. They didn't say anything to each other; not even good morning. My father sat in the kitchen and ate cold bread and milk. He ate noisily. My mother set out her pasting things again. She used to put them away when she went to bed, and take them out again in the morning.

Then my father went, still without saying anything. The stairs creaked under him. It was quiet in the house. It was quiet in the street too. Downstairs in the passage he found his clogs; then he went out through the gateway. I could hear him along the pavement. Heavy steps, slow steps. Tired, although it was morning. I could hear him for a long time, for he didn't have to turn the corner. I could hear him until he was a mile away, it seemed to me.

In the living-room my mother had begun her work. She kept up her rhythm the same as yesterday, the day before that and every day.

Soon afterwards Klyver the carrier started work in the yard

below. The horses had to be fed. They had to be watered. The two carts had to be brought out from the open shed. Then the beer-merchant coughed his morning cough in the gateway. Each time he sounded as if he were going to suffocate. Factory-hooters sounded; there was the tramp of horses in the yard; hooves through the gateway. Klyver was driving out. There were more and more people in the street, most of them in clogs.

I dozed off again and slept until mother woke me. She showed no shadow of the night, no trace of what had happened the evening before. A strip of eastern sunlight slanted in through the window, across the platform and over to the opposite corner of the room.

'Was father sad last night?' I asked.

'We won't talk about that,' said my mother. 'Not now or any other time.'

She began straightening my blouse.

'Try to look like other boys. What a sight you are . . .'

'There's the train,' she said. 'You'll have to hurry.'

4

M Y sister came that summer. She came by train and we met her at the station. She was a big girl; five years older than me and prettier than any girl I had ever seen. Even prettier than Lydia. But we didn't know what to say to each other.

'I don't know what to say to you,' she said, 'although I've been longing to meet you ever since I first knew I had you.'

'No,' I said, feeling a great tenderness. But I couldn't get anything out except No.

'Haven't you been looking forward a bit to seeing me too?'

'I didn't know I had you,' I said.

We sat on the green ottoman in the bedroom, whispering to each other. Sometimes my mother came in and stroked our hair, and sometimes my father came in and said,

'Why Kirstine . . . but Kirstine,' he said, and 'How you've grown.'

'Yes,' she said, and looked grave. She had a brown-eyed look, slow and serious.

'Are you going to live with me for good now?' I asked.

'N-no,' she said, hesitating. 'No, I can't do that. I promised to go home to father and mother . . . To father and mother . . .'

'But if you're my sister –'

'She is your sister,' said my mother. 'She'll be going back to her foster-parents, but we won't think about that yet.'

'I'm so glad I've got you,' she said, moving closer to me on the ottoman. 'Aren't you?' she said. Her brown eyes looked into mine and she took my wrist.

'I wouldn't go down into the yard with the others if I were you,' said my mother. 'Better not.'

I couldn't see why it was better not. Neither of us could.

'Kids get such notions,' said my father. 'You never know what they might say to you. Tomorrow, perhaps, or some other day, but not just now.'

I would have liked to show all of them that I had a sister, and at once. But I sat there with her hand round my wrist and her brown eyes looking into mine, and would cheerfully have given up the world.

My mother had her pasting to do, but she couldn't attend to her work as usual. Each time she finished a stack of twenty-five she had to pause. Or rather, she didn't exactly pause; she just had to keep coming into the bedroom for some reason or another. She had suddenly to look for something in the chest of drawers – something she'd been searching for for a long time. She couldn't think where she'd put it.

'It just struck me it might be in the top drawer,' she said.

'But what is it?' asked my father, who had followed her.

'Oh, nothing special. I just thought it must be somewhere or other.'

Next time it was a duster she wanted, and that was tucked behind the wash-stand. And then a handkerchief. She wiped her nose and her eyes were moist and her mouth gentle.

'You all right in here?' she said. And 'Wouldn't you rather come into the living-room with your father and me?'

'Maybe they like it better in there,' said my father.

He hadn't gone to work, although from that point of view it was an ordinary day. And nobody said anything about his not being at work. He didn't sit down idly with his matchbox and his pipe, and he didn't brood over his Bible. He walked about being father. Rather restless, perhaps, and rather empty-handed. He couldn't settle anywhere. And he couldn't make up his mind where to go.

'Why don't you two take a walk in the woods?' said my

mother. 'If you went as far as the fountain you'd be back by dinner-time.'

'I might come too, and keep an eye on you,' said my father.

'Keep an eye on us –' I said.

'On the time, I mean. To see it didn't get too late.'

My mother came in from the kitchen.

'Go on, now's your time,' she said. 'There's nobody on the stairs.'

What does it matter, I thought, whether there's anybody on the stairs or not? I would rather there had been; I wanted to meet them all and show them my sister. But there was nobody. Only Rudolf and Else at the gate. I don't know what they were playing.

'This is my sister,' I said.

Kirstine looked rather embarrassed.

'Oh,' said Rudolf.

'So you got a sister now, have you?' said Else, peeping at us over her shoulder.

'Why couldn't you hold your tongue?' said my father. 'You oughtn't to have said anything.'

My mother was standing up at an open window, looking after us and waving. But she didn't see that there were women watching us from some of the other windows. And in the shop. And at the baker's. Lots and lots of people saw my sister. But we walked along with our father just like everybody else, and were quite ordinary people.

We passed the sports-ground, which was bright yellow with dandelions.

'Look, down there's where the summer theatre burned down,' I said. 'And that green house by the ice-ponds is where Stougård lives. Not at night,' I said, 'but he might be there now.'

'Yes, you take a good look, Kirstine,' said my father. 'Take a good look round so you'll know your way about if they let you come again.'

There was a big pond where the woods began. It was full of

26

white flowers and when we passed it, it breathed on us. It breathed a smell of honey. I often passed it, but I'd never noticed before that it smelt of honey. Perhaps it didn't as a rule; only today, because of my sister.

'If you go up that path there,' I told her, 'you get to a place where perhaps one day we shall have a garden.'

'Oh?' said my sister.

'That's just his talk,' my father said. 'But we did think about it.'

'Oh, yes?' said Kirstine. But she said it as if she weren't interested, or as if it didn't concern her.

The fjord lay on our right, glittering in the sun, with belts of shadow across it; green shadows and black shadows. And on the other side of the fjord were meadows and Sønder Woods and a red house hiding at the edge of the trees, peeping out with one gable, a chimney and a window.

'They say it's pretty here,' said my father. 'I don't know much about those things. But people who know say it's pretty.'

'It's charming,' said Kirstine. 'Charming,' she said. Like a grown-up lady.

'But there are no mountains here. Or rivers,' he said.

'Miss Nissen says the road up Jelling Hill is as steep as a mountain road,' I said. 'She says it's like a mountain, and lots of mountains aren't any higher. And we've got a river too – a little one,' I said.

But that didn't interest my sister, nor my father. They walked along together in silence. Then suddenly she took me by the wrist. She took my wrist in one hand and with the other she held on to my father's jacket. My sister did that sort of thing. She would do it quite of her own accord. She held me firmly and we walked in step, and I was made a partaker of the silence. It was good. Everything was good.

The woodland paths wound zigzag over the slopes, in and out among the trees. There were green cushions of moss on the floor of the woods, and brown, withered leaves, and flowers –

27

lots of flowers, whose names I didn't know – and quaking-grass.

It was all good.

Long nights. Peaceful nights. My mother slept and my father slept. I woke and saw them lying with a hand on the eiderdown. The skylight held a blue glimmer from the night outside. And on the couch in the sitting-room a bed was made up for my sister. I crept out of bed and peeped through the crack of the door, and saw that she was asleep. She slept with her hair spread out over the pillow and her cheek against a rounded, girl's arm.

'Sh,' said my mother. 'You mustn't wake Kirstine. What are you doing there? Why are you up?'

'Just wanted the pot,' I said. But I didn't; I only wanted to see my sister sleeping. I wanted to make sure she was still there, and that it wasn't just something I'd dreamt.

'Come back into bed,' said my mother.

So I got back into bed and lay looking up at the skylight; I heard the birds beginning to sing in the woods, and saw that the blue of the night was growing paler and that golden splashes and streaks were coming into it. And I heard the signal-bell at the level-crossing, and the trains going by and the church clock striking. Other birds and more birds began to sing.

My father's hand lay quietly on the eiderdown. And my mother's hand. And the scarlet cloak in the picture of Jesus with the crown of thorns began to turn red, and the drops of blood on his forehead began to turn red. The flowers on the wallpaper opened and were filled with colour, as if they really were flowers, and the green ottoman turned green. Far away a horse and cart were trotting along; you could hear the clip-clop, clip-clop of the hooves, and hear them for a long time before they died away.

And I had a sister who lay asleep in the next room.

'You oughtn't ever to have gone away,' I said to her one day.

28

'I didn't,' she said. 'They gave me away. But I didn't know anything about it, so it doesn't matter. They gave me away when father went to Sweden to be a soldier, and then he never came back.'

'You must remember I'm illegitimate,' she said. 'You're not. And it's no fun being illegitimate. If I hadn't got my father and mother it would be awful. But now hardly anybody knows.'

She was always grave. I can't remember that she was ever not grave. She was always quiet and always grave, but sometimes she smiled just a little – a brief smile that came and went in a moment. And she had her brown eyes, and her hands and her tenderness.

'I don't want you to go away again,' I said, 'ever.'

'It's never been so nice as since you came,' I said.

'I don't want to stay here, though,' she said, 'because I don't know anybody here – nobody except you. I'd like to take you with me. Perhaps when we're grown up,' she added.

She sat there beside me, knowing everything in the world and thinking about everything in the world, making clever plans and understanding things. She was thinking so hard that a little furrow came between her eyes and her face was grown-up.

'You've been so stuck up since your sister came,' said Lydia. 'If she really is your sister.'

'What d'you mean, if she really is – ?'

'Well, she's not your whole sister. Else and Marie both say so. Their mother says so. She just can't be your whole sister, she says.'

'And you're all halves,' I said. 'Stupid old halves, all of you.'

'Is she going to live here?' asked Lydia.

I didn't want to answer that. It was far too sad to answer.

'There you are, you see,' said Lydia. 'Look at you, all red in the face.'

'Perhaps we'll both go away,' I said. 'It isn't quite fixed up yet. But I can tell you one thing; we don't either of us want to stay here because you're all so stupid, and so we might quite likely go away.'

'Wish you joy,' said Lydia. 'Wish you joy, that's all. Nobody'll miss you, I can tell you that.'

And one day we went to the station again. This time my father couldn't come. We left home in Jesus' name and slipped the key under the mat, and mother carried Kirstine's little box. People we met said,

'Goodbye, Kirstine.' And 'Coming again soon?'

They hadn't spoken to her the whole time she'd been there, and yet they said,

'Come again soon, Kirstine.'

'Thank you,' she said, and bobbed.

My sister bobbed so prettily.

We walked to the station and arrived there too early, and we sat on a bench to wait. The rails looked shiny in the sun, and the gravel between the sleepers was raked like the gravel on a garden path. Porters slipped in and out among the coaches, whistling, and the engine answered them with little hoots. But it had nothing to do with us. It was happening in almost another world. We sat waiting for the train and my sister was going away, and the sunshine made it no better. Worse, if anything.

'But I'll write to you,' she said. 'I'll write you a nice letter for Christmas and for your birthday.'

'There's only five weeks between,' said my mother. 'But you've got good handwriting already, Kirstine, and I'm sure he'll be able to read it.'

In that other world they were whistling and hooting and shunting, and the sun was shining on the rails. The gravel was so neatly raked. Then the train was signalled.

My mother had fidgety thumbs. She twiddled them in the hollow of her hands, not knowing it; her mouth quivered and she had to bite her cheek. But she made her voice ordinary.

'You've got good handwriting already, Kirstine,' she said.

Kirstine was silent now, with grown-up features and a line

between her eyes. She just gripped my wrist. But people were coming out of the waiting-room. They put their luggage on the seat beside us. A postman came, pushing a low truck in front of him. Lydia's father was walking beside him. He looked at us but gave no greeting.

'You can't if you're in state service,' said my mother. 'People in uniform don't say good morning.'

'But he wasn't in uniform,' said Kirstine. 'Only a cap.'

Then the train came in and there was a bustle. My sister gave me a silken kiss on my cheek; she breathed on me and touched me with her lips. A summer breeze – a silken kiss. I thought of Gertrud, who once said I looked so ugly when I cried.

'If you knew how ugly you look when you cry,' she said, 'you'd never do it again.'

Kirstine stood at the open window of the carriage and sent me a look that was even browner than usual.

'Hope you have a good journey, Kirstine,' said my mother. 'Give my regards . . . and thank them for letting you come.'

'Yes,' she said, like a saint from her frame. 'And I'll be writing. Goodbye,' she called, as the train began to move. 'Goodbye, brother.'

We could see her hand for a long time; her hand and a white embroidered handkerchief. I stood and was unrestrainedly ugly.

'We must go,' said my mother. 'We can't stand here till the next time she comes. But I've always got you,' she said. 'I must be as thankful for you as if you were both. If only I had a handkerchief,' she said.

5

'I'M disappointed in you,' said Miss Nissen one day. She was holding me by the ear with her little claw-hand. 'You began well, because you knew it all before you came, but now it's really dreadful.'

'Oh,' I said, wanting to leave with the others.

'No, you're not to go; you're to stay here with me for a little.'

She had grey hair and a grey face. Her whole person seemed somehow strewn with ashes.

'You're inattentive,' she said. 'You don't follow the lesson.'

'Am I being kept in?' I asked, but Miss Nissen didn't answer. She went to dismiss the rest.

I stood there, thinking that today it was my turn to catch it – my turn, although I hadn't done anything. But someone always got into trouble in Miss Nissen's classes. She sat at her desk with thin lips, ruler in hand and with steel spectacles in front of her ashy eyes, and said,

'What's the matter with you? And what's that you've got under the table?'

One of us was half-asleep, and another kept turning round. Now it was my turn.

'You did so well at first,' she said again when she came back. 'Oh.'

'How is it one can never get anything out of you but "oh"?'

'I didn't know,' I said. 'You never told me before.'

'What – that you were doing well?'

'Yes.'

'It oughtn't to be necessary to tell you a thing like that. You could see it for yourself . . . Didn't I say that your mother had taught it all to you at home?'

'Yes,' I said.

Miss Nissen had picked up the ruler. I thought I was to have one over the fingers, as she called it. I didn't mind that, for then it was over and done with. There wouldn't be anything to explain.

'I want to know why it is you don't pay attention,' she said. 'Is it that you're lazy – or perhaps a little stupid?' She waved the ruler in the air, invisibly underlining some of the words, though which of them I wasn't quite sure. 'I want to know why you're so sulky and obstinate, and why you keep to yourself and don't play with the others.'

'I expect I'm stupid,' I said. I said it because others had said it about me. They said it at home in the yard.

'Don't be impertinent,' said Miss Nissen. 'I want to find out what's the matter with you. I want to talk to you; and I may talk to your mother too. But I won't have impertinence.'

'No,' I said.

'You're so queer; you don't follow properly in your book when we read, and you don't finish your sums. Frankly,' said Miss Nissen, 'your reading and writing and arithmetic seem to me worse now than when you first came.'

Lydia was in the gateway playing with her ball. The others were there too. So I knew I was late home.

'They say you stand gaping at me every day, in the photographer's show-case,' said Lydia. 'I won't have it.'

'It's not true – I don't stand there every day,' I said.

'Anyway I won't have it. I don't want you to gape at me.'

'I s'pose you think you're pretty,' I said.

'I don't know whether I'm pretty or not,' she said, 'but I do know I won't have you standing there and gaping.'

'He's so stupid,' said Gertrud. 'And he's cross-eyed, too.

That's why. He can't help it, Lydia. He doesn't mean to. But you oughtn't to put up with it, all the same.'

'I'm not going to,' said Lydia.

'If he doesn't stop it, we can get Rudolf to thrash him. He's been so stuck-up since he got that sister all of a sudden,' said Else.

I said,

'I only stare at you because I think you're so ugly. You're the ugliest girl I've ever seen in all my life. And stuck-up. And stupid. I shall go into the photographer's tomorrow and say "Who's that ugly girl hanging out there in your show-case?" That's what I'll say. And then he'll take you inside. Because nobody wants to look at you. People walk past and turn their heads away. I've seen them. They turn their heads away so's not to have to look at you. That's how ugly you are.'

In the passage I took off my clogs. The butcher's dead dog, which was called Rolf, had been sick on the mat. We called it the butcher's dead dog because it was always lying down asleep, and it slept so heavily that one might easily have trodden on it. It slept as if it was dead. When I was nearly at the top of the stairs I had to stand still for a moment. I was very nearly crying. I couldn't think why, for there was nothing to cry about, except that business with Lydia. I was so fond of her, and now that my sister had gone I didn't feel I had anyone else. I didn't care about Else either way. What was it Else had said: 'He's cross-eyed.'

'You weren't kept in, were you?' said my mother.

'No, I wasn't kept in.'

'You look as if you're not telling the truth,' she said. 'But I hope I shall never catch you lying to your mother.'

'No,' I said.

My father and mother had begun to talk about me in the evenings, when they thought I was asleep. For they weren't always silent now. They had worries. It seemed to me we'd always had them, but now it was my fault. The school. Miss

34

Nissen. How could mother bring herself to talk to Miss Nissen behind my back? They seemed to have banded together against me. They asked question after question, and whatever I said to one got round to the other. So I said nothing. They shouldn't get a word out of me about what they were so anxious to know.

'He goes about alone so much,' said my mother.

'Alone?' said my father. 'Well, where's the harm in that?'

'I mean he must always be awkward and different. He's not like the other boys. Miss Nissen says so too. He's got an old-fashioned way with him and he's awkward, and backward in his work. She thinks it's because he goes about alone too much.'

'When I was a boy, the nearest kids of my age were twelve miles away,' said my father.

'But everything's so different now.'

'Yes, it's different all right. But only here.'

'Only here! But this is where we are,' said my mother. 'The boy ought to be like the people here.'

I lay listening to them, and was glad that they were talking together. I was glad to hear something besides the pasting-rhythm – to hear voices, and not just silence.

'Well, there's that Marentcius boy,' said my father.

'Yes, Marentcius is a fine boy. Miss Nissen says so too.'

'And there's Lydia, and the Ravns' little girls.'

'But he can't be with girls all the time.'

My father knocked out his pipe. It was some time before he answered.

'Suppose you let him look after himself a bit more,' he said.

Next morning my mother asked,

'What was all that about a mouse you were pestering us for – a white mouse?'

'Marentcius won't take less than five øre for it.'

A minute's pause and suspense.

'Your father and I were talking,' she said at last. 'You go about alone too much. We thought it might be a good thing if you had a mouse like that. Company for you.'

'Yes,' I answered. 'Marentcius says you can talk to it. It understands what you say. Not everything, of course. But you can train it.'

'Your father's promised to make a box for it. It could stand over there on the platform.'

So I got the mouse. I bought it from Marentcius for five øre, and it had a little box with wire-netting over it, which stood on the platform under the window. It brought a new smell to the room, a special smell of wet bran and mouse-droppings. The whole room smelt of animal.

The mouse was rather timid by nature. If one happened to touch the box, or if one scratched the wire-netting gently with one's nails, it was scared and dashed round and round so quickly that it looked like a white ring at the bottom of the box. But it was true that one could talk to it, and if one did no more than that, it sniffed about and drank water and ate a little and behaved like a mouse. My father would sit and watch it too. He tried taking it out in his hand and letting it run up inside his sleeve. He did lots of things with it, but mostly he just sat and watched.

'May we see your mouse?' asked the others in the yard. And I let them come up. I wasn't 'no good' as they called it any more; there was something *to* me now. Else and Marie even came in in the evenings and watched my father send the mouse running up his sleeve until it popped out again at his neck. Afterwards I went back with them.

There were lots of people at the Ravns'. Else and Marie had two grown-up brothers who lived in a room in the loft, and a sister who sewed. There was no silence or quietness at the Ravns'. They played ludo and lotteries and drank coffee and talked. Old Ravn always sat bolt upright in a chair and slept. He was tired when he came home from the foundry. He sat in a chair rather outside the circle of light and let his head fall backwards, and he snored with his mouth open. Black shadows ran together in the hollows of his face like little pools of molten iron. But when the cups were put on the table he woke

36

up. We could play all round him, and talk, and it made no difference to him; but when Mrs Ravn or Birgitte set the cups out he woke at once.

'Coffee-time already?' he would say, yawning and stretching. 'Late as that, is it?'

He had a hoarse voice, which sounded as if fine casting-sand had drifted in to his throat. The Ravns' place smelt of coffee and peat-smoke and sour dish-cloths, but all in all it was a good smell, a warm smell. If it got too late my mother came to fetch me. She wouldn't stay; she just wanted to get me home and into bed. My father never came.

It was all on account of the mouse. Because of the mouse Marentcius and I took to being together during break at school, and sometimes we walked there and back together. Because of it Rudolf came up now and then to ask whether I would go and do this or that with him. Because of that mouse I was some good, and in time I became almost ordinary. But later that winter it died. One morning it was lying in its box with its nose stretched out straight and its little pink paws in the air. And then it wasn't long before I was no good again.

'Well, now it's your own fault,' said my mother. 'It's you – you're so awkward. We shall have to see if you do better in a new form, with a master.'

But by now we had acquired a taste for pets. My father too. My father especially, perhaps. And there was the empty dove-cot over the coach-house. One evening he brought a pair of pigeons home. The female was white, chalk-white, with a yellow beak. The male was blue with little white flecks among the blue and a bit of red round the beak. At first they had to be shut in, or they would have flown away and found their way home again.

'They're like that,' said my father. 'If you don't shut them in and watch them they fly away back to the place they came from.'

We stood quite still in the coach-house between the landau

37

and the wagonette, and waited to see whether the pigeons would start cooing, as pigeons do. But they didn't. Neither that day, nor the next, nor the next. We stood there listening every evening, my father and I, thinking that surely they would start now. But they sat like china doves on their landing-board, staring with little red-rimmed, beady eyes. They didn't eat and they didn't drink. Sometimes they would peck a little at the chicken-wire to see if they could get out.

'Animals are like people,' said my father. 'They get home-sick. And that's a bad sickness; it lasts a long time.'

Of course it was nice having pigeons, I thought; but when they won't coo and mayn't fly, what use were they? They didn't make me interesting.

'Pigeons!' said Rudolf. 'And little white mice,' he said – as if he hadn't been glad enough to know my white mouse. 'That's for kids,' he said. 'Give me adders.'

'But you can only have those when they're dead, and pickled in spirit,' I said.

'Ah, go on – as if I didn't know lots of boys – grown-up boys who keep adders loose in their rooms. I've thought of having some myself. But pigeons – !'

I looked up at the white hen and the blue cock as they pecked at the chicken-wire, and felt I didn't care whether they cooed or not. 'Don't bother on my account,' I thought. 'Coo or not as you like – it's all the same to me.' Rudolf was a magician who could turn everything pale and dull and rob it of its brightness.

'It's only envy,' someone said. 'He's jealous because they're not his.'

But that didn't help.

Marentcius came in one day with a fine, new, shiny knife; it had two blades and a corkscrew.

'Let me see,' said Rudolf. '*That* thing,' he said, holding it in his hand. 'I wouldn't want a thing like that. Give me a swan knife.[1] And if I couldn't afford a swan knife –' and he made a

[1] A strong, short-bladed clasp-knife, very popular with Danish boys.

fart. That was another thing one admired about Rudolf: not only did he dare say everything, but he could fart at the right moment.

But it was Marentcius's knife, and Marentcius needn't have minded. He didn't live in our yard and he didn't have to meet Rudolf if he didn't want to. All the same he came along a few days later and asked me if I would buy his knife for ten øre.

'That's a lot of money,' I said.

'You had the mouse for five, and it's a good knife. It cost fifty.'

'Maybe,' I said. 'But I haven't got ten øre.'

'Can't you even get ten øre from your mother?'

'I could get much more than that,' I told him, 'but I don't want to.'

I'd been standing with the knife in my hand, wanting it, but Marentcius took it and threw it over the board fence, far into the neighbour's garden.

'I don't want it,' he said. 'If I can't have a swan knife I won't have one at all.'

Marentcius would have liked to do as Rudolf did and put a full stop in the right place, but it was an art he hadn't learnt.

'You might have given the knife to me,' I said. 'If you didn't want it anyhow you could have let me have it.'

'I'm not such a fool as to give away a brand new knife,' he said. 'It can stay where it is and rust to bits.'

I looked at Marentcius and was surprised that he still looked like Marentcius. I expected his face to look different.

'Come on,' he said. 'Let's go over to Pilke Hill.'

We played together all that day, and I thought of the knife. I could think of nothing else. It was lying rusting to bits now – on purpose. It wasn't lost. It was just thrown away. I thought of it that evening, and once when I woke up in the night. After all, it was a good knife.

Next day I went to look for it. I couldn't help it. I wanted to find it and hide it away so that Marentcius shouldn't see it. I went along a strange path and through a strange yard, looking

39

as if I were used to coming into the yard and into the garden too. I looked as if it were the most natural thing in the world.

'What are you looking for?' cried a voice from an open kitchen-window.

'Only a knife,' I said. 'I chucked it in here last night.'

'A knife? But Marentcius has been in for it already, surely.'

So I went away again, and nobody ever knew I'd been there. Long afterwards Marentcius happened to show me the knife.

'Isn't that the one you chucked over the fence?' I asked. 'The one you were going to leave to rust to bits?'

'No,' said Marentcius, turning red.

'Let me see,' I said. 'But that's not a swan knife. That's the one you threw away.'

'It isn't quite that one,' he said. 'You wouldn't understand. You're not even allowed to carry a knife yet.'

I felt I had won somehow, and got the better of Marentcius. But he bore me a grudge after that, and we didn't go about together as much as before.

One day the pigeons really did begin to coo. It was lovely to hear them. They didn't coo like other pigeons I knew; they had their own throat-noises.

'Those are my pigeons cooing,' I told Lydia.

'I dare say.'

'You can hear they're mine.'

'I can't,' she said.

'When they've laid eggs and the hen's begun sitting they'll be allowed to fly free,' I said. 'You can train pigeons so they'll come and sit on your shoulders or on your head.'

'How nasty,' said Lydia.

No, pigeons don't help, I thought. They don't make me interesting.

'But you can sit quiet and look at them,' said my father. 'You can go up into Klyver's loft and talk to them through the shutter.'

He did that himself. He sat on a cart-tail, peering at them and watching them as they flew in and out. Sometimes he went up into the loft, and then I think he talked to them.

'I should have thought you could find something better to do,' said my mother.

'Yes,' he said.

'Next year we'll have a plot of land in Nørremarken,' she said.

'Suits me,' he said. 'Only I think it would be best to get it now.'

But the pigeons could get along without me. They hatched their young and were set free, and the young ones began to fly too. One fine day a strange pair arrived, and they stayed.

'We could kill the old ones now, really,' said my mother. 'If you leave them too long they get tough.'

I said no, but my father didn't hear.

'*You* needn't talk,' my mother told me. 'You never take any notice of them.'

A few days later she spoke of it again.

'Shall we have the pigeons on Sunday?' she asked.

'On Sunday,' said my father, putting down his paper. 'I wonder if Sunday's really the best day,' he said, staring in front of him.

'I think it ought to be Sunday,' said my mother. 'Who'd have pigeon on any other day – a week-day?' she said.

The trains came and went. The signal bell rang at the level-crossing and the lights changed. There were red signal-lights and yellow and green and white, a whole illumination, when one looked along the rails towards the station. Life went on. Everything went on.

'I think we'll have those pigeons,' said my mother.

When she said it in that way we knew it would be so. It was something she had made up her mind about; perhaps because she really thought the birds ought to be eaten now – because her mouth was watering, as it were. My mother had tasted pigeon before, and perhaps it was something not easily forgotten. But she also resented them. She disliked my father

41

watching them so continually – going up into Klyver's loft to chat to them. When my mother made up her mind to anything it came to pass. She never said much about it – just an odd word now and then. But she went on wanting it: she went quietly about with it in her mind; one could see it. One had to give in at last – one had to say yes and do what she wanted. Or else she did it herself. She might take it into her head to want a dozen cups, for instance – some she had seen at the iron-monger's.

'They had little sprays of roses on them,' she said, 'and such pretty little gold rims.'

'What do we want with more cups than we got out there?' my father might ask.

'Well, for one thing I wouldn't keep these in the kitchen,' said my mother. 'I shall put them in the cupboard – the little cupboard in the best room. And as for needing them – suppose the Nielsens in Cross Street were to come in one evening, or Abeline, or anybody – well . . .'

'Vanity,' said my father.

Pasting went on and wanting went on, with narrow lips, and hands that allowed themselves no rest but kept time incessantly, whatever was being discussed. The decision was made.

One day the cups were there, and silver teaspoons to match. Little miracles of art, with gold on the bowls. Father hid behind his paper or turned his back; he just couldn't fix his eye on anything. The same thing happened when the two new plush chairs appeared. He walked past them and round them. He even bumped into them, but he never saw them. He never noticed them at all until Mrs Ravn came in, clapped her hands and said,

'Bless my soul, new chairs! Easy to see who's got money – wherever it comes from . . .'

'New chairs, eh?' said my father. 'I heard some talk about it, but I never noticed them.'

'Else and Marie said there was talk of cups too. And tea-spoons.'

42

'You're welcome to see them all,' said my mother. 'There's no secret about it.'

'No. She just wishes things into the place,' my father said. 'She asks for them to drop from heaven and she won't give in till she gets what she wants.'

'I get them by working,' said my mother. 'With brush and spreader and paper – so a blessing comes with them. I can't see anyone sitting on a cart-tail and staring pigeons down from heaven ready-roasted.'

'N-no,' said my father, twiddling the matchbox in his fingers and staring in front of him. 'N-no,' he said, and sighed. 'That's true enough. Vanity,' he said.

But one evening – it was a Saturday – he went down to fetch the pigeons. He went because he could see that it had to be. There was no getting out of it. Especially as mother, who always remembered everything, had strangely enough forgotten to plan anything for Sunday dinner.

'Well,' he said. 'I'm off.'

A little later he came up again. He had brought the white hen with him. He came in holding her by the wings and legs; she blinked at the lamplight with her little red-rimmed beady eyes, and moved her head in little jerks, now this way, now that.

'Doodle-doodle-doodle,' said my father.

'Do you know how to do it?' my mother asked. 'You ought to have done it downstairs,' she said.

'Seems there's two hollows under her wings,' said my father. 'That's what the butcher said.'

'All the same, you ought to have done it downstairs,' said my mother. 'And what about the cock?'

'That fine blue cock,' said my father. 'Yes, well – got to start with one of them, I suppose.'

He went into the kitchen and shut the door behind him.

My mother sat with light on her forehead and light on her hands. She drew her brush along and used her spreader. Her fingers were moving at a different, faster tempo than usual.

43

'If you'd rather go over to the Ravns,' she said. 'Or get to bed.'

The crying in me reached from the bottom of my chest to my collar-bones.

'Need we have any dinner tomorrow?' I asked.

'Well, we wouldn't die if we didn't,' she said, 'but –'

It was quiet in the kitchen. Deathly quiet. One would never have guessed that my father was out there, far less that he held a live pigeon in his hand and was going to kill it.

'Find something to do,' said my mother, and I found something to do.

A long time afterwards we heard my father going downstairs again. He must be going to fetch the cock-bird. That handsome bird with white flecks in the blue, and a little red near the beak. Trains were passing below. But trains always went by at this time of day. The Copenhagen express. The signal-lights changed and showed that the line was clear, and the bell announced the goods train from the north.

My father came up again and went into the kitchen. There was nothing to be heard. One couldn't hear him breathing, one couldn't hear him moving. After a long interval I was told to open the door. Carefully. I pressed down the handle. I opened the door. My father was sitting on the stove looking out of the kitchen-window. There were no pigeons lying on the table as I had expected. No slain birds with dead wings and a head hanging on a thin, limp neck. There was nothing there.

'What!' said my mother as she rose and came in. 'No pigeons?'

My father sat where he was on the stove without moving. The half-open door cast a triangle of yellow light on the floor and up over the kitchen table, but he was sitting almost in darkness.

There we stood looking at him, not understanding, waiting.

'Couldn't you find that place under the wings?' asked my mother.

44

A long pause. The yellow triangle on the floor and up over the kitchen table to the row of plates stood still too.

'Yes,' said my father slowly. 'It wasn't that. I found the place all right. Yes,' he said. 'But it's hard to kill a dove with one's hands, with one's head full of hymns and the Song of Solomon. She was so very white,' he said.

'If that's how it is, then it was meant to be,' said my mother. And 'In Jesus' name, then let them live,' she said.

There was healing in that moment. There was infinite relief.

'You've got a good father,' said my mother. She looked at me. She laid one hand on my head and the other on my father's hand. 'You've got a good father,' she said, and looked at me in a curious way.

When it came to the point my father had been incapable of killing a pigeon. But he must have frightened it. It would be timid now and wouldn't venture to eat out of his hand, even though he hadn't been able to harm it.

I stood and thought about the pigeon being afraid and not daring to come to us. From a dim past I knew something about that pigeon. Something nobody else knew.

'Well, we won't say anything more about it,' said my mother. She said it in the voice one uses when one comes back after being far away in thought.

'We won't say anything about it,' she said. 'Come on in again.'

6

WE had a new schoolmaster whose name was Vester-strøm. We had him for history and arithmetic. He was good at history. So was I now. He wrote names up on the board and told us about them. He told us so well that one never had to read at home. But he was strict. He wouldn't have any whispering, or the least disturbance in class. There had to be absolute silence. He wanted it even quieter than it was with Miss Nissen. It was difficult.

He wrote some sums upon the board for us to work out. I whispered to Paulus that I couldn't see them. He didn't answer.

'I can't see the figures,' I whispered. 'Tell me what's written up there.'

'That's because you're stupid,' said Paulus. 'You're so stupid that soon you won't be able to see out of your eyes.'

'Quiet,' shouted the master, and banged his ruler on the desk.

We were quiet.

Paulus worked. I did nothing.

'You might tell me what it is,' I whispered after a time. 'Just the first one. I can do the sum all right.'

Paulus didn't answer. He just minded his own business and went on working. So I got nowhere. Soon we should have to go up and show our sums, and Mr Vesterstrøm would see that I hadn't done anything.

I rocked back and forth in my seat. I whispered to Paulus again. But Paulus wouldn't answer.

'Monitor, fetch me the rod, please,' said Mr Vesterstrøm suddenly.

I wasn't sure what a rod was. I wasn't sure either why the monitor had to fetch one. Presently he came back with a cane which he'd borrowed from the class next door.

Mr Vesterstrøm called me.

'Come up here,' he said. 'Let's see if we can teach you to hold your tongue in class.'

I rose and went up to him. I was horribly frightened. I was afraid of being caned. If it had been a box on the ear I wouldn't have been quite so frightened, but I had never tried a cane. They all said it was awful unless one had time to put something inside one's trousers. They all said so except Wesly. He was to go to a reformatory as soon as there was room for him. Wesly didn't care.

'Bend over,' said Mr Vesterstrøm.

He didn't ask why I had whispered. He wasn't interested in knowing what I had asked Paulus, and Paulus didn't tell him.

'Bend right over,' said Mr Vesterstrøm. 'You're going to have three cuts, the kind you'll feel and remember. I don't usually thrash a boy more than once. Once is generally enough – he remembers it. And so will you. Further over,' said Mr Vesterstrøm, and he held the back of my neck with his left hand.

I was frightened. I don't know what I imagined. I knew that others had been thrashed. I'd often seen others getting caned; Wesly, for instance. But I'd never thought about it and never been sorry for them; I don't believe it had even struck me that they were to be pitied. And they didn't look any different afterwards. Most of them wouldn't admit they'd been hurt. They said,

'He can't even cane properly.'

But Vesterstrøm could.

I was frightened. So frightened that I wetted my trousers before he hit me. I was so terrified that I forgot to notice whether it hurt. But I wetted myself, though not enough for the others to see. It was only I who felt the warm trickle down my thighs.

'There,' said Mr Vesterstrøm. 'Monitor, take the rod back

with my thanks for the loan. It's done its work. Hasn't it?' he said to me. 'You and I understand each other now. You'll stay in and finish your sums after school, and in future you'll hold your tongue in class, eh?'

'Yes,' I said.

'Yes what?' said Mr Vesterstrøm.

'Yes, thank you.'

'Very well.'

I was afraid someone might have seen that I'd wetted my trousers.

'*I* saw you press your legs together!' said Paulus. 'D'you think I didn't?' he said. But he didn't talk about the wetting. He hadn't seen it. Nobody had. They didn't even talk about my being caned. That was disappointing; but most of them were used to it. I was the only one who hadn't had it before. And now it didn't seem to me to have been so bad; the worst bit was just before. It hadn't hurt as much as I'd expected. The fear was the worst thing about it. But I should have to get used to that. I should have to get used to being thrashed in Mr Vesterstrøm's arithmetic lessons. How could I find out what was on the board without whispering to Paulus, or without somebody telling me?

Outside the windows the chestnut trees were murmuring. They murmured as they always did in this wind. The sun was shining but a wind was blowing, and in among the dark leaves, if one were lucky, one could spy a chestnut, spiky and green. It was all just as it had been before I was thrashed. Nothing had changed. The pretty little houses opposite had flowers on their window-sills. Stone steps which were always swept and clean, and curtains. White curtains in the windows, and the sills full of all kinds of flowers. The world was as it had always been. It was almost as if nothing had happened. As if I'd never been caned by Mr Vesterstrøm at all. How was it possible . . .

The sums were easy. When the others had gone and I was alone in the classroom I went up to the blackboard to see what was on it, and worked them out. I could do them in my head. But I was still wet; I unbuttoned to look. I had red garters and they had stained my shirt.

Mr Vesterstrøm came in and looked through my sums.

'Quite right,' he said. 'Cut along home.'

When I'd reached the door he called me back.

'Why do you talk in class?' he asked.

'I don't know.'

'But you know I don't allow it.'

'Yes,' I answered.

'Well then, can you stop doing it, do you think?'

'No,' I said.

'What? Why not?'

'I don't know,' I said. I couldn't explain.

'What was it you were whispering about?'

'I was asking what was on the board.'

'Can't you see?'

'Sometimes I can't. Sometimes I can't get my eye on it,' I answered.

'But then you must tell me,' he said.

'Yes,' I answered. But I didn't want to. I didn't want the others laughing at me for asking the master what was on the board.

'Is that a promise?' he said.

'Yes.'

I couldn't explain to my mother why I'd been kept in. She asked what I'd been up to. I said I hadn't been up to anything. She asked if I hadn't known my lesson. I wanted to say I had but that made it too difficult, for what was I to say next? I said I hadn't known my lesson.

'There now,' said my mother. 'You must study more. That's what I've always said.'

'But I don't need to,' I said. 'Mr Vesterstrøm tells us everything. He tells us much more than there is in the book.'

'All the same you must study,' said my mother. 'From now on you'll read every day.'

When I undressed that night she saw that the red garters had stained my shirt.

'Good gracious!' she said. 'Don't tell me you've wetted yourself – and you in the third form!'

I said yes. Anything else would have needed far too long an explanation. It seemed easier just to say yes. But I hated my mother. I hated everybody. Mr Vesterstrøm. Paulus. The others. I hated them all, and I hated my mother too.

Down in the yard and in the gateway and out in the street they were playing. I could hear Lydia laughing. And Rudolf. And Gertrud was there. And Silly Anders was asking if somebody would play horses with him, but nobody would. And I had to go to bed. I had to go to bed because I'd been kept in. I hadn't known my lesson and I'd wetted my trousers, although I was in the third form.

'What would Lydia say if she knew?' asked my mother.

I made up my mind to hate everybody from now on, until I died. I determined to hate my mother too, and it wasn't difficult. It would have been difficult not to. I could kill, too. I could be a matricide. And I could kill Mr Vesterstrøm. But anyhow I would hate everybody. And in case I forgot I would say to myself every morning when I got up:

'Today you must remember to hate. You must remember to hate them all – except Lydia . . .'

My father came home from work and I heard my mother tell him that I'd been kept in and that I'd wetted myself.

'Well, well,' he said.

That was all. He had his meal and clearly never gave the matter another thought. He ate in silence. Then he took his book – the little book in the red cloth cover. I could hear it was that one when he laid it on the table.

'What are we to do?' my mother asked.

'What about?'

'About the boy . . .'

My father didn't answer. He read. He read, thinking that something must have happened to the people since last he had the book in his hands. But he made no answer as to what was to be done about me. I decided I wouldn't hate my father.

'Don't you think you could find something better to do than read novels?' said my mother.

Long silence.

'Heeling my shoes, for instance.'

My mother pasted her paper bags, keeping steady time even when she was talking.

'I shan't be fit to be seen soon,' she said.

My father said nothing. He turned a page of the book, but he didn't answer her.

'How did you get that bump?' asked Mr Vesterstrøm.

'I don't know,' I said. 'I just bumped myself.'

It was a window I had run into. An open window that I hadn't had my eye on. Somebody's living-room window, and I'd been walking close to the houses.

'So you bumped yourself, did you. How?'

'I don't know. I just did.'

I didn't want to tell him I'd run into a window; he'd simply have told me to look where I was going. I always looked where I was going, but sometimes I couldn't spot things until I hit them, or until somebody pointed them out. I couldn't explain.

'Why don't you look where you're going?' my mother said.

'Catch the ball, can't you?' said Lydia. 'Why are you so stupid? Why can't you see it?'

I could see the ball all right. Of course I could. It was just that I was looking another way. It always happened when I was looking at something else. That was how I ran into the window.

'When you were whispering to Paulus yesterday,' said Mr Vesterstrøm, 'was it because you couldn't see what was on the board?'

'I couldn't see it from where I sit,' I said. 'But I could see it all right afterwards.'

'How do you mean – afterwards?'

'Afterwards, when I came up to your desk.'

Mr Vesterstrøm looked at me hard. He looked right into my face.

'I believe you squint a little,' he said.

At break they all shouted 'cross-eyes' after me, and pinched me behind. They snatched off my cap and threw it up into the chestnut trees. But that didn't matter, for even if I couldn't get my eye on it I knew it must be up in the big chestnut.

'Hoo, what a squint!' they shouted.

Once one of them came and yelled it right into my ear.

'Cross-eyes!' he shouted. 'I've never seen anybody so cross-eyed in all my life.'

I hated Mr Vesterstrøm. I hated them all.

In the next break I went and sat in the lavatory. The master on duty went past.

'Why are you sitting there?' he asked.

'I've got a stomach-ache,' I said.

I thought that was a good thing to have. I thought one could perfectly well have that. But one couldn't have a squint.

'Oh,' he said. 'Well, hurry up and finish. The bell will soon be ringing.'

'Yes,' I said.

I was sitting with my trousers up.

It was nice sitting there in the lavatory. I knew that now. I would do it every day, at every break. I didn't mind living here. There was always somebody talking next door, and one could hear them. One could hear them running past, too, and playing outside. I didn't mind not being with them. I didn't want to be. I would much rather sit here in peace.

'Would you like to come up to my desk and copy down the problems?' asked Mr Vesterstrøm in the next arithmetic lesson.

'No,' I answered.

'You might at least say thank you,' he said.

'No thank you,' I said, and I stayed where I was. But at the end of the lesson I hadn't done a single one of the sums.

'That's because he's so cross-eyed,' said Paulus.

Marentcius said,

'And he's such a funk he hides in the jakes during break.'

'Oh,' said Mr Vesterstrøm. But he didn't say anything about a rod. I wasn't going to be caned. I'd expected it. I'd been so sure of it that I was almost disappointed. But I hurried down to the lavatories.

Things went on like this for a time. Some days or some weeks. I don't know for how long. I only know it went on for a long time.

One evening when I came in my mother said,

'It's tiresome, all this bother over you at school.'

'There isn't any bother over me at school,' I said.

'What about arithmetic?' she asked.

'I can do it as well as anybody else.'

'Can you!' she said. 'Then why don't you?'

I didn't answer that.

'Is there anything the matter with your stomach?' she asked.

'No,' I said. 'Nothing.'

'Do your homework now, anyway,' she said. 'I don't like to hear of your being behind the others.'

'But I'm not.'

'I don't like to hear of your behaving different from the others,' said my mother.

I fetched my book and sat up on the platform.

Far away the windmill was slowly turning its sails, with the evening sky behind. The signal-lights by the station and along the line changed from white to red to green and to clear again. Soon the ten-o'clock train would come. Soon my father would come home from work. My mother sat pasting paper bags.

'Why aren't you reading?' she asked.

I couldn't make out whether she was cross or just sad about something. Sometimes I thought she looked the same for both.

You thought she was sad and she turned out to be cross. Or you thought she was cross, when really something had gone wrong and made her unhappy. Her face went smaller when something was wrong. Her eyes went too close together. Her mouth became small and her nose pointed; but this happened too when she was cross.

The train came and the signals changed again. And the evening sky grew darker. One couldn't see now whether the sails of the windmill were turning or standing still. Up in Freden Street lights appeared, first in one window and then in another. Little yellow lights. Klyver the carrier shut the half-door of the stable, and he shut the coach-house. The loft-shutter above was open. It was dark in the garden behind the stables and the coach-house. The trees stood there whispering with darkness, it seemed to me. They whispered with rain and darkness, but it was not raining.

My mother sighed. She sighed and got up and lit the lamp, and sighed and sat down to paste again. And my father came home. He ate his meal out in the kitchen, and while he was eating my mother told him that there'd been some bother over me at school. She told him that a schoolmaster had been to see her. She told him that I didn't do my sums – that I wouldn't do them. I could do them very well, the master said. But I wouldn't.

'Oh,' said my father, and went on eating.

'But we shall have to do something,' my mother said.

He didn't answer.

'We shall have to see the doctor about it,' she said.

'Doctor . . . Are you going running to the doctor again?'

'I say it's not normal. Other children aren't like that.'

My father said nothing.

'There may be something wrong with the boy,' said my mother.

My father still said not a word.

I had come down from the platform to the table, where the lamp was, and was sitting where my father usually sat when he read the Bible or his book. I was sitting there with my book exactly like him when they came in. I hadn't read anything yet, for I had no need to; I knew it. I knew it better than the book did. But I opened it at a place further on. I found a place I didn't know because we hadn't had it yet. I could settle down to reading that, since mother was so keen for me to stick to my book.

They came in and my mother sat down to make more bags. My father stood and looked at me. I could see that he was standing looking at me and I felt rather afraid of him. He said nothing; he just stood watching me to see whether I was reading or not. I dared not look up from my book. I dared not ask him anything. I could smell his clothes – his tobacco-y breath. I could smell the sweat which had chilled and dried into his skin. He stood close beside me and I was so frightened I couldn't read. Or I couldn't keep my mind on what I was reading, and understand it.

Suddenly my father slapped my face.

'Stop making faces, boy!' he said. 'Mimicking the blind girls!'

'You've no need to hit him,' said my mother, pushing her bags away. 'No need to hit him till we hear what's wrong.'

'I don't know what should be wrong,' said my father. 'But he's not to sit mimicking the blind girls.'

'No,' said my mother. 'But I won't have you hitting him. I won't have you doing anything until we've had a talk with the doctor.'

I was let off reading any more. I wasn't to stay there in my father's place; I could count some bags, and when I'd counted some bags I could go to bed. I hadn't cried. I hadn't done anything to attract attention. But I didn't want to count bags.

'Well then, you can go to bed right away,' said my mother.

'You've given us worries enough for one day,' she said. 'You can go to bed and shut the door.'

'Yes,' I said.

'Remember to say your prayers,' said my mother.

'Yes,' I said again. But I didn't want to say my prayers.

'I think he's getting hard,' my father said. 'He's taking after you and getting hard. But he's not to make faces and mimic the blind girls.'

Mother didn't answer.

I shut the bedroom door. I knew they were going to talk about me and that I mustn't hear. I undressed in the dark and got into bed. I didn't say my prayers. It didn't matter. Nothing mattered. I lay there getting hard. I would show them all how hard I could get. I'd be as hard as a stone.

There was a star in one pane of the skylight.

7

THE doctor said there was nothing wrong with me as far as he could see. He opened first one of my eyes and then the other. He lifted my eyelids with his thumb and peered at each eye for a long time.

'No,' he said. 'What should be the matter?'

'I don't know,' my mother said. 'It seems as if he can't see things when they're right under his nose.'

'Well, he must learn to look what he's doing,' said the doctor.

'And sometimes he runs into things,' said my mother.

'Does boys good to take a few knocks,' said the doctor. 'They need a few knocks,' he said. 'Do you fight a lot at school?'

'No,' I said, and it was true.

'Perhaps you've been coddled,' said the doctor. 'Boys mustn't be pampered,' he said. 'They must take knocks and learn to keep their eyes open; and it'll do him good to be knocked about a bit until he learns to look what he's doing. If you're worried about him go to Kolding; there's a specialist there. But I can't see anything wrong.'

We didn't go to Kolding. We wouldn't have gone even if we'd been worried. We would have gone if anything had been wrong. But nothing was.

My mother thanked God because nothing was wrong. She knelt by the green ottoman in the bedroom and thanked God.

'I'm glad there's nothing wrong,' she said. 'And I thank Thee, God. But I will bear whatever Thou sendest me. I will bear it because Thou wilt gave me strength and because I know Thou sendest me pain and sorrow to purify me and make me a temple.'

That is what my mother said to God when she came home. She said it aloud in the bedroom by the green ottoman. I sat carving my block of wood with a knife that father had found. My father was good at finding things. I wanted a fret-saw, and wondered what mother meant by all that sorrow and pain she was talking to God about, and what it was she would be given strength to bear.

'Don't you think you ought to thank God too?' she asked when she came in. Her eyes were red. She had been crying.

'What for?' I asked.

'Because there was nothing wrong.'

'No,' I said, and went on carving. 'I want to make a girl out of this block of wood.'

'You must practise for Abeline on Sunday, and you must count some bags for me,' said my mother.

'I do so want a fret-saw,' I said.

'Why?'

'I want to make my block of wood into a girl,' I said.

'You know you can't do that. Come along now and count some bags, and afterwards you must practise.'

I'd been given a guitar which I'd never asked for and never even wanted. Wedell had given it to me. He came to speak sometimes at the Friends'[1] meetings in Tønnes Street on Sunday afternoon. He brought it from Copenhagen, and it was strung according to his own system.

'The seven system,' he said. 'The divine number seven.'

Baron Wedell looked at me and said,

'God has plans for that boy. I can tell that from his forehead. It's radiant.'

Next time he came he brought me the guitar. But I wanted a forehead like everybody else's.

My mother wanted me to go to Abeline's house to learn to play the guitar, and to practise in the evenings and sit beside

[1] No connection with the Society of Friends.

58

Abeline on Sundays in the Tønnes Street hall, and play for the songs they sang. But I didn't want to. I wanted a fiddle. I wanted a ten-crown fiddle, without case.

'What would you do with it?' asked my mother.

'Play it.'

'But you can't.'

'One day I'm going to have a fiddle,' I said.

Then I sat down to count bags. Down in the yard the others were playing. I could hear their voices. I could hear what they were playing.

'Another hundred and you can go down to them,' said my mother.

I didn't care about going down – not when there were so many of them. When my mother thought I'd gone out to play with the others I sat on the stone steps drawing with chalk. Then Christensen the moulder's wife came and told me I mustn't draw on the step and that I must wash it off again and go away. So I found a rag and wiped it off and went out into the street. Sometimes the butcher's dead dog went with me. He was a very good dog. Sometimes I talked to Anders.

'If you must be awkward and can't play with the other children,' said my mother, 'go for a good brisk walk in the woods.'

So I went off towards the woods. I didn't go into them. I went as far as the brewery ponds. The brewery had three ponds where they cut ice in winter. We called them the ice-ponds. When there was thick ice on them it was cut and carted away. A green-painted wooden house stood by the ice ponds, and in this were some huge troughs or vats. I didn't know what they were for. But there was a man there named Stougård, who looked after them. He looked after the vats and the ice-ponds and all the things belonging to the brewery. In the morning when he went to work he bought two bottles of *braendevin* from the shop. One bottle to each pocket. That was so that he could walk straight, he said. He lived on *braendevin* and potatoes, which he baked on a fireplace he had. He baked them in their jackets and dipped them in salt.

'You can have one if you like,' he said. 'But you must dip it in salt and wash it down with *braendevin* and beer.'

I tasted one and liked it. It tasted burnt. It tasted charred and salt, but I liked it.

'Now try the *braendevin*,' he said. 'Drink from the bottle and take as much or as little as you can get down. It'll do you good.'

I tried to put the bottle to my mouth. I tasted a few drops too, but I couldn't get them down.

'It'll come,' said Stougård. 'You'll learn. You're the kind that can learn anything they wants to. And later on the thirst comes,' he said. 'I don't know how it is but it always happens: poor people are always thirsty. There's their own thirst they can't get rid of, can't get to the bottom of – and then there's their father's and grandfathers' thirst. That comes down to them because their fathers and grandfathers couldn't get to the bottom of theirs neither – couldn't ever quench it for good. When a man's poor he's got a thirst in his bones and in the marrow of his bones. You'll learn,' said Stougård. 'I can see you're the kind that can do whatever they want.'

'That's because God's got plans for me,' I said.

'What the hell –' said Stougård, and stopped gnawing his potato. 'What the hell's that you're saying?' he said. 'Who the devil's been telling you that nonsense?'

He rubbed his charred potato well into the white salt and ate it, and washed it down with *braendevin* and beer.

'Who the devil's been spinning you that yarn?' he asked.

'Baron Wedell said so. The man who gave me the guitar.'

'I might have known it was somebody like that. God may have plans for counts and barons and rich people like that, but not for you and me. Don't you believe it, you little cuckoo.'

Stougård took another gulp. Then he began to sing. He always sang hymns. He sang 'Who knoweth when my end shall come . . .' He sang so that at first one thought it was a

60

foreign language – a language one couldn't understand. But gradually one could understand it after all.

'Don't you go swallowing rubbish like that, you little cuckoo,' he said.

I didn't mind Stougård calling me a little cuckoo.

'God don't give *that* for you or me. But you're the kind that can learn anything. You might easily come to look after the ice-ponds and caulk the vats and have a good time here when I'm dead.'

Outside there was a wind blowing. A raw, wet wind from the fjord. But the embers on Stougård's hearth made the place cosy. They smoked, too. And behind the green-painted wooden house were the woods. My mother sat at home thinking I was going for a brisk walk and getting rosy cheeks, as she said. But I never got rosy cheeks because I sat here with Stougård, sharing his potatoes until I was so full I couldn't eat anything when I got home.

'But a guitar . . . That's a funny thing to play, unless you want to be a Salvation lass. Why don't your dad buy you an accordion, if you've got a turn that way?'

I didn't want an accordion.

'Then you could play at dances as well,' said Stougård.

'I want a fiddle.'

'A fiddle's good too. You can play that at dances. You can get a calfskin bag for it, and carry it on your back. Then you can stroll from place to place and all the girls will come to meet you with flowers in their hair, all of a fidget to get dancing. Perhaps a fiddle's even better than an accordion, now I come to think of it. You stick to that,' said Stougård.

He hiccupped, and took a good draught of beer to push down the hiccup.

'Stick to the fiddle, mind,' he said. 'Though it's all the same what you choose, so far's that goes. It's all the same to you. You can learn whatever you want.'

The sky was low and grey, and the rain streaked down the panes. And the grass round the ice-ponds was withered. I

61

ought to have been going for a brisk walk in the woods to get rosy cheeks, but I was sitting here with Stougård, enjoying myself.

When I got home Mr Vesterstrøm and Miss Nissen were there having coffee. So there was more bother over me. My mother looked grave.

'You'd better go out again for a bit,' said Mr Vesterstrøm. 'Miss Nissen and I have something to say to your mother.'

So I went out again. It was getting dark. It was raining too. None of the others was there and I went into Klyver's coach-house. There was the landau. I got into it and shut the door. It was almost like a room, and a handsome room at that. I thought of what Mr Vesterstrøm and Miss Nissen could be talking to my mother about, and of there being more bother over me at school. But I liked being here. I liked it almost as much as being at Stougård's. I wished there had been a landau at school. Then I could have sat in it at break instead of the lavatories. I had been chased out of the lavatories, so I stayed by Marentcius. Marentcius kept to himself a good deal; it was because he was so clever. I walked beside Marentcius and sometimes I held on to him.

'Don't touch me,' he said. 'I don't like you hanging on to my blouse.'

I touched him or hung on to his blouse because then I seemed able to see better.

'You can go on your own,' he said, 'or stay in the jakes, but I don't like you pawing me.'

'All right,' I said.

So I went on my own until I began hiding in the jakes again because somebody pinched me or spat on me or snatched away what I had in my hand. I let my cap stay up there.

But if there'd been a landau at school, to creep into and hide in! That would have been fine. And if Lydia would come it would be fine. And if only there needn't be more bother over me.

I couldn't think why they were so frightened when they

found me. I'd only fallen asleep. I'd been lying asleep on the back seat of Klyver's landau. I was a bit cold, but nothing had happened to me.

'You know very well I don't want you kids in my carriages,' said Klyver.

Christensen the moulder was there too, and Ravn and my mother. My mother cried and scolded at the same time.

'The things you do!' she said. 'Why can't you behave like other children?'

I didn't know why not, but I was sorry about it.

'We've been hunting everywhere,' she said. 'Your father's been all round the town. Now he's gone to the woods to look for you there . . .'

I thought it was funny they should run about looking for me in the town and in the woods when I hadn't been anywhere except Stougård's and here in Klyver's landau. But I didn't say anything. I went upstairs with my mother.

'We're going to Kolding tomorrow,' she said.

For the moment I couldn't think what we were going to Kolding for, but then I remembered. It was to see that specialist the doctor had talked about. If we were worried.

So we were worried, I thought. I wasn't. But I didn't mind going to Kolding.

Over in Freden Street there were lights in the windows. The lights twinkled because it was raining. The signal-lights up by the station winked red and green and yellow.

'You must go to bed right away,' said my mother, 'because tomorrow we go to Kolding.'

So I lay and looked at the strip of light from the door, which stood ajar, and at the square of the skylight. My mother was pasting, and keeping up her tempo. She gave herself time to sigh when she gathered the paper bags and 'tapped them up' as we called it. She sighed, but she kept time. Then I could hear the tramp of my father's clogs. I could hear it from a long way off – from right over by the woods. I could recognize it. He was walking more quickly than usual and not as if he were tired or sad. I could hear him coming nearer. I could hear him come through the yard gate and up the stairs. My mother went out to meet him. They stood out in the passage for some time, and then in the kitchen. At last my father came in. I wondered if he was angry. But he wasn't angry. He said only,

'So you're off tomorrow, then.'

'Yes,' I said.

'Going on a journey.'

'Yes.'

'But there's nothing to be afraid of.'

'No,' I said. It had never entered my head that there might be anything to be afraid of.

My father bent over the bed. He smelt of tobacco. He stroked my hair.

'Nothing to be afraid of,' he repeated. 'You're just going on a journey.'

'Yes,' I said, and fell asleep.

So we went to Kolding. I was washed all over, although my father said,

'Where's the sense in that? The specialist's not going to look at the boy's neck, or his back or his legs.'

But I had to be washed just the same. We put on our best clothes, too. And my mother made sandwiches, a big packet of them, tied up in a handkerchief.

We reached Kolding too early and we didn't know anybody there. We wandered about the streets and looked at the houses. There was a ruin there. I had never seen a ruin before. It was a burnt-out house. Jagged end-walls. Empty squares of windows through which one saw the sky.

We arrived at the specialist's too early, too. He had gone out to lunch, said the lady who opened the door to us. But he'd be back, she said. We were to come in and sit down.

So we came in and sat down. It was better than wandering about the streets.

'We shall feel easier in our minds afterwards, for walking about,' said my mother.

I wasn't uneasy. I was just bored. There was no one but us to see the specialist, and no more would come, the lady thought.

'There are never so many to see a specialist as there are to see a real doctor,' she said.

No. We could understand that. We had often been to a real doctor, but never to a specialist.

'Is it the boy?' asked the lady.

'Yes,' said my mother.

'He doesn't look as if he had anything wrong with him,' said the lady. 'But for all that he may be blind before the year's out.'

'I don't like to hear you say that,' said my mother.

I neither liked nor disliked it.

'Just sit down and wait,' said the lady. 'If he's not back soon I'll ring up the Club.'

There weren't many things in the specialist's room. A couple of chairs; a table with a case of spectacle-lenses on it. A funny lamp. A card with letters on it on the wall. The top one was a big B. I could see the next one too. And the next again. I went right up close to the card so that I could read all the letters.

'You must sit still on your chair,' said my mother.

'Let him look round if he likes,' said the lady. 'There's nothing he could break except the lenses and the lamp. Let him have a look round,' she said again. 'See as much as he can, while he can.'

'Yes,' said my mother, no doubt pondering what this might mean.

'For even if children don't look as if there's anything wrong with them,' said the lady, 'all the same . . .'

I stood reading the card.

I stood reading the card just as I'd been allowed to do in Mr Vesterstrøm's maths lessons. I'd been allowed to go up to the board and look at the problems, and then afterwards I could go back to my place and work them out. I could always remember a sum until I got back to my place. I could remember lots of sums.

'A man buys three barrels of corn at 10 crowns a barrel. He sells one barrel for 15 crowns. For the second he receives 12 crowns, and he has to let the third go for 8. What is his total profit? How much per cent.? What is the average price of the corn per barrel?'

'I think I'd better ring through to the Club,' said the lady.

'We can wait,' said my mother. 'We shall have to wait anyway until our train goes.'

'Still, I'd better ring him up,' said the lady. 'Let him know someone's here. Otherwise he'll just stay on and have too many drinks. And then he'll be sleepy or irritable when he comes in. Men need looking after like children,' she said, 'or there's trouble. He needs it, anyway,' she said.

I thought that perhaps he was like my uncle Anton. I thought perhaps he tasted his drinks as Uncle Anton tasted wine in Copenhagen, and forgot to spit them out.

We heard the lady telephoning next door. We couldn't hear what she was saying, but it sounded like scolding. It sounded as if she were giving the specialist a thorough good scolding, my mother said.

'But you'd hardly think she would,' she said.

I imagined the specialist as a little man with close-clipped red hair and a shirt open at the neck, and a shabby old jacket frayed at the wrists. I imagined he must be like Uncle Anton.

The lady came in again. She told us that she had rung up for the specialist and that he would be here any minute.

'I'll get you a cup of coffee in the meantime,' she said.

'No, please don't do that,' my mother said.

'But of course I shall,' said the lady. 'You must have a cup while you're waiting.'

'They'll charge us for it,' said my mother when the lady had gone out into the kitchen. 'It'll be an expensive cup of coffee, I'm afraid.'

I peeped out of the window. I saw the strange houses on the

opposite side of the street. I looked at the spectacle-lenses, which lay in long rows in the glass case on the table.

'Don't touch,' said my mother.

'No, I won't touch. I'm only looking.'

'That's right,' she said, and yawned.

She'd been pasting bags nearly all night.

Then the lady brought us the coffee. She brought it on a big tray with a cup for herself too.

'And what are you going to be when you grow up?' she asked.

'I'm going to play the violin,' I said.

'Are you!' said the lady. 'Well, it's nice when children know what they want. Plenty of them don't.'

'But that's just his nonsense,' said my mother. 'He can't play at all.'

'Still, it's not a bad idea,' said the lady.

'That may be,' my mother answered. 'But it's not for a boy like him. We haven't begun to think about it yet, anyhow.'

'No,' said the lady, 'there's plenty of time. And one never knows.'

'No, one never knows,' said my mother.

Then the specialist came. He was a big fat man. He wasn't a bit like Uncle Anton. He was very red in the face. One could see all the veins under his skin, a close network of red blood-vessels. I could see this when he drew me between his knees saying he was going to have a look at me.

'Take my hat and hang it outside, Miss Poulsen,' he said.

So the lady's name was Miss Poulsen. She took his hat off. Ash from his cigar showered down over his waistcoat.

'Pooh,' he said. His breath smelt like Stougård, by the ice-ponds at home.

'Pooh,' he said, opening my eyes with his thumbs as the doctor had done. 'Turn round,' he said, 'and read what's on the card over there. Let's see how far you can get,' he said.

I turned and read out what was on the card. I read all the way from the big B at the top to a tiny z at the bottom.

'What the hell's supposed to be wrong with him?' he asked. 'He's got eyes like a hawk.'

'I don't know,' said my mother. 'It's the teachers at his school.'

'School-teachers know nothing about it. What do they say?'

'They thought there was something wrong and he couldn't see properly.'

'Well, now you've heard him for yourself. He could read the whole thing.'

'Yes,' said my mother.

They didn't know I'd learnt the card by heart. The specialist didn't know and my mother didn't either. They didn't know I'd got into the way of memorizing what was written on the board at school, once I'd been allowed to go up and look at it.

The specialist turned me round to him again. He pressed my eyes through the lids. He pulled down the blinds and lit the lamp beside his chair. He took out a big glass from his drawer. He peered into my eyes. The lamp was reflected in the big glass or whatever it was.

'There may be a structural defect in the right eye,' he said, narrowing his own eyes to see better. His mouth pulled itself crooked. 'There may be a structural defect. But that's something he was born with. If it gets any worse he can wear spectacles. Come again in a year's time and I'll prescribe some for him. But if he's just lazy, spectacles won't help.'

'He's not lazy, I don't think,' said my mother. 'But he never seems to look where he's going.'

'Then he must just learn to look where he's going,' said the specialist.

It cost two crowns.

'That was easily earned,' my mother said when we came out into the street. 'I wish your father could earn two crowns as easily.'

'Yes,' I said, thinking that it would take my father a whole day to earn two crowns.

'Still, I'd gladly have given five to hear what he told us,' she said.

'Why would you?' I asked.

It was raining. Dead leaves lay all about, wherever there were trees. And even where there weren't trees. We went to the ruin. There was a little lake there, and a park. We sat on a bench and ate the food mother had brought in her handkerchief.

'We ought to thank God,' she said. 'We ought to thank God before we start eating.'

'Do you think so . . .'

'Yes,' said my mother. 'We'll give thanks first.'

We knelt on the bench. This was wrong, of course; we ought to have knelt on the ground, but the ground was so wet. We knelt on the bench and clasped our hands on the back of it, and my mother thanked God because the specialist had said it was only a structural defect – whatever that might be. She thanked God because He had given her a normal child, and because I could have spectacles if it got worse.

'But remember,' said my mother, 'spectacles are no good if you're lazy, or awkward.'

'No,' I said. 'But I'm not lazy.'

'No, I don't think you are,' she said.

It was raining and our food got wet and dead leaves lay all about us. One could see the grey sky through the empty window-holes of the ruin with the red jagged walls.

'How silly of us,' said my mother. 'We could have gone straight to the station and sat in the waiting-room.'

'We couldn't have prayed then,' I said.

'We can pray anywhere,' my mother answered. 'Remember that. It doesn't matter where you are, you can always pray.'

'Yes,' I said.

We bought an ash-tray for my father. It was made of glass and had a picture of the ruin gummed to the bottom, with the words 'Greetings from Kolding'. We had never had an ash-tray before and we unpacked it twice on the way home. We thought it was so pretty. We would put it in the best room. It should lie in the middle of the oval table so that everybody could see it as soon as they came in.

'So it was all for nothing,' said my father.

'Yes, all for nothing,' my mother admitted. 'Except we needn't worry any more.'

'Well, you had your way.'

They said no more. They didn't talk any more about the specialist or about there being anything wrong with me. We pasted paper bags to earn the money it had cost. My father was at 'the Ground'. He had been there the whole summer. It was almost like a regular job, but it wasn't regular, because on days when there was no work for him there was no money either. He drove horses to the station. He carted dung. He cut chaff. But it wasn't good work. It was bad, for the pay was poor and there was always a long way to walk and it was twelve hours a day. But one had to be thankful for it, all the same. One had to thank God for it.

One day my father came home in a cab. It was the horse-dealer's own fine carriage that brought him. He was sitting in his dirty working-clothes. He was very pale. His left hand and arm were bandaged.

The driver helped him down and he was sick on the pavement.

'That's the anæsthetic,' said the driver. 'It's nothing to worry about. He's not tight,' he told some people who had stopped to look, and others at the windows. 'He's not tight. He's just been under an anæsthetic.'

My father had caught his hand in the chaff-cutter. His index-finger had been cut off. He told us how it happened. He lay on his back in bed, very white, and told us how he'd been pushing with his left hand and suddenly the blade came. But it hadn't hurt. He hadn't felt anything.

'It was just like – that!' He struck a quick blow with his right hand. 'Just like that, and the finger was gone.' There'd been a thin stream of blood, but not too much for him to stop by pressing the stump against his blouse.

'Like this,' he said, and he showed us how he had held his finger.

He'd been taken to hospital in a cab and brought home in a cab.

'And I'll get the insurance,' he said. 'Everybody says I'll get the insurance.'

People from the rest of the house came in to hear what had happened, since my father had come home in a cab and been sick on the pavement. Christensen the moulder came, and Klyver the carrier, and Ravn.

'Almost lucky, really,' said Ravn. 'You're bound to get the insurance,' he said. 'Mortensen got enough to buy a tobacconist's. But then it was three fingers he lost. You wouldn't get so much for one. And it's your left hand too; that makes a difference. But you'll get the insurance all right.'

Ravn stood in his grimy foundry-clothes at the foot of the bed, working out how much insurance we should get.

'You'd have got more for the right hand,' said Ravn.

Ravn went on reckoning up our insurance-money, and it was clear that he envied my father his good luck.

'But it won't be enough for a tobacconist's,' he said as he went.

So my father stayed at home for a bit. He stayed at home and got wages all the same. If it had been summer he could have gone out and done one or two jobs in the allotment with his right hand. But it wasn't summer, and he couldn't find anything to do but read the Bible. And it made him queer.

'Seems strange,' my mother said to Laursen the builder one Sunday in the Tønnes Street hall, 'that a man can get queer from reading the word of God.'

'Perhaps it's too strong for him,' said Laursen the builder. 'God's word is mighty strong. It's like being chastized with scorpions and burnt with hell-fire,' he said. 'Specially if you've got a soul with no skin to it.'

71

So my father had a soul with no skin to it, I thought.

'Tell him to keep off Revelations,' said Laursen. He said it as if it were *braendevin* or some other poison.

'That's just what he broods over,' said my mother.

'I once turned queer myself from reading Revelations,' Laursen said. 'I used to see horsemen on black horses, and white horses with golden snaffle-rings, and fire coming from their nostrils. And the stars in the sky turned into shining images, and one night I saw a golden cross, a shining cross, planted out in the middle of the sea and reaching right up to the Milky Way. I was living in Esbjerg then,' Laursen added, to explain the sea part of it.

'Yes, well, it's not like that with him,' my mother said.

My father slipped away from the meeting after a little while. He had been sitting by the door, and when the singing and speaking was going on he slipped out. He went down and sat in one of the privies. He was like me at school, now. And yet here there was no break and nobody he need be afraid of. All the same he slipped out and down the stairs and over to the privy. He sat there smoking. Sometimes he stayed there for the whole meeting. You could see the smoke coming out between the planks.

'Is there something the matter with you?' my mother asked when we left.

He didn't answer.

'There must be something the matter, to make you like that.'

He still didn't answer. As usual, he walked a little behind my mother and me, in silence. When we got home he remained standing in the gateway. And he didn't come up. I had to go down and tell him supper was ready. But he was no longer in the gateway. He wasn't in the yard either, nor in the coach-house nor in the garden behind the stables.

'I wonder whether perhaps your dad didn't go for a turn in the woods,' said Klyver. 'He went off that way, anyhow. He was blubbering a bit. I couldn't see him, but I could hear him.'

It was dark. The lamps were lit. I thought I'd go as far as

where the woods began. I wanted to see whether my father was there. He wasn't. There was only the black wood and the road and the footpath which disappeared into the darkness. I stood there for a bit, hearing the wind rushing in the trees and the branches grinding hard together. Once I called him, but no answer came.

'Father!' I shouted.

Once I thought I smelt his tobacco. I thought perhaps he might be standing behind one of the tree-trunks, and just not wanting to answer. He was like that sometimes. But I was afraid of the dark. I dared not stay there and I dared not call again, so I started home. But on the way home I noticed something queer. I noticed that round all the lights there was a rainbow shimmer. And when I went on looking at the light it arranged itself in three rings: one red, one green and one yellow. I thought of Laursen the builder and of what he saw after he'd been reading the Book of Revelation. But I had never read Revelations. Yet all the same I saw rainbow rings round all the lights.

I wanted to tell my mother about it when I got in, but she didn't want to listen. She asked what had become of my father. I said that Klyver thought he'd gone into the woods.

'So it's happened again, then,' said my mother. 'I'm afraid it's happened all over again,' she said quietly, as if nobody must be allowed to hear.

8

My mother hit on a thousand things to keep me out of the house. Wouldn't I like to go and see Marentcius? Or have a chat with Stougård? Had I ever been right round the wood? Perhaps Lydia would go with me . . . Wouldn't I like to go and see Valborg's chamber-organ?

There wasn't time to answer one suggestion before she made another.

The truth was that my father couldn't bear to see me. But at the same time he couldn't bear me to be away. He sat bolt upright on his chair all day long, just staring in front of him. He sat staring with wide-open eyes, and yet he saw nothing. The most he ever did was to move his chair up on to the platform, rest his elbows on the window-sill and watch the trains as they came and went – watch them with his chin in his hand, motionless.

My mother did her pasting. She pasted and tapped up and pasted again. She didn't say anything. If I came in she turned her face towards me. She nodded or made a sign that I was to go out again. She never stopped pasting.

'Will you play horses?' said Anders.

'All right,' I said, and we played horses.

'See those two half-wits?' cried Else. 'They're playing horses.'

'He's not a half-wit,' said Rudolf. 'He's mad. That's much worse.'

'You can come up to my place if you like,' said Lydia. 'I've got some pictures to show you.'

So I went up to Lydia's place.

Lydia had no pictures. She found some old magazines and we looked at those. Not for very long.

'You mustn't mind them teasing you,' she said.

'No,' I answered.

'I mean – about your father.'

'There's nothing the matter with my father,' I said.

'No, of course not,' said Lydia.

Pause.

'They tease me too, about my mother,' she said.

I looked away. I loved Lydia. Especially when we were alone together. But I didn't want to talk to her about my father. And I was embarrassed when she said anything about her mother; I didn't know how to answer.

'You oughtn't to play with Anders,' she said, 'or they'll tease you about that too.'

'They can tease me if they want to. I don't care.'

We could hear Lydia's mother singing in the kitchen. She sang loud and shrill in a voice that sometimes cracked. She talked to herself too.

'Don't listen,' said Lydia. 'You're not to listen.'

'I'm not listening.'

I looked at the rooms. They were quite different from ours. They were bigger and grander. There were carpets on the floors. There were two armchairs. There was an aspidistra in the middle of the table. There was a palm on a pillar. The place smelt of cigar-smoke and flowers. It smelt of flowers although it was winter. Lydia's father was a post-office clerk.

Lydia's mother came in. She was in a smart frock but it was undone at the back. Her petticoat hung below it. Her face was blotchy red.

'Billing and cooing, eh?' she said.

'Go to your room, mother,' said Lydia. 'We don't want you here.'

'Oh, so you don't want me here . . .'

Lydia's mother came up to me. She bent over me. She smelt

75

of *braendevin*. She kissed me suddenly on the forehead – a big, wet kiss.

'Go to your room, mother,' said Lydia. She said it louder than before.

'Dear me, dear me. I'm intruding I see . . .'

She stood looking at us with swimmy eyes. She swayed a little. Then she turned on her heel and went.

'Now you've seen my mother drunk,' said Lydia. 'Now I don't like you.'

I thought that was funny, because I'd seen Lydia's mother drunk before. But perhaps she didn't know about that.

'I'll go, then,' I said.

'Yes,' said Lydia.

But when I was putting on my cap in the hall she came out to me.

'It's only today I don't like you,' she said.

'Oh.'

'And only if you tell the others. If you tell the others I shall hate you till I die.'

'Yes,' I said, for I could understand that very well. 'But I won't,' I said.

Lydia looked at me for a moment. Then she came up and kissed my cheek. I thought it was odd, this way they had of kissing. But I was glad. I was glad that Lydia kissed me.

'Will you shake hands on it?' she asked.

'All right,' I said, but I didn't know how I was going to manage this.

I went downstairs and at the street door I met Lydia's father. He was coming home from the post office.

'Where have you been?' he asked.

'Up with Lydia.'

'I thought as much,' he said. 'But don't do it again.'

'It was Lydia who asked me to come.'

'I dare say, but you're not to do it. You're not fit company for my daughter,' he said.

He shoved me aside and went past me up the stairs.

I looked at the coffee-mill in the shop-window. And at the *kringle*-bread at the baker's. I went to the ice-ponds to look for Stougård, but he wasn't there and I could see through the window that he hadn't been there. There was no fire in his fireplace and his work-blouse hung thin and limp and cold on a nail. So I went to find Marentcius. On the way I met Anders' mother.

'Anders likes being with you so much,' she said. 'He says you're so good at playing with him.'

'No I'm not,' I said.

'You might all of you be a little kinder to Anders,' she said. She hid her hands under a blue check apron. 'You might all play with him a bit now and then,' she said. 'He's always so grateful.'

'Yes,' I said.

Marentcius' mother asked,

'Do they want you out of the way at home?' She had a way of smiling that I didn't like.

'They said I could come and play with Marentcius,' I told her.

'I daresay they did. But Marentcius has homework to do,' she said, 'and he'd rather do that. But you can go into the wood-shed if you like. You can play with his toy theatre so long as you don't break anything.'

'Thank you,' I said, and I did. But after a time I got bored with sitting by myself in the woodshed, and I went to see Valborg.

Valborg and her mother came to the Sunday meetings too. They lived in a villa. It stood high up on a hill at the edge of the woods. You had to go in through the kitchen so as not to disturb her father, who was a master at the grammar school. Sometimes he had pupils with him, and when he hadn't got pupils he read.

'Valborg and her sister are playing duets; that's what you can hear,' said Mrs Thomsen. She was frying something on the stove. She sat down to do this because she suffered from rheumatism. 'Go on in if you like,' she said.

I had never seen anybody play duets before. I thought it looked nice. It looked nice when it was two girls – and all those hands on the keyboard.

'We're playing Beethoven,' said Valborg.

'Oh,' I said. But I wasn't sure what Beethoven was.

'I'm glad you've come,' said Valborg. Her sister said nothing; she just stood there tidying some music. Soon afterwards she went away, looking annoyed.

'Don't take any notice of her,' said Valborg.

I could hear her father next door talking in a schoolmastery voice.

'Now, are you sure you understand?' he was saying. 'Because unless you do you won't be able to do the next one. Look, we'll go through it again.' You could hear him writing on the board with chalk.

'Father's got a pupil,' she said. 'It's one of the masters from the free school. His name's Vesterstrøm or something. Would you like to see the organ?'

'Yes, please,' I answered. I was thinking that now I knew something about Mr Vesterstrøm – something that nobody else knew.

Valborg showed me their chamber-organ. She explained the stops.

'I'll teach you the notes if you like,' she said.

'I could never learn them.'

'Of course you could.'

I thought I could too, really.

She began looking for a book.

'We might as well start at once,' she said.

Valborg was twelve years old, or thirteen, but she wasn't like any other girl. She was prettier and more grown-up. She was different, too.

'What's Beethoven?' I asked suddenly, while she was explaining to me about the lines and the spaces between the lines.

'Beethoven?' she repeated. 'Why, you know that. Everybody knows.'

'Yes,' I said.

'Then why do you ask?'

'I just thought you might explain it another way.'

'Another way . . .? He was a great composer.'

'Yes,' I said. But I didn't know what a composer was, and I didn't want to ask.

I learned my notes that afternoon. There was nothing difficult about it. I learned the notes and I'd found out something about Mr Vesterstrøm – something that nobody else knew. I thought that if I'd known it before I wouldn't have let him flog me. I should have told him I knew something about him.

It was dark when I went home. It was dark, but the street lamps were lit. They shone with the rainbow shimmer round the yellow core of light. When I'd been walking for a bit the shimmer arranged itself in three rings. I had told my mother about it again and she thought it was rubbish. I thought that if it was rubbish, then what Laursen the builder said was rubbish too, with his white horses and his black horses and the golden cross planted out in the middle of the sea. That was rubbish, even if he had lived in Esbjerg.

'Where have you been?' my mother asked when I got home.

I told her. I didn't tell her I'd been to Lydia's, and to Marentcius's place; I said I'd been to see Valborg, and learnt my notes.

My father was asleep on the couch, and we talked quietly so as not to wake him.

'What did Sister Thomsen say?'

'Nothing.'

'And Valborg?'

'She played Beethoven with her sister and then she taught me my notes.'

'What's Beethoven?' asked my mother.

'Everybody knows that,' I said.

There was a smell of paste, I thought, and stale tobacco, and all the rubbish we burned in the stove.

'Have you done your homework?' my mother asked.

'Yes,' I answered. I hadn't, but I didn't need to.

We ate alone. My father lay asleep on the couch beside us, but we ate alone. He was sleeping heavily. He snored. Now and then he turned and said something in his sleep which we couldn't understand. My mother had left her pasting-things on the table; we sat at one corner and ate off an old newspaper. When we had nearly finished my father suddenly woke up.

'Queer how I can lie here and sleep, with you two eating close beside me.'

'You were tired,' my mother said. 'It's only natural when you can't sleep at night.'

'I wonder. Wonder if you put some sort of muck into my dinner,' he said, looking at her sharply.

'Put something in your dinner?'

'It can't be natural to sleep the way I do.'

'I don't know how you sleep,' said my mother.

'You were doing something in the kitchen when you were making the porridge.'

'What I was doing was making the porridge.'

He looked darkly at us both.

'A man can't get anywhere with you two,' he said. 'You gang up against me.'

'You're ill,' said my mother. 'If I hadn't thought all along that you were ill – that it comes hardest on you – I'd be really angry.'

'Don't sit there making faces!' my father shouted suddenly. He hit the table so that the brass shade of the lamp rattled and my mother's bowl of paste jumped.

'You'd better go to bed,' said my mother.

'Already?'

'Go to bed,' she said. 'D'you hear me? Do I have to say everything twice before you understand it?'

I went into the bedroom and shut the door after me. But I didn't go to bed. I sat in the dark and thought that perhaps at this moment they were playing duets up at Valborg's. I thought that if one lived like that one could easily be good.

80

I thought about Lydia too. But she had her mother, and I wasn't fit company for her, whatever that might mean.

Next door my mother was pasting paper bags. Sometimes I could hear my father sighing. But they didn't say anything to each other. Outside it rained and hailed now and again, and the wind sent it dashing across the skylight. Below us the Christensens were laughing. They were always laughing. Up here we never laughed.

Sometimes people would come to my mother and say they thought she ought to get my father into hospital. They thought it would be best.

'If I hadn't been a night-nurse there myself,' said my mother, 'perhaps I'd have thought so too. Now I know it's the worst thing that can happen to anybody.'

She had often told us how they were put into strait-jackets or into a cell, or were beaten up by the male nurses if they were violent.

'I wouldn't send my worst enemy there,' said my mother.

They were laughing below at Christensen's, and the rain and hail dashed across the skylight. But in the room next door my father and mother sat in silence. My mother pasted paper bags and my father sighed now and then, but they didn't speak.

I undressed and got into bed. I undressed without them hearing me and got into bed and lay looking up into the darkness, and fell asleep. Once during the night I woke up. I don't know why – I hadn't heard anything. I was just suddenly awake. I could see something at the foot of my bed. Something big. A person. My father. I could hear him breathing and bending forward. My mother lay asleep beside me. My father wasn't where he ought to have been, on the other side.

'Father,' I said.

He said nothing.

'Father, are you cross with me . . .?'

The dark form at the foot of the bed didn't stir. It was my father. He didn't stir. He didn't say anything. He just stood there.

'Father,' I said again. 'I'm getting so frightened.'

'If I was really your father,' he said, in quite a faint voice, 'blood would tell. You wouldn't be frightened then.'

My mother woke up.

'Why have you put out the night-lamp?' she asked, groping for matches. 'And why have you taken away the matches?'

My father didn't answer. He just stood at the end of our bed. He stood there without moving. My mother wanted to get up and find the matches and light the lamp again.

'No need,' he said suddenly. 'I'm getting into bed now.'

And he did. He still had his left arm in a sling. He used to go to the doctor to have the dressing changed. But we didn't ever mention that there might be something else the matter.

'I'm getting into bed now,' he said, and sighed. And he did. He lay down slowly on his back. But he lay with his eyes open, I noticed. He didn't shut his eyes; he just lay looking up into the darkness. My mother fetched some matches; she lay with her eyes open too and looked up into the darkness. None of us dared sleep. It went on for the rest of the night. It went on until Klyver began racketing about down in the yard, feeding the horses and leading them out and putting them to. It went on until people began going to work and the spinning-mills hooted six o'clock.

ABELINE came now and then in the evenings and showed me the fingering on the guitar. She came with a brooch and white ruching at the neck and pince-nez on a cord pinned to her chest. She showed me the fingering and we sat twanging away together, for she brought her own guitar with her. It had a mother-of-pearl peg for each string, and little flowers, and a green embroidered ribbon which she slung round her neck. It was more than an instrument; it was something she put on and became grand by wearing. My father sat and watched us and my mother watched us until she almost forgot to paste, and there was brightness in both their faces. They brightened as soon as Abeline got inside the door and took her fine guitar out of its oilskin bag. 'He's not so bad, you know,' my father might suddenly remark, after he'd been watching Abeline placing my fingers. 'I don't think I could learn all that – not so quickly, anyhow,' he said, trying to place his fingers in the air. 'Fingers have got too stiff for it now,' he said.

'It sounds really beautiful,' said my mother. 'Like a string band,' she said.

'Yes, he soon picks it up. It won't be long now before I have to pass him on to someone else,' said Abeline.

'There can't be anybody better at it than you, Abeline,' said my father. 'I can't imagine anybody in the world could play better than you do.'

'Some people can do something like this, with the hand loose across the strings.' Abeline showed what she meant. It sounded just like harps.

But it was difficult to go on twanging the guitar without anybody to sing to it. We just had to sing.

'We're not blessed with much talent that way, you know,' my father said. 'But if it will help the boy we'll have a go.'

My mother found the song-book we used on Sundays, and we sang from that. My mother had to stop pasting to sing, and my father sang rolling his r's, in a strange, unfamiliar voice. I forgot to watch Abeline's fingers and follow her through the positions because I was listening to my father's voice and my mother's voice, as they sat there in our own room round our own table and the little lamp, singing.

'That must be how it'll sound in heaven,' said my father. 'All joyfulness and songs of jubilation.'

Abeline said, 'Scripture tells us it will be harps, but I've never seen a harp.'

'Have there been any since the days of King David?' asked my father.

'I've never heard of any,' said Abeline.

'They couldn't ever sound more beautiful than two guitars like this,' said my mother.

We drank coffee out of the best cups with the sprays of roses and the gold rims, and the silver tea-spoons.

'Now I know what you were thinking of when you bought them,' said my father. 'But who'd have thought it then? We'll get a new lamp – another bigger one – before you come next time, Abeline. This poor light won't do for you. It's all right for us, but not for when you got to play with your fingers on the strings and your eyes on the book at the same time. We'll get a lamp, Abeline, so you don't need to wear those glasses; they don't suit you.'

My mother was silent. So she was probably making up her mind about something else. We had talked about a new lamp before my father was ill. We had talked about lots of things we were going to have when at last the insurance-money came through, including a new lamp. But now it seemed as if my mother were deciding something else.

There was no bother over me at school now. I didn't know why there wasn't, but it was nice, I thought. We had another new master. He wore dark glasses. His name was Lieutenant Christensen. Marentcius didn't like him.

'You can't tell what he's thinking,' said Marentcius. 'It's because he wears those glasses.'

I felt I understood quite well what he was thinking.

Mr Vesterstrøm let me have an arithmetic book in front of me now, so I didn't have to go up to the board and copy down the problems. This made it easy. So easy that I did too many of them. And Lieutenant Christensen said I needn't read aloud in the Danish lessons; I could just follow in my book. That wasn't difficult either.

The only bother came when we had singing, and I didn't mind about that. There was trouble because I would always make up a second part. I made up second parts to all the songs, and the exercises too. I tried to put seconds to everything, and sometimes it was difficult. Sometimes my seconds wouldn't fit the songs we sang.

'Who's that growling?' asked the singing-master.

His name was Herskind and he always seemed to be in a rage. He had a yellow-brown skin like a mulatto, and curly hair, but he wasn't a mulatto. He just came from Holbaek.

'Who's that growling?' he shouted again.

Marentcius stood up and told him I was the one.

'I don't want to tell tales,' said Marentcius, 'but he's got an awful voice and he growls in my ear the whole time, and that makes me growl too,' said Marentcius.

I was told just to listen and not sing with the others. I tried. But I couldn't help singing, and I couldn't help making up a second part.

Marentcius stood up and asked if he might move.

85

'No,' said Mr Herskind. 'You're not the one to move – you're so musical. You've got a voice like an angel.'

I was told to go and sit on the growler's bench, where I wouldn't put Marentcius off, or the others who could sing. I didn't care. It wasn't a thing that mattered.

'It's fun being a growler, isn't it?' asked a boy called Oluf. Only five minutes had passed.

'I don't know quite,' I whispered.

'It'll be fun now there's two of us,' said Oluf. He had always been alone there before.

'Why's it fun?' I asked.

'Well,' said Oluf. 'You can idle.'

So we idled, and Oluf thought it was fun. But I made up second parts all the same. I made them up inside me. Nobody could hear – not even Oluf, although he sat beside me. And Marentcius who sat a long way away couldn't hear. He just looked at my mouth now and then to see if I was singing. But I didn't move my lips. I was singing my second part quite inside. And even if I hadn't Mr Herskind couldn't have heard me, for he was walking up and down and playing his fiddle out of tune. Sometimes he played so much out of tune that it sounded like a slate-pencil on a slate. Or else he stood at his desk beating time with the cane. Mr Herskind wouldn't have been able to hear me even if I'd sung at the top of my voice. Once he came up and prodded me in the hair with his fiddle-bow.

'It's a pity you're a growler,' he said. 'But there's nothing we can do about it.'

'No,' I said.

'Don't let it worry you,' he said. 'A chap can be a decent person even if he is unmusical. And you don't look as stupid as Oluf.'

Oluf heard this, but he didn't care. Neither of us cared. We sat side by side, not caring.

One day Lieutenant Christensen told me to stay behind when the others went out for break. He wanted to know if I went to an oculist.

'No,' I said.

'Have you ever been to one?'

'I went to a specialist,' I said.

'And didn't he say you ought to wear spectacles?'

'No,' I said. 'He said it was a structural defect.'

Then he asked how long ago this was, and whether we'd thought of seeing another specialist. I knew what he was getting at. He wanted me to wear dark glasses too, of course, so that then there'd be two of us and he wouldn't have to be the only one. But I wasn't having that.

'If you'd rather stay in for break, you can,' he said. 'You can go out into the playground or into the street or stay up in the classroom – whichever you like.'

'Thank you,' I said. 'I was afraid there was going to be some more bother over me.'

'No bother, but we may have to talk to your father and mother about another specialist.'

I thought he could if he liked, and that I could quite well wear dark glasses if he didn't want to be the only one.

'Oo, what a funk!' said Marentcius. 'Just because you're cross-eyed they let you stay in the classroom. But we'll make up for it on the way home.'

Outside it was snowing. The snow was tumbling down; it was like a white curtain in front of the windows. Oluf was kept in. He was always being kept in. I stayed behind with him and helped him do his sums.

'I wish I could do them like you,' he said. But he just couldn't understand them. He could write down the figures as he was told, but he didn't understand. It seemed to him any other figures would do as well.

Oluf had glands. He had been at the sanatorium. He was nearly two years older than the rest of us. Two years in the sanatorium had set him back, and he found everything difficult.

'I'll help you,' I said. 'I'll do all your sums for you from now on, for ever.' I didn't say that out of kindness. I said it because I was suddenly conceited. But Oluf thought I was decent. He had four øre which we spent on sugar-toads. Sugar-toads were stick-jaw toffee in a little cornet.

'I hope there hasn't been any more bother over you,' said my mother when I got home. I had a bump on my forehead because I'd run into a lamp-post.

'I suppose you expected it to get out of your way,' said Gertrud, who had come up to borrow something or other.

'How silly you are,' I said.

'Not so silly as to think lamp-posts will make way for me, anyhow.'

'Oh well, so long as there hasn't been any more bother over you,' my mother said.

My father didn't have his hand bound up any more. He just wore a leather finger-stall lined with cotton-wool on the stump. He could help to clear snow, if he was careful, and he could gather firewood. He wasn't frightening any more. In the evenings he went out to gather firewood in the woods. One couldn't do that as a rule. Only really poor people were allowed to. But since the firewood was lying there anyway, doing no good to anybody . . . When he came home he settled down to read. My mother pasted paper bags, and sometimes I helped her, and my father sat reading and we had a nice time again. Now and then he would ask me to play the guitar. Could I play this or that song? But the guitar was nothing on its own, and now that I was a growler . . .

'You're always so obstinate,' said my mother. 'You never want to do the things you can do.'

My father sat twiddling his matchbox between the fingers of his right hand.

'I was thinking maybe we could get hold of one of those violins some time,' he said. 'If that would be better,' he added after a pause.

'So that's what you're thinking about, is it?' said my mother.

It was that winter that my father made a sled for me. He built it out of some old boards that were much too thick and the

88

sled was far too heavy, and it had no iron on its runners. It was no good for anything but dragging behind you.

He had made it one day when my mother and I came back from Horsens. We'd been to see a new specialist. He didn't think there was a structural defect. He didn't think I should have spectacles, not even dark ones. But on the other hand I must have drops. I must have drops every night when I went to bed, and he wanted to see me again in a month.

'Any better this time?' my father asked.

'I don't know,' my mother answered. 'He can still read just as many letters on the card – no more and no less. It was just the same, and the oculist says it don't fit in with other things.'

'Well now,' said my father. 'That's queer. Well . . .'

'Aren't you going down into the yard with the others?' he asked.

'There's no children down there now,' said my mother.

'No, maybe not, but he ought to have a breath of fresh air.'

'Why, we've just walked from the station!'

'I might go with him,' said my father, as if he hadn't heard my mother's protest.

So we went downstairs. I didn't know why, but I wasn't afraid. We went right down into the cellar, where we had a place for fuel. And there was the sled. I saw it by the light of the stable lantern. It looked huge. It was so big one might have hauled timber with it.

'It's yours,' my father told me.

I said nothing.

'It's a solid job,' he said. 'It won't break even if you run into something with it.'

'No,' I said.

'Different from the gimcrack things the others have.'

'I'd rather have had one like those,' I said.

'I been working on it all day so you could have it when you came home,' said my father. He picked up the front of it and held it in the air. 'It's a solid job,' he said. And he let it drop so one could hear what a solid job it was.

'Well, there it is, and it's yours,' he said. 'We'll see if the snow keeps on, so you can take it out to the hill.'

I didn't say anything, but I didn't want to take it to the hill and I could have done without the snow.

'Well, we'd better go up again,' said my father. 'I thought you'd like it, but now we'll go up again.'

The stable lantern hung from a hook in the ceiling. Dust lay thick on the glass. My father blew out the light and then struck a match so that we could see our way up. Shadows flickered like big spiders' webs under the ceiling and in between the boards.

'You've got a kind father,' said my mother, when she heard that he'd made me a sled.

'Yes,' I said. 'But it isn't any good.'

'No good?'

'It isn't like the others'.'

'There's no pleasing you,' said my mother. 'You ought to be glad to have something the others haven't got.'

'Not when it's a sled. It ought to be like all the other sleds.'

We were standing in the bedroom and my father couldn't hear what we were saying. He had sat down with his Bible as soon as we came in.

'You must thank your father for the sled,' said my mother. 'You must thank him and tell him you like it.'

'Even when it isn't true?'

'Yes, because it will be true. Perhaps not tonight nor to-morrow, but one day, when you understand, you'll be glad he gave it to you . . .'

I couldn't see what there was to understand about a sled. It just had to be a good one, and like all the other sleds in the world.

I didn't think about the sled any more that night. I thought about the new specialist and how he guessed that I saw rainbow-coloured rings round the lights outdoors at night.

'I suppose you don't see coloured rings round the street lights at night?' he asked.

'Yes I do,' I said, and I thought it was extraordinary.

'Didn't he ever tell you this?' he asked my mother.

'I don't think so,' she said. 'He's funny that way. He doesn't talk much about things he doesn't want to talk about.'

'But I did tell you about this,' I said.

'I don't remember it,' said my mother.

'Does he run into things much?' the specialist asked.

'Not much, I don't think,' said my mother. 'Sometimes he does. The other specialist said he must learn to look where he's going.'

'Yes, of course he must,' he said, 'if he can.'

'Foggy vision?' he asked.

I didn't know what foggy vision was. Nor did my mother.

'So he hasn't got that,' said the specialist. 'But I must see him again soon. I must see him at least once a month.'

In the waiting-room my mother talked to other women who had come either for themselves or for their children. There were never very many; usually two or three. They talked about how expensive it was to see a specialist and about the sickness-fund not paying anything towards it and about it being hard for working-people.

I disliked them. They were so miserable. I didn't care for miserable women, and I knew quite a lot.

I thought it was extraordinary that the specialist could guess all those things, and next time we went there he had a new card for me to read from. The card had figures on it. I hadn't seen it before and I couldn't read very many. Then he brought out the one with the letters. I did better with that.

'Do you know it by heart?' he asked.

'Yes,' I said.

So he'd guessed that too.

'It's worse than I thought,' he said.

My mother said, 'And he's getting worse about running into things. Soon he'll have no skin left on his nose, and he's always got bumps on his forehead. He runs into everything.'

'Hm,' said the specialist.

'It didn't really get bad until after you asked about it,' said my mother. As if that was the reason. As if I ran into things because the specialist wanted me to.

Sometimes Oluf came to see us. He didn't ask if he might. He just came and sat and hung about.

'I think he's a nice boy,' said my mother, 'but there's no go in him. He's not clever like Marentcius. I'd rather you went about with Marentcius,' she said. 'You can learn from him. You must try to be like him.'

I didn't tell her it was Marentcius who had made me a growler. I didn't say either that, more than any of the others, he threw snowballs and hid so that I couldn't get my eye on where they came from. I just said that Marentcius's mother would rather he studied. He was always studying when I went there to ask if he could come out and play.

'And you'll soon be too old for that sort of nonsense,' said Marentcius's mother. 'Marentcius is, anyhow. How are things at home, by the way?' she asked.

'All right,' I said.

'Didn't your father have some sort of trouble?'

'No,' I said.

'Surely he lost a finger in the chaff-cutter.'

But I knew very well it wasn't that she was thinking of.

'And doesn't your mother take you to a specialist . . .?'

'Yes, she does,' I said.

'Well, then . . . And you say everything's all right!' she said. 'But Marentcius would rather get on with his work. He doesn't want to come out today.'

So I went away. I went down into Marentcius's yard and looked into their woodshed and saw that his toy theatre and other things were all neat and tidy. It was always neat and tidy in there. It looked as if each separate piece of firewood had been laid in place. And paths had been dug through the snow. One path to the gate and one across to the lavatories and one to the dustbin. It was a fine, big yard and everything was tidy.

I lingered a little in the gateway and watched people passing in the street. Then Marentcius came.

'What are you gaping at there?' he asked.

'I'm just looking,' I said.

'I don't want you looking in my gateway.'

'No,' I said. 'But I was waiting to see if you'd come down and play.'

'I don't want to play with you,' said Marentcius. 'You're too stupid and too cross-eyed.'

It was almost as it was with Oluf. I thought Oluf was too stupid, and he had glands too. My mother didn't like it. She was afraid they were catching. And sometimes glands gave one bad eyes. Sometimes people stopped my mother and me in the street just to ask.

'Is it glands?' they asked.

'No,' my mother would say. 'We don't quite know what it is.'

'But it must be something.'

'Yes, of course it's something. We just don't know what it's called. The specialist never said the name.'

'What a shame,' they said. 'It's hard on you and your husband. You've got worries enough as it is.'

'Yes,' my mother said.

'Strange to think that a child like this should live, when so many strong and healthy ones die. They die of diphtheria and scarlet fever and all sorts of things, and yet a boy like him – he'll go on living, you'll see.'

'Yes,' said my mother.

'Glands can be catching,' she said. 'And they've had scabies too.'

I didn't know what scabies was.

'I don't like him hanging about here,' said my mother, 'but he's a nice boy. It's just that there's no go in him like there is in Marentcius.'

I liked playing with Anders best. He was quite willing to be harnessed to my sled and pull me. And I went for walks with

93

the butcher's dead dog, so that he didn't always have to lie on the wet mat and sleep. And I visited Stougård in his house and ate baked potatoes.

My mother had taken a morning job as charwoman. She began the day early and pasted bags. Then she went over to the lawyer's and cleaned the house. Then she came home and cooked dinner. Then she pasted bags again. She pasted until late at night. It was because I was costing so much money. And I had to have decent clothes on when I went to the specialist every month. And my father was out of work. Sometimes he went down to the docks, but there was hardly anything doing there in the winter; and sometimes he found some job or other with a carter, but nothing steady.

'If you had any go in you,' my mother said, 'I know you could get a steadier job.'

For my father had no go in him either. He thought we were well off. He had nothing to complain of. He was quite satisfied.

'I'd like to have a sofa in the best room, for instance,' my mother said. 'And a clock, and the new lamp you were talking to Abeline about.'

'Vanity,' said my father. 'It is written . . .' he said.

Sometimes I went up to Valborg's and was allowed to play her organ. I knew my notes. She helped me to place my fingers properly. I learned a song out of a book. First it had two voices and then three. Sometimes I didn't want to go on; I stayed at the same place because I thought that particular harmony was so lovely. There was one place in the song that I always looked forward to. Now and then I stopped before I got to it. I didn't want to wear it out.

'If you came a bit oftener,' said Valborg, 'and if only you'd practise, you'd be very good.'

With the organ it didn't matter about being a growler.

'But you must look up at the music,' said Valborg. 'Not down at your fingers all the time.'

I looked at the music when Valborg was out of the room.

After that I knew it; I could sort of see the notes in my head.

'Remember to keep pedalling, too,' she said, 'so that the wind comes evenly.'

I forgot to pedal. I was bewitched by the sound. Sometimes it sounded exactly as I'd expected, and at other times quite different.

'Come again tomorrow. Come every day,' said Valborg.

But I didn't come again tomorrow, and it was often a long time before I did come. I didn't want Marentcius to know about it. And I didn't want Oluf to know either. I never talked about going up there, and I only went now and then when I couldn't find anything else to do. When Stougård wasn't in his house, or when I didn't feel like playing horses with Anders or going for a walk with the butcher's dead dog.

'I don't see you using the sled much,' said my father. 'I made it for you, though, and it's a solid job.'

'It's no good for sliding downhill on,' I said, 'and you can't steer it.'

'It don't matter if you run it into things. I made it strong so it wouldn't hurt,' said my father. 'If you like we'll try it out.'

I didn't want to, but I said yes all the same. And we tried it out. My father set off, pulling me. It was evening, and there were rainbow rings round all the cores of light. And in some places the pavement had been scraped bare of snow, but my father pulled me along just the same. Anders was standing by his street-door.

'Can I come and play horses too?' he asked, but my father didn't answer.

We went into the woods. We went up the steep path to the allotment gardens. You couldn't slide on that path; it was too steep and the snow was too soft. When we got right to the top my father sat down behind me on the sled.

'Now I'll show you how we did it back home in Sweden,' he said, and tried to get going. 'We sat like this and steered with our feet.'

My father tried to get the sled to move, but it wouldn't. Some people came along; they stopped to watch us. But it wouldn't.

'You need some iron on those runners,' said a man.

'Back in Sweden you can do it all right without,' my father said. 'But of course we've got mountains there.'

We moved a little way and stopped again. The man who was watching us laughed. Snow lay fine and white between the black stems, and above the network of branches the stars were twinkling. Out on the fjord people were skating.

'I'll pull you for a bit,' said my father. 'But I must wrap you up better first.'

He took off his jacket and wrapped me up. Then he harnessed himself and set off. We went along the path. We passed the bench where he sometimes sat in the summer, when the young trees were leafy. Now there was just a web of bare, sticking-out branches. We went past the great oak and the forester's lodge. There to the left lay the gardens, windswept and snow-covered. Then came the dark spruce forest with a few beeches in amongst it. My father said nothing. He just pulled. Now and again I could see his big hand on the rope. He held it behind his back. Most of the time I could see nothing at all. But there were stars in the sky. Lots of stars. Pale stars. And the snow creaked under my father's footsteps and under the sled-runners. And at times he trod on brittle ice which broke with a noise like glass, and at other times a dry twig snapped. And although there was no wind the woods rustled. The rustling sounded like a long, deep breath. My father just walked. He went by ways I didn't know at all; he came to places I had never seen. And if I had I would never have recognized them now because it was almost night, and because the woods were bare and there was snow and darkness and stars. My father was thinking, I suppose, and he never noticed the sled, which ran very well here. He walked, and the sled with me on it followed, and he never gave it a thought. He walked as if he were alone.

We followed the edge of the woods. Out to the left lay wide, open land. As vast as steppes. I began wondering what I should do if wolves came. But no wolves came. I heard them howling in the distance – unless it was dogs. But we saw no wolves. The path turned to the right and lost itself in the darkness of the woods where one couldn't see anything, and my father was still silent. I remembered the story of Abraham and Isaac, and wondered whether my father wanted to take me out and sacrifice me. But he hadn't brought a knife with him – not so far as I knew. I could well imagine that my father might want to sacrifice me, but he had to have a knife and he had to have fire for the burnt-offering. I didn't know what kind of fire that was – whether perhaps it was different from ordinary fire that came from a match. I supposed it was . . .

'Father,' I said, 'am I going to be sacrificed? Am I going to be a burnt-offering like Isaac?'

My father didn't hear me speaking to him. He didn't hear anything. He just walked and pulled the sled with me on it, and he had no idea that he was pulling the sled and me. He was walking as he walked when he was alone.

Once he stopped to light his pipe. I heard him take it out of his pocket. I heard him crumble tobacco in his fingers and fill his pipe. I saw the flame which he shielded in his hands, and the red glow on his face every time he pulled at the pipe. But we didn't say anything. I heard the noises of the woods and the fields, and the noises of the fjord. The fjord was frozen right out to its mouth, and above it were stars, as in an arctic night.

My father went on walking and walking. Mile after mile he walked, dragging the sled behind him – or so it seemed to me. We met nobody. There was nobody but us in the whole world. All the others were frozen to death. Buried under mountains of snow. Dead. From time to time I dozed, woke up and saw that I didn't know where I was, and shut my eyes again. I don't remember being cold. I don't remember being frightened. I thought that this must be my father's own special way, which he wanted to show me; and that it was a good way but much too long for me and much too difficult to find. I couldn't think

97

how my father could find it either, but I wasn't afraid that he would get lost.

My mother was standing waiting for us. She was standing in the gateway looking and not knowing which direction to look in. She had been to the lawyer's house to help in the kitchen because they were having a party. But she hadn't spent half the night there. She was angry. She was angry because my father had been pulling me through the woods at night. And she was angry because she had had to stand there in the gateway looking out for us, and because passers-by asked her what she was waiting and watching for.

'Well,' said my father, 'I just thought we might try the sled.'

'Couldn't you have done that in the daytime? Other men take their children out on Sundays. But on Sundays you just sleep.'

'Yes, unless we're at the meeting,' said my father. 'But I thought I'd let him see the woods.'

'At this time of night?'

'Have you ever seen them now, I wonder?'

'I got other things to do,' said my mother. 'And other things to do besides waiting and not knowing whether you've fallen off the dock with the boy, or what . . .'

We put the sled away and went upstairs. The butcher's dead dog was sleeping on the mat, which was wet with melted snow. The little lamps were burning on their shelves, so I knew that everybody hadn't gone to bed. But the house was quiet.

'Never do anything like that again,' my mother said when I was undressed.

'No,' I said.

'You must tell me where you're going and how long for,' she said.

My father had sat down with his book. I could hear him turning the pages to find the place he had got to last time. I could hear Christensen's voice below, and Gertrud's, and her mother's. They were talking. There were thick frost-flowers on the skylight. But I wasn't cold. On the contrary it was cosy, I thought. There was a cosy sound from the rest of the house, where people were talking about going to bed, and it was cosy with us too. My mother pasted paper bags and my father read. The door stood ajar and the yellow strip of light fell across the wash-stand that we never used and across the green ottoman. It bent and ran up the wall to the slanting window, which was quite blocked out with frost-flowers.

'It was a grand night out,' said my father in a low voice. He talked quietly because they thought I was asleep. 'It was a grand night with frosty stars, and snow creaking underfoot, and the woods. And quite still . . .'

'Twenty-two – twenty-three – twenty-four – twenty-five,' counted my mother.

She was pasting bags. There had to be twenty-five in each bundle. She was checking them.

'You can talk while I'm tapping up,' she said, 'not while I'm pasting.'

'All right,' said my father. 'I thought he ought to see the woods and the snow and the stars.'

'And couldn't he do that in the daytime?' asked my mother.

'Stars,' said my father. 'Stars, in the daytime . . .?'

99

10

THE specialist had asked whether I ran into things
much. I didn't – it was only now and again. Perhaps
I wasn't very good at looking where I was going, but
other people ran their heads against doors too sometimes, or
didn't see a ladder propped against a wall, or a slack clothes-
line. It happened to people who were half-asleep. I was always
half-asleep, my mother said. I was half-asleep when I counted
bags, or when I was sitting with something in my hands which
I didn't need to look at.

'I'm not asleep,' I would say. 'I'm just thinking.'

'And what great thoughts might *you* have?' my mother
would ask.

'I don't know,' I said.

It was so difficult to explain. Most things were much too
difficult to explain. It was better to say 'I don't know' at once,
and then as a rule there were no more questions.

I used to think in the street too. That was part of my oddness,
my mother said. I wasn't so alert as other boys of my age, and
that was probably why I ran into things. But it didn't really get
bad until after the specialist had asked about it.

'You'd almost fancy he'd told you to run into things,' said
my mother. 'If it's because you can't get your eye on them,
then walk a bit slower, do. You rush off so – you're so wild.
You either rush off,' she said, 'or you go sleep-walking and day-
dreaming and getting nowhere.'

He'd asked about something called 'foggy vision'. We didn't
know what foggy vision was. But one day it struck me that

sometimes when I came indoors after playing outside I couldn't see anything. Things had no outlines. They melted into each other. Pictures became part of the wall. The paper bags on the table became part of the table-top. I might over-turn a chair because I hadn't seen it was there. It wasn't as it had been before when I couldn't get my eye on it. Now I simply didn't see it.

I didn't think it was anything to talk about.

'How did you come to knock over the chair?' my mother asked. 'Didn't you see it?'

'No, I didn't see it,' I said.

'Couldn't you get your eye on it?'

'Yes, but I just didn't see it.'

I knew where everything was. I knew where my belongings were. I could find them in the dark if necessary. I could count paper bags without looking. There was no reason to talk about something that went away by itself after I'd sat down for a bit.

'Look, there must be something wrong,' said my mother one day. 'You've often run into things, but you've never tried to pick up things that aren't on the table, or not seen the plate of food in front of you . . .'

'It's because everything goes muzzy when I've been out,' I said. I didn't say foggy, I just said muzzy.

'You must have been out too long,' said my mother. 'Maybe the snow has dazzled you. Try not to be so wild. And I don't much like your going on the fjord.'

I was given skates that winter. I was given them on condi-tion I never skated on the fjord. I would willingly have promised not to go on the ice at all if they'd wanted me to. I was given skates and I learned to use them on the ice-ponds with Stougård. Men cut the ice there every day and Klyver carted it away. But it froze so hard and for so long that there was always a part where one could skate without danger of falling in. And if one did there was so little water that one could barely have got a wetting. At first Stougård helped me on and off with my skates. Then he stood on the bank telling me what to do and conducting me with big gestures. He never came on to the ice himself. The three little ponds were for him as perilous as oceans. Gales might arise and huge waves wash over him if ever he left the safe shore.

'Not too far over on that side,' shouted Stougård. 'We cut ice there last Wednesday. For God's sake!' he shouted. 'You'll drown! You'll go down with all hands if you don't keep to the eastern end.'

It was true that they had cut ice there last Wednesday, but it had frozen solid again already. And it was difficult to keep within so small a space as he would have liked.

The edge of the woods was powdered grey with snow. The meadows lay like boundless white plains, and where at last they did come to an end the fjord began. A black stream of people poured ceaselessly along the fjord all the way from the lime-kiln; a steady movement of people cruising in and out between each other along paths that were daily swept free of snow. A sort of town had sprung up on the ice of Skyttehus Bay: a town with streets and market-places and squares, bordered by banks of snow, and there was as much coming and going and as big a crowd as if there were a fire or a Christmas exhibition. I had been there with Oluf and with Marentcius and with Lydia, but only on foot, without skates on my shoes, and that was no fun. The icebreaker had cut a channel up the middle of the fjord, where an occasional steamer came in with coal or cattle-cake. Or a ship bringing timber or lime. You could go right out to this channel. You could stand close by it and watch the chunks of ice turning over at the bows and along the vessel's sides. You could shout to the seamen who walked the deck or stood by the rail. And the sun shone on the broken surfaces of the ice, and on the snow, and all round you there was a flashing like diamonds. The air was pierced through and through by sharp glints of light. They dazzled, and the snow dazzled. No wonder you sometimes ran into somebody.

'It's not that,' said Stougård. 'What's it matter if you run into people? That won't hurt you or them. It's the eel-fishers I'm thinking about. It's those devils, those damned eel-fishers that come and cut holes in the ice every night, and fish with flares, and never think that next day some little idiot like you might come along and tumble in. If you did, you'd have to walk home under the ice; we'd never get you out. What do you want to go out there for, anyhow?' asked Stougård. 'Where do you want to get to? There's no sense in it. If you skate round this pond a hundred thousand times you'll have been as far as the world's end, and seen just as much.'

So I set myself to skate round the pond a hundred thousand times. Systematically. Grimly. Every tenth time Stougård made a mark in the snow. When I reached a hundred he made a big mark. At a thousand he'd make a cross.

Fire and smoke rose from the tall, thin chimney of the lime-kiln. Trains came and went: the three o'clock, the three-thirty and the four-thirty. Lights went on in the carriage-windows. The grey-powdered fringe of the woods darkened. And I sped on towards the world's end. But Stougård got cold standing there, though he'd been shouting and conducting the whole time. He got cold and needed a hot potato and a dram. He went into his little house and lit the lamp – a little train-oil lamp that had been converted to paraffin.

The skates cut into the ice. And the dry, stiff-frozen reeds rustled each time a little gust of wind came. Far away one could hear voices on the fjord. And I was on my way to the world's end. But before darkness came to put a stop to the journey I was overtaken by the fog. It came from the fjord but it also came from the woods. It began somewhere or other very far away and stole nearer, closer and closer upon me. It rose up from the snow round the ponds, up out of the ice, and at last it seemed to come out of my own eyes. Fog. Thick, dense, impenetrable fog on all sides. Sky, earth and all sank beneath this grey wool.

For a bit I could get along all right in spite of it. I had the rhythm in my body, and knew pretty well how many kicks it was along each side of the pond. I had a fairly sure sense of distance; all the same, there was to be no reaching the end of the world that day. For I began to run into the reeds and into the banks, and plunge elbow-deep in snow. I wasn't quite so sure where the fjord was, and Stougård's house, and the woods and the road.

I sat down where I was on the ice and unscrewed my skates.
'Well,' said Stougård. 'I'm glad you've had enough at last.'
'I haven't,' I said.
'But it's evening now,' said Stougård. 'It'll soon be so dark we shall have to think about getting home.'
'It's not the dark,' I said, 'it's the fog.'
'Fog?' said Stougård. 'Is it foggy? Can't be much.'
He stood at the open door and looked out. It had got so foggy that I nearly hadn't found his house.
'Fog – well, we may get some,' said Stougård. 'We get it most mornings and evenings, but there's nothing much yet.'
There was a smell of sweet malt and sour yeast, and there were the scorched potatoes and Stougård's quid of tobacco and his wet clothes. But there was fog inside the house too. Just at first I couldn't even get my eye on the lamp – the old tin lamp that had been converted from train-oil to paraffin. But when I'd been standing for a bit, there it was after all. It was like a yellow brightness in the fog. A yellow patch without firm outlines. Something bright swimming in the fog.
On the way home I held on to Stougård's jacket, stealthily. Not hard. I didn't think he'd noticed it.
'Are you afraid I can't walk straight?' he asked. ' 'cause you needn't be. I can walk straighter than you can.'
Stougård came upstairs with me.
'There's something wrong,' he said. 'I don't know what it is, but he keeps talking about fog. He says it's so foggy he can't see, and that the fog follows him into the house.'
'Yes,' said my mother. She was pasting. 'Yes,' she said. 'We've noticed there's been something the matter.'

My father said I'd better go to bed. But I didn't want to go to bed because I wasn't tired and I wasn't ill and it wasn't very late.

'Still, you'd better go and lie down for a bit,' said my father.

So I went into the bedroom and undressed. I could quite well undress in the dark or without looking. I'd always been able to do that. I undressed feeling that the world was wicked and my mother and father were wicked. I went to bed and lay with my eyes open and noticed that by degrees the fog was lifting and the room was getting properly dark. In the other room Stougård was talking to my father and mother. Talking about me. He told them a whole lot of things. I wouldn't have believed he'd tell tales like that.

The darkness went nice and black. It was right close up to my eyeballs, and there was no fog any more. And I could see a yellow strip of light at the bottom of the door, where the step was worn. There wasn't anything that needed talking about any more. And in the dark I could see the skylight with the frost-flowers on it. There was nothing to lie in bed for; I was only here because my father and mother were wicked. And Stougård. And the whole world. It had got foggy on the fjord and in the meadows. Sometimes it got foggy down in the yard. And the fog didn't go when I came indoors. Was it my fault? Must I be ordered to bed just because it was foggy? Next thing would be, they'd shoo me into bed when it rained, or when there was a thunder-storm, or in the summer when the sun kept on shining and we needed rain.

I lay looking at the yellow light between the worn step and the door, and at the skylight where the crystals of the ice-flowers sometimes caught a glint of starlight or moonlight, or whatever it was. I lay listening to the voices in the next room, where Stougård was talking to my father and mother. And voices down in the street. And people dragging sleds, and a horse with sleigh-bells. And a man coughing. But there was no more fog. There was only darkness, and different coloured lights in the darkness. And there was nothing anyone need talk about any more, and no reason for me to lie here.

Next day we went to the specialist. We went although it was a fortnight too early. My mother told the people in the train about me. They came into the carriage and asked where we were going and she told them. She told them about the coloured rings I saw round the gaslamps in the street at night. She told them how the specialist had asked whether I ran into things much. And how he'd talked about foggy vision and none of us knew what foggy vision was, but now I'd got that too. I crouched and squeezed myself up small and wished I could disappear altogether. They talked about me as if I weren't there, or as if I could neither hear nor see. They talked about me as if I were a thing.

'That's queer,' said a woman. 'Almost seems as if the specialist himself brought it all on, just when he wanted it.'

My mother had never thought of this.

'Perhaps he can cure colour vision and foggy vision,' said the woman, 'so of course he takes care the boy gets them.'

'But that's just it: he can't cure him,' said my mother.

'If he can't be cured,' said the woman, 'let's hope he dies before it gets too bad, and before you've paid out too much money for nothing.'

'Yes,' said my mother.

'You could always try another specialist,' a man said. 'There's a professor in Copenhagen . . .'

'Costs a lot to get to Copenhagen,' said the woman. 'Nearly five crowns. And on top of that, what would he charge? And you got to think whether it's worth it in the end.'

'Luckily my husband thinks we should do the best we can for him,' said my mother. Usually she said 'his father' or 'the boy's father'. It was funny to hear her say 'my husband'. 'My husband thinks we ought to try everything. If only we knew who was best and what was best.'

'The best would be a professor in Copenhagen,' said the man.

'No specialist who's any good is going to bury himself in Horsens. I'll get the address and send it you.'

'Thank you,' said my mother; but I could tell she didn't think he meant it. We'll never get that address, she thought.

Then we came to Horsens. There was the square with the fountain in it in front of the station. There was the grey, dreary street. There was the specialist's waiting-room.

'What, here again already?' he said when he saw me. 'Couldn't you bear to stay away from me any longer?'

My mother didn't like him talking like that.

'You said something once about foggy vision, doctor,' she said. 'We didn't know what it was then, but now I'm afraid we do.'

'Didn't you know what it was? You ought to have asked me,' said the specialist. 'But as a rule when you've got it you aren't in any doubt.'

'I suppose it isn't your questions that brings these things on, doctor, is it?'

'How do you mean?'

'Well, first you asked if he kept running into things. He never used to, but after that he did. Then you asked about foggy vision and we didn't know what it was – and now it's come.'

He pulled down the blind so that the room became quite dark. He lit the lamp and brought out his mirrors. I had to look past his left ear and past his right ear. I had to look up and I had to look down. I had to look over at the doorhandle.

'Yes,' he said, 'there can be no mistake.'

'Do you often have headaches?' he asked. 'Not just a little bit of one, but really bad – so bad you can hardly stand it?'

'Doctor, please don't ask questions like that,' said my mother. 'I'd rather you didn't ask any more about anything, after what's happened.'

So he asked no more questions. He pressed one eye and then the other. I had to read with one eye and then the other. With the right eye I couldn't read at all.

'There, that's all,' he said. 'Now will you wait in the waiting-room for a little while? I want a word with your mother.'

So I sat down and waited. The window opened on to a yard, a paved yard with a little garden. And there was a tarred fence. And the backs of some other houses which had big, grand-looking windows. It was neat and clean in the specialist's yard, and in the other yards on each side.

I sat and waited. There was an old man waiting too. He was reading a paper. He didn't say anything. I could hear the specialist's voice and now and then my mother's voice: it sounded as if she was crying.

'It would be a miracle,' I heard him say, 'and miracles don't happen nowadays.'

'Copenhagen,' he said. 'Yes, you could always try, but who . . .?'

I couldn't hear what my mother was saying; I could only hear her voice. I could hear the tone she was talking in: it was the one she used for sad things. I could hear that she was crying.

'It's bad,' said the specialist. 'But I've been afraid of it all along.'

'You've never mentioned it before!' said my mother suddenly, loudly and rather sharply. 'You never mentioned the word before today; if you had we might have gone to Copenhagen long ago.'

'Copenhagen, Copenhagen!' said the specialist. 'Everybody thinks it's just a matter of going to Copenhagen. It's a miracle we need here,' he said.

Mother said nothing on the way to the station. She held me by the hand. She almost always did. We walked along the dreary grey street where the specialist lived. We crossed the square with the fountain immediately opposite the station. But she didn't say anything. She was silent, as she usually was when she was angry.

'I can't help it,' I said.

'No,' said my mother.

'Then why are you so angry with me?'

'I'm not.'

'But you're not saying anything. Just like when you're angry.'

She was crying.

'It isn't my fault,' I said.

'No,' said my mother. 'If it's anyone's fault it's mine. God visits the sins of the fathers upon the children,' she said.

'But you're not the fathers,' I said.

'You don't understand.'

'Can't I know what the specialist said to you while I was waiting?'

'He said that you . . . He said you might – go blind,' said my mother.

'Oh,' I said. 'And what else?'

'Nothing else.'

'Is that what you're crying about?'

'Yes,' she said.

'You were talking about a miracle, too.'

'I don't know,' said my mother. 'I want to talk to builder Laursen about that.'

'Why, is he the person who has to do with miracles?'

'You do ask silly questions sometimes,' said my mother. She spoke rather irritably.

But I would rather she should be irritated than that she should cry. I couldn't see there was anything to cry about. I shut my eyes and tried to walk with them shut. I thought it was interesting. It was interesting until I stumbled over a kerb-stone.

'There you go again, not looking where you're going,' said my mother. 'If I hadn't been holding your hand you'd have fallen.'

So I didn't play that game again until we got into the train. I sat by the window and shut my eyes and counted to ten or twenty or even more before opening them again. I had made this journey so often that I knew lots of the houses and copses and farms and fields. The game was to guess how far we would have come by the time I'd counted to thirty or fifty. I never could. I thought every time that we'd come much further than we had. I thought it was exciting to play at being blind.

'Don't sit like that with your eyes shut,' said my mother.

She couldn't know that I was only playing at being blind.

'You're not to keep your eyes shut like that,' she said. 'I can't bear it.'

'Oh,' I said; and I thought it was funny that my mother couldn't bear even that.

The fields spun round, and the little woods, and the farms and level-crossing boxes, and snow lay everywhere. The telegraph-wires rose and sank, and I could see it all when I wanted to, and I could see the sky over it, and sometimes a bird having a rest on a telegraph-wire. Presently, when it began to get dark, I should be able to see little lights lit in the windows, and the lanterns at the entrances of the stations we stopped at. I should be able to see everything. What was there in that to cry about or be irritated by or not be able to bear . . .

Foggy vision – the specialist's funny word . . .

The fog only came if I stayed out of doors too long. I had noticed that myself. I just mustn't be out for so long at a time, that was all. I could play indoors. It was nothing to cry about.

Next evening we went out to builder Laursen's, to talk to him about the chances of a miracle. My father and mother had talked about it all night and all day. I don't believe either of them slept. My mother had pasted bags all night, and between-whiles – whenever she tapped them up – they talked about miracles, and my father had read the Bible. But now all three of us were going to talk to Laursen about it. We had on our Sunday clothes. This wasn't on Laursen's account, nor his wife's; it was because one couldn't somehow talk about miracles in one's ordinary clothes.

It was a long way to Laursen's place, and for the first time the air was soft and mild. The sun shone all day and my father had heard the sawfinch.

'Back in Sweden we called it the sawfinch,' he said. 'But I dare say they've got another name for it here; they mostly do. When the sawfinch starts sawing it means there's warmth coming up from the ground too,' he said. 'The fire in the earth and the fire in the sky have equal power then. Of course I don't know if it's true,' he said, 'but that's what the old folk said.'

Roofs and gutters dripped, and the wind smelt different. It didn't smell of sulphur any more – or perhaps it wasn't sulphur the wind had smelt of while the frost lasted. It had smelt like the sparks struck from paving-stones by clog-irons at dusk. Now it smelt of water. Of water and mouldering leaves and a tiny bit of earth. But ice still lay on the river, and there was snow in the gardens and on the road.

'We'll be hearing the sawfinch tomorrow too,' my father said.

'Is that what you've been thinking about all this time?' my mother asked. 'Don't you think we ought to turn our minds to something else just now?'

'I'm thinking of that and other things,' said my father. He wasn't walking behind as he usually did; he walked with us and held my other hand. 'Doesn't do any harm to remember the sawfinch, and think maybe the frost's over for this winter.'

My mother didn't answer. I knew she was wondering how best to put it to builder Laursen. All of a sudden he'd become as important a person as the specialist.

I was playing my own game of shutting my eyes and counting to some number and seeing where we'd got to when I opened them again.

Over on the other side of the river there was a wood, and there were woods up on the hill too.

On the right the houses came to an end, and fields and meadows ran down towards the river. On the left there were little houses and gardens. At one place the wood crawled down from the crest of the hill and came as far as the highway. But there it stopped. The trees stood by the road and dared not cross to the other side. At one bend there was a water-mill, but it wasn't working. And then at last we caught sight of Laursen's cement-works.

Only a year or two before there'd been just a wooden shed here. Now he had built himself a house with outbuildings, and the works.

He was walking about in his builder's clothes and was a perfectly ordinary man. There was no alleluia about him here in his own place. If one hadn't known one might think he was just builder Laursen, neither more nor less. It was the way he showed us round, and showed us how they made tiles and cement pipes and pillars and lots of other ingenious things. He was quite proud of how he was doing. Not once, not for a moment, did he mention God or blessing or anything like that. He was simply proud of how he himself had made things prosper for builder Laursen, and of all the things they could do – he and the boys and Stinmai and the whole family. And in the summer, or as soon as the frost was out of the ground, he was going to dig the foundations for yet another building with two little flats in it which he could let.

'H'm,' said my father. And 'Ah,' he said.

He knew something about cement-casting, and could ask questions now and then, which gave Laursen the chance of telling him more about his boys, and Stinmai, and his plans for the future. And my mother took care that we didn't go too near the wet cement or anything else in our best clothes.

'How mild the weather's turned,' said my father. 'And the sawfinch has started. So now –'

'And if we could manage to borrow a bit of money,' said builder Laursen, 'we might get the land on the other side of the stream. My property only goes as far as the stream now, and the price is sure to rise –'

He stood and pointed and explained and calculated what might be done. But there was no sign of any alleluia or praise be to God. If it hadn't been for the beard and the voice I wouldn't have recognized him; but for those he would have been just an ordinary builder who happened to be called Laursen.

'We've come on rather serious business really,' my mother said. 'There's something we wanted to talk to you about. Ask your advice about,' she said, correcting herself.

My father said, 'To tell you the truth we've been wondering about the possibility of a miracle.'

Yes, he really said that. But afterwards there was a peculiar silence. It was as quiet as if he'd said something improper.

When we went into the house and sat down at the scrubbed table my mother told him about me. She told him about my always running into things, about the rings of colour and about the foggy vision – all the things I knew already. Builder Laursen had sat down on the other side of the table, and was listening with his hands folded in front of him.

'We've thought about taking him to Copenhagen,' said my mother. 'But the specialist thought that wouldn't be enough. He thought we'd need more than that. A miracle, he said.'

My father said nothing. He wasn't listening, any more than I was. Perhaps he was still thinking about the sawfinch, and heard its rasping pipe inside his head.

'Things aren't the same now as they were in the days of Jesus,' said Laursen. 'We've got doctors and specialists. They weren't known in those days.'

'I seem to have read somewhere about men with special power in their hands,' said my father. 'And I wondered if maybe Ullnes or Staff was like that.'

Ullnes and Staff were from Norway. They came sometimes with Baron Wedell, and held jubilee-meetings for the Friends in the Tønnes Street hall.

'Ullnes and Staff,' Laursen repeated. 'They're good men, both of them. Strong in proclaiming the Word. Strong in testimony. But they're no more than God made them, and God made them Ullnes and Staff, neither more nor less.'

I thought it was clever of my father to mention Ullnes and Staff. If there had to be a miracle for me, it was more likely that Ullness and Staff could do it than an ordinary Dane like Laursen. But perhaps he felt hurt at being put in the shade like that.

'We mustn't forget,' said Laursen, 'that things are no longer what they were in the days of Jesus.'

In the kitchen his wife Stinmai was getting the coffee ready; we could hear her.

'H'm,' said my father.

My mother had fidgety thumbs. She moved a saucer on the table before her, and moved it back again.

'I'm just wondering whether perhaps God would give us a sign,' said Laursen. 'More than once in my life God has given me a sign, but that was mostly when we were living in Esbjerg.'

'Yes, if only we might have a sign,' said my mother.

I saw white horses in front of me, and black horses with golden snaffle-rings, and fire coming out of their nostrils, and mighty flaming crosses between earth and heaven. But I couldn't imagine that such marvels would be brought about just for my sake.

'We often overlook God's little signs, you know,' said builder Laursen, 'and I'm wondering whether He hasn't already shown you what His will is.'

'How –' My mother looked up. 'How?' she asked.

'You were saying it costs a lot to go to Copenhagen,' said Laursen. 'But now supposing God in His heaven thought that that was the way He could best do miracles today, and made you a present of the journey –'

'Then there could be no doubt about it,' my father thought.

'I've never heard of it snowing railway-tickets,' said my mother, rather tartly.

She thought Laursen was trying to slide out of it. He was talking himself out of the miracle, she thought.

Stinmai set out cups and we had coffee. We talked about other things too; about the cement-works and about the land on the other side of the stream. It was a relief.

'I see you still wear a finger-stall on that stump of yours,' Laursen said to my father.

'Yes.'

'I don't know how it is,' he said. 'Suddenly it seems to me as if there was some link between God's finger and yours – the one the chaff-cutter took. I suppose you got compensation,' he said.

'I haven't had it yet,' said my father. 'But from what we hear it should be along any day now.'

Laursen pondered for a time, looking before him with the Sunday look that went with the meetings in the hall.

'How blind the children of men can be,' he said. 'How blind we can all be and of how little faith – until the Spirit lets the scales fall from our eyes and we behold God's finger in all things.'

'Yes,' said my mother, but she didn't understand. One could hear from her 'yes' that she didn't know what Laursen meant.

'God took your finger so that you could afford to do His will,' he told my father. 'It's all so simple, when God of His mercy vouchsafes to breathe on our eyes and make us to see.'

I thought about the new sofa we'd been going to have, and the lamp, and all the things we had talked about. They faded away now and vanished as we sat talking about miracle-working with Laursen.

'God has His own ways of performing miracles,' he said. 'It doesn't always happen in the way you think it will. We're not living in the time of Jesus now. Today it can be a miracle to take the train to Copenhagen and see a famous professor. For what is a professor but God's instrument for performing miracles? That's what he is, even if he doesn't know it himself.'

'What a wise fellow that Laursen is,' said my father as we went home. 'He sees everything so clearly,' he said. 'He looks right into the middle of God's most secret thoughts.'

'Let's hope so,' said my mother. 'Anyhow we'll go. We'll go as soon as I've finished those coloured bags. We'll go next week,' she said.

II

'W HY didn't you bring him to me before?' asked the professor, without looking at my mother and without stopping even for a moment. I had his white forehead and snowy hair in front of me all the time, and a white hand moved first to one side and then to the other. It came back with a pipette or a lens or another pipette.

'Don't turn your head,' he said. 'Look at me all the time.'

The hand shot up and pulled a blind-cord. It lit a lamp.

'Why didn't you come a year ago, or two years?' he asked. 'Now I'm afraid it's too late. Look at me,' he said. 'How many fingers am I holding up? And now? And now?'

'You're cheating,' I said; for the moment I said two there were three or four. 'I shan't do it if you cheat.'

'Look at me again,' he said. 'Don't move your eyes. Tell me when you can see my hands.'

He stretched out his arms, I could see by his shoulders that he was doing something or other, but it was some time before I could see his hands, those white, professor's hands, moving up and down or in a circle, and coming a tiny bit closer together each time.

'Now,' I said.

'Not before? We'll try again.'

So we tried again, but it was the same as the first time so long as I didn't turn my head, and that I wasn't allowed to do.

'Highly restricted field of vision,' said the professor. 'You find it hard to spot things,' he said, 'little things – a ball, for instance, when you're playing, don't you? But once you've

caught sight of it – once it's come into your field of vision –
you can see it perfectly well.'

I said nothing, for he knew. He knew all about it.

'I can't think why you didn't bring the boy to me earlier,' he
said again to my mother.

It went on for a long time. It was endless. And I knew my
mother was thinking of all the people outside in the waiting-
room. They must be getting angry with us now, for wasting so
much of the professor's time and their time. When it was no
good. When we had come too late.

'Sit down on that chair,' he said to me. 'And would you come
with me a moment?' he said to my mother. 'I must have a word
with you alone.'

It was like the specialist in Horsens: he wanted to talk to my
mother alone. So there wasn't going to be any miracle, I
thought. A miracle must surely be something which happened
easily, without hurting – a word or two spoken in the right
way. And it hadn't been easy, and it had hurt. I was all
confused by the way it had hurt and by all the stuff he had
dripped into my eyes. I was so confused that I was sick where
I sat.

'You ought to have told me,' said the nurse who was tidying
up and putting things to rights. 'You must have felt it coming
on,' she said, 'and you should have told me.'

The professor came back with my mother. I couldn't see her
face. I couldn't see anything clearly now. I had foggy vision
from all the professor had done to me.

'Come back this afternoon, then,' he said. 'I must get him in
at once. You can quite well go home then, if you'd rather.'

My mother just said yes – an almost inaudible yes. But from
that one word I knew exactly what she was looking like. I
couldn't see her face, but I knew what it was like.

The nurse hadn't finished wiping up after me. The professor
came to the door with us.

'Next, please,' he said.

I expected a scolding for being sick, but my mother didn't

scold me. She didn't say anything. She just walked beside me holding my hand, down the wide stairs, out into the street and along towards Kongens Nytorv. She said nothing. She just squeezed my hand.

'Why are you cross?' I asked.

She didn't answer. She only squeezed harder.

We went out to Aunt Jane, who had a dairy in Marstal Street. We walked for the sake of getting some fresh air, but also to save the tramfare. I still had foggy vision. It had never been worse. I didn't say anything about it; I just walked and let myself be led, as I'd seen the blind girls doing. Once I was sick again. After that we took a tram, so we hadn't saved anything after all.

Aunt Jane had a sitting-room behind her shop. We sat there drinking coffee and eating stale Vienna bread.

'That's all I can offer you,' she said, 'but you can have as much stale Vienna bread as you like. When you've finished the day before yesterday's you can start on yesterday's.'

She never had time to sit with us for more than a moment. There were always customers in the shop – people she knew and had to talk to. But in between-whiles she ran up the two or three steps into the back room and asked questions.

'Well, the professor's right,' she said. 'Why did you put off coming till it was too late?'

'But we'd been to a specialist,' said my mother.

'A specialist!' she sneered. 'A specialist in the provinces is about the same as a vet here. Specialist!' she said.

Outside the trams rattled by, and the shop bell rang every time the door opened or shut, and my aunt had a telephone. That rang too.

'My nerves wouldn't stand it,' said my mother. 'I just couldn't stand living like this.'

People came and went, and aunt said pretty well the same things to all of them. But they didn't sound like the same things.

'Spring will soon be here,' she said, and 'A little milder

today, isn't it? We've had a bit of sunshine. A pound of butter was it? Oh, a half.'

To the next one she began by saying that we'd had a bit of sunshine, that it was milder and that spring would soon be here.

'How you can keep talking like that, Jane . . .' said my mother. 'How you can think what to say to all those people . . .'

'When are they going to operate on him?' she asked, next time she came in.

'Tomorrow,' said my mother. 'Early tomorrow,' she said. This frightened me rather. I hadn't heard I was to have an operation; but it seemed I was.

'Isn't Anton coming home for dinner?' asked my mother.

'No one comes home for dinner here. That's only in the provinces and the country. He'll be in this evening,' she said. 'Drunk, most likely.'

'Don't talk like that,' my mother said. 'Anton was always a good boy.'

'It's no more than the truth. He's all right,' said Aunt Jane, 'but he forgets to spit it out.'

'It's hard to have to do with wine and such-like if you're like that,' my mother thought.

'It's hard for me, living with him,' said Aunt Jane. 'But why's the boy to have an operation if it won't cure him?' she asked.

'I don't know,' my mother answered. 'The professor wanted it. It's not easy to argue with a professor. But I shall be sorry to miss Anton.'

The foggy vision had passed off, and so had the sick feeling. The Vienna bread must have helped. I could see my aunt with her long horse-face and red hands, and her American rocking-chair and the porcelain stove and all the things hanging on it to dry.

Then my Uncle Anton came. He'd looked in to welcome us that morning, he told us, but had come just too late. He'd been to the professor's too, but we'd just left.

'In the hell of a hurry, weren't you?' he said. 'Hell of a hurry.'

His face was rather red and blotchy. His shirt was open at the neck and his sleeves were frayed at the wrist.

'Had a bit of business to attend to on the way, of course,' he said, 'but even so –'

'I can guess where that business took you,' said my aunt.

'God, how dreary you look, both of you,' he said. 'You look as if you had cirrhosis of the kidneys and cancer of the liver. Come along, son – you come with me; we'll push off and leave these two miseries to themselves.'

I was startled by the things he dared to say, but I wasn't afraid of him.

'And what's he had to eat?' he asked. 'Warmed-up coffee and stale bread. I'll take him out and give him some lunch. If you like to come along, Lisbeth, you're welcome; if not, I know a little place where only men go.'

Uncle Anton took me by the hand and away we strolled.

'It's a damn shame about you,' he said. 'I popped up and had a word with the nurse at the clinic. A damn shame, that's what it is. And so you're going in this afternoon. Else I thought we might have a real good day together, just the two of us. Now it'll only be a potty little lunch. But you're sure to be coming to Copenhagen later, and then we'll show 'em – then we'll have our day, you'll see.'

We went to an eating-place my uncle knew. They knew him too. He told them what I had come to Copenhagen for, and that I was to go in that afternoon.

'So mind you do him really well,' he said. 'Bring us the best you have.'

'Too bad he's such a little fellow, damn it,' said one man, 'or I'd have stood him a good stiff schnapps.'

'I've tasted that at home, with Stougård,' I said.

'D'you hear that?' said my uncle. 'The little ruffian, he's started already!'

In a way they were all like Stougård. I liked being there. Their voices weren't sad. But it was a good thing my mother wasn't with us. I kept thinking the whole time what a good thing it was my mother wasn't with us.

In the afternoon we went back to the professor. Uncle Anton came too.

'But you're not to come in with us,' said my mother. 'You smell of *braendevin*, and you're not to come with us.'

'I've just had one teeny little schnapps,' he said. 'Why should that embarrass you? I feel all the better for it.'

'I'm sorry you're like this,' said my mother. 'Think what you might have been if only you didn't drink so much. You could have worn good clothes from morning till night.'

'And been all mildewy inside,' he said. 'Yes, you're right there, sister Lisbeth. I'll come and fetch you in a couple of hours,' he said. 'Meanwhile I'll find you a nice, sour-faced missiony place to stay in. You can't stay with Jane – you'd go out of your mind. I'm the only one strong enough to stand it.'

He began walking away.

'Hold on,' he said. 'Wait a bit, son. I promised you this.' He came back and dropped a whole crown into the breast-pocket of my sailor-blouse.

'Don't spend it all on drink,' he said.

My mother shook her head. I could feel her doing it. I could feel from her hand what she was looking like. I didn't need to look up into her face to know.

I was to share a room with a quarryman from Bornholm. He was lying in bed with a bandage round his head. He had got splinters in his eyes – stone splinters.

'Good day,' we said.

But he just lay there groaning and wouldn't say good day to anybody. His face looked like a stone. He was as grey as granite, and his two hands on the eiderdown were as grey as granite.

'You won't have anything more to eat,' the nurse said to me. 'Not until tomorrow, after it's all over.'

My mother stayed and put me to bed. She stayed until the nurse came and said she must go, and that a man was waiting

121

for her. 'Someone I couldn't allow further than the waiting-room,' she said.

That was Uncle Anton, who'd been to find a nice, sour-faced, missiony place for my mother.

Strange voices out in the passage, in the other rooms, everywhere. The clatter of crockery in the kitchen. Windows being opened and shut. A church clock striking. Striking with forlornness and homesickness. The quarryman complained and groaned.

The light was put out. The nurse said good night. Laughter and voices down in the courtyard and out through a gateway. But it wasn't the yard at home. It wasn't our gateway. It wasn't laughter I knew, and the voices were strange. This was a strange land, a strange world. I thought about where my mother was now, and my father, and my sister Kirstine.

I must tell you that I'm second in school now, and getting on well. And I want you to know that I'm thinking about our living together when I'm grown-up and you're blind. They say it may not be for a long time but I don't think we shall have very many years to wait.

Your affectionate sister,

Kirstine.

Dronningborg School, No. 2.

That's what she had written last, in the fine, big, round writing that was so easy to read. I had learnt it by heart. I learned all my sister's letters by heart. I could remember the last one until the next one came. There was always a long time between.

The Holmen church clock struck again, and the bells of the Raadhus could be heard from far away.

'You must get to sleep,' said the quarryman. 'Make haste and go to sleep; you can't stick it otherwise. That's the only thing you've got to think of. If you don't sleep you can't get through it. We ought to be able to sleep from the time we understand anything to the time we go back into the earth we came from. Sleep like a stone,' he said.

He turned and moaned: 'Oh – ho, oh – ho,' he moaned; but a little while later he was snoring, all the same. And the Raadhus bells chimed again with more homesickness and more forlornness. You could hear how big the town was, and how strange, and how uncaring. It didn't know me. It didn't know my mother. It didn't know I had a sister with brown eyes; a sister who would sometimes take me by the wrist, and who wrote to me in big, round writing. The people, the streets, the houses didn't care.

Once during the night I woke to find the quarryman out of bed. He wanted a pot.

'Can't anybody help me?' he said. 'Have I got to go on knocking myself black and blue?'

I could hear him rubbing his shin.

'You awake, boy?'

'Yes,' I said.

'Well then, get up and help me, can't you? You got nothing the matter with you yet. You've got your sight – you're all right until you come under the knife tomorrow.'

It was pitch dark, but I didn't mind darkness. In a way one could see very well in the dark. One couldn't see in fog. Foggy vision made one lose the sense of how far it was from one place to another, one thing to another. In the dark it was all right.

'There was a chair here last evening, and a table here,' I said. The quarryman had taken me by the arm with his granite hand. 'So we must go over to the wardrobe,' I said.

'What the hell do I want with the wardrobe? I can't piss into that.'

But in the end we both found the wash-stand, got into bed again, and went to sleep again.

'It's hard luck on you,' he said next morning. 'If I was you I think I'd run away. You shouldn't let them take a knife to you,' he said. 'First they suffocate you, then they cut you open, and you wake up before they've finished. If I was you I'd run away. You're not like me – you haven't got stone-dust and bits of flint and urgent things like that in your eyes.'

But I didn't run away, and it all happened more or less as he had said. He lay and waved to me in a tired way with one of his grey granite hands when they came and fetched me.

My mother wasn't allowed to stay in there. She saw the white operating-table. She saw the powerful lights. She saw the professor getting himself ready. Afterwards she told me all about it. She went out and waited in the passage.

'I waited,' she said, 'and waited and waited. It was the longest eternity I've ever known,' she said.

But at last the nurse came. The professor sent her out. He knew that my mother was waiting and he sent the nurse to tell her that the operation had gone well; better than he had dared to hope.

'Your boy won't go blind,' she said. 'From the way it's gone, the professor doesn't think he'll be blind.'

'Thank you,' said my mother. She said it to the nurse, but she was thinking of the professor and builder Laursen and God. She missed the green ottoman in the bedroom at home. She missed being alone. She was saying thank you for a miracle.

My mother didn't go home. She stayed, and spent every day with me. The nurse brought her a book to read; she read it aloud to the quarryman and me. It was a novel. The people in it had names you couldn't pronounce, but it didn't matter. It was a good book. The quarryman was out of bed, and he sat on a chair most of the time. I had bandages over my eyes, so I couldn't see him, but I could hear him sitting on his chair and sighing and rubbing his hands together with a horny sound. He listened when my mother read aloud, and in the evenings we talked about what might happen in the next chapter. We talked about the people in the book as if we knew them, and I thought of my father and his red book, which he never quite finished with.

My mother read, and when she was tired of reading she knitted. She was never idle, and at first she only read because the nurse had brought the book. She felt obliged to, she said. But as time went on it was different; as time went on she too got to know the people. But things happened which her reason couldn't accept.

'It says here that she sat by herself dreaming in the moonlight,' she said. 'Then how can anybody know what she was dreaming about or thinking about?'

'She must have told somebody afterwards, and they told somebody else,' said the quarryman. 'That often happens. If you don't want a thing to get about it's best to keep it to yourself.'

'It doesn't say here that she told anybody anything,' said my mother. 'I just don't believe it,' she said.

In the late afternoons my uncle Anton came. He had his frayed jacket on but my mother had made him wear a tie. He brought a little bottle in his pocket. It wasn't hidden; everybody could see he had a bottle in his pocket.

'It's madeira,' he said. 'There's no better medicine for a sick person. Drink up, little mole,' he said, and he brought a glass from the wash-stand. 'It tastes of nuts and honey. Here's health,' he said.

But I wasn't allowed to drink nuts and honey. My mother tasted it.

'It's a shame,' said Uncle Anton. 'By God it's a shame. It would do him good, and if he got used to it in time he'd make a fine taster. You taste best when you shut your eyes and don't look at anything.'

Then he went over to the quarryman.

'This isn't much good to you,' he said. 'You're used to dynamite. This'll seem like slops. But we can kill time with it. It's very good for killing time.'

'I'm afraid you forget to spit it out sometimes,' my mother said.

'I hope that was a nice, sour-faced missiony place I found for you,' said Uncle Anton.

'I don't complain. All I complain of is the price. How anybody has the face to ask two crowns for a bed . . .'

'It's cheap, when you think what you've been spared with Jane.'

The church clocks struck and the Raadhus clock struck, and nothing was quite as strange any more. One day they took off the bandages. One day I could see again, further and more clearly than ever before. That's what it felt like. I could stand at the high window and see Gammel Strand and some yellow house-fronts with early spring sunshine on them, and the rounded tower of St Nicholas. I could look deep into the sky until it swam; it swam with sun-fire and blue in a mile-deep spring sky.

'But we must give him some dark glasses,' said the professor. 'He'll have to wear dark glasses for the time being.'

So I was like Lieutenant Christensen. There were two of us with dark glasses now. I didn't want to wear them, but being two made it easier. Perhaps they wouldn't dare to laugh at me then. They could hardly tease me when the other one was Lieutenant Christensen.

A fortnight had been a long time to think of beforehand. It had lain ahead of us as something we couldn't see beyond. An ocean of time. The days were hard to get through – and the nights. Especially at first. Afterwards the hours passed more easily, and the last days weren't so bad. Once the two weeks lay behind us, they were nothing. Nothing to look back upon. I had been in Copenhagen a fortnight, I'd had an operation and been given dark glasses like Lieutenant Christensen. A fortnight. That was the time it took to work a miracle nowadays.

'But you must keep an eye on him,' the professor told my mother. 'Notice everything carefully. If he gets that foggy vision again, or the coloured rings round the lights, or headaches, you must bring him to me at once. I'll see him again in six months, anyhow.'

'Yes,' said my mother, thinking perhaps that there were limits to this miracle. But we were allowed to go home. We could go home, so long as we were careful to drip Pilocarpin into my eyes, morning, noon and night.

'If that's all that's needed,' said my mother. 'If just that will get him right –'

'We must see,' said the professor. 'But in any case you must bring him to me again some time in the autumn.'

We had left home at night. Everybody had gone to bed. We came back so early in the morning that nobody had got up. Nobody saw us go or come back. It was as if I'd never been to Copenhagen at all.

'Prove it,' said Rudolf. 'Show us something to prove it. A swan knife, for instance, or an air-gun.'

'Well, he's got blue glasses anyhow,' said Lydia, 'and they're so blue they're almost black.'

'That's only to hide how cross-eyed he is. Take them off,' said Rudolf, 'and let's see you squinting.'

Later, when Rudolf had gone and there was nobody else in the gateway, she came up and said,

'Don't take any notice. There's nothing you can do about it. My mother says that things you can't help you mustn't bother about.'

'Oh,' I said, because I didn't see it made things any better, and because I remembered that I wasn't fit company for Lydia.

I went about in my dark glasses and saw the world in a new light. A blue light.

'Sucking up to Lieutenant Christensen, that's what you're doing,' said Marentcius. 'Or are you trying to look like the blind girls . . .?'

Sometimes I peeped secretly over the top of the spectacles, or to the side of them, or put them in my pocket and marvelled at how pure and bright everything was; almost dazzling. I went about seeing. I looked at the chestnut-candles that were lit now, and at the faces behind the windows of L. Pode's Home for Blind Women. I looked at the knitting-bags and the grey knitting and the pale ovals of the faces, and heard the stringed instrument every time the door opened or shut. I looked at the meadows and the fjord, and at the white line of steam that the southbound train trailed after it far away towards Munkebjerg. I went about seeing, and was a perfectly ordinary boy. But when I put the dark glasses on again, far-away things disappeared, things not so far away grew fainter, and only things close to me were sharp and clear. I never got foggy vision now, even when I'd been out for a long time, and in the evenings there were no coloured rings round the street-lamps.

Sometimes in the evenings I went to Valborg's and learned new tunes on her chamber-organ. I played the music in front of me, or so she thought; really I still used to learn by heart. It wasn't cheating. I didn't mind Valborg knowing that I couldn't do more than one thing at a time: read first and then play. Then one could hear what was happening. Or one could look out of the window and play about wistaria instead of about a whole lot of black dots that flickered up and down on the lines and between the lines.

'What a pity you've got nothing to practise on at home,' said Valborg. 'You'd be very good, you know. Better than me.'

But I didn't particularly want to practise. I would rather come up to Valborg's. There was the piano that one was allowed to touch too. There was a fine, clean smell. It was all nice to look at, and they talked about other things. They talked about Beethoven and the Septet and about a book that Valborg's mother had read: things I didn't know about. But they just let me sit there, and didn't ask me any questions. I was allowed to sit and listen when Valborg and her sister played the Septet as a duet. I began to know it.

There were lots of plush chairs which always stood in the same places, and there was an embroidered table-centre. And on the linoleum floor in front of each window lay a pool of sunlight. Vases of daffodils stood on the window-sills, and they smelt sweet. Valborg's rheumatic mother had a rubber tip to her stick so that she shouldn't slip. They talked quietly so as not to disturb her father, who was asleep or reading in the next room behind a closed door. Playing didn't matter; he slept and read quite well to music.

I went to see Valborg and sat listening to them talk quietly about things I didn't know about; I listened to them playing and smelt the scent of daffodils, and they didn't ask any questions. Not even Valborg's mother asked whether a miracle had happened to me, although she came to the meeting in the hall on Sundays.

I came and I went, and when I went they said I must come again soon. But there were many days when I didn't go to see Valborg or Marentcius or anybody else. There were days when I just went about seeing.

12

B<small>UT</small> on Sundays there was church. There was the service, and Sunday-school and the meeting in Tønnes Street. Church with variations from morning till night. A ceiling lay over the day: a low, heavy ceiling of chiming bronze, of church bells.

In the mornings we went to church. This was not for the sake of the pastor or the sermon.

'He's blinded by the old Covenant,' said my mother, 'by learning and theology. He knows nothing of the new, joyful message, as builder Laursen says. The Spirit doesn't reveal itself in cassock and bands.'

'But there's the music,' said my father. 'The organist, sitting up there and playing . . .'

You could see his shoulders and the back of his head under the great organ-pipes in the gallery.

'The music's beautiful to hear,' said my father.

Then I went to Methodist Sunday-school. I went with Marentcius. We had always gone to Sunday-school together. We had texts read and explained to us by Madsen from the gasworks and Bentsen the joiner. We went to Sunday-school so that one day we should be good, God-fearing men. It was like a long-term medicine; it didn't work at once. It didn't make us good, God-fearing boys. But on the way home one could learn quite a lot about swearing and how to treat girls. This was knowledge one could use at once; one didn't have to wait for it to take effect.

'The Embankment's like a street in Amsterdam,' said our

geography master. 'With the river flowing along the rows of houses, and the bridges and the trees and the roadway, you can imagine it's a street in Amsterdam.'

One could play away a lot of time on the Embankment. In the yards, and on the bridges over the black waters of the river. And Marentcius had the whole day to himself – a long, endless Sunday afternoon. But I had to hurry home and go with my father and mother to the meeting in Tønnes Street. For it was on my account we had to go. There had been something of a miracle, after all, and builder Laursen had played his part in it. We had always gone there, really, but now it had become impossible to miss a single meeting. It would have shown ingratitude to Laursen and to God.

The worst part of it was that I had to take my guitar, so that everybody saw me walking along with my father and mother and a guitar. A fiddle, now; one could walk with that, or with a trumpet or a trombone . . . I should have been proud to walk along with a trombone on my arm and belong to a band. But a guitar . . .

'Learning to be a Salvation girl, are you?' asked Rudolf.

But he only asked this when my mother and father weren't there. He asked on Mondays. When we left home on Sunday afternoon nobody said anything. I just knew they were tittering. I could see it by their backs. The girls too. Lydia too.

We left home, and I had my guitar to carry, and the top part of the song-book stuck up out of my father's jacket-pocket. It was red and was called *Joy of Salvation. Joy of Salvation* in winding golden writing stuck up out of my father's jacket-pocket.

The people who met in the hall called themselves The Friends.[1] They called each other brother and sister. They said alleluia, Brother Laursen, and alleluia, Sister Thomsen. They would clap each other on the shoulder or hug each other and say alleluia as other people said good morning or goodbye.

'Alleluia,' they said, and 'Praise be.'

On ordinary Sundays there were seldom many there: fifteen

[1] See footnote on p. 58.

or twenty, perhaps, not more. They were the ones who lived in the same house: the Høyers, the Christensens and Sister Thora, who did dressmaking and had fine white hands; and Anna, radiant and transparent with T.B. And the Nielsens from Cross Street and a smiling little chemist. His name was Ludvigs.

'Alleluia,' they said to each other. 'How are you?'

'Very well, God be thanked and praised,' they said.

'God is good,' they said.

'Yes, praise be to Him.'

The hall smelt of shavings because it had once been a cabinet-maker's workshop. It smelt of glue and stain. Sometimes it also smelt of the wet coats which the Friends took off and hung on the row of pegs just inside the door, but always of glue and stain and fresh wood. That smell was in the walls.

On ordinary Sundays no children came. There was only me. I sat and played the guitar with Abeline, and was supposed to be doing it out of thankfulness. I didn't want to play the guitar, and I wasn't thankful. At times I had growing-pains in my legs and couldn't sit still on my chair. At times I fell asleep while builder Laursen was testifying.

But when the Norwegians came – Ullnes and Staff – and when Wedell came from Copenhagen, a 'jubilee-meeting' was announced. It was announced in the newspaper. Joy of Salvation, it said, and Coffee. All are Welcome.

Brothers Ullnes and Staff from Norway and Wedell from Copenhagen will testify. Music, it said.

Many people came then. There were faces one hardly knew. Every kind of person. They drove in from the west and all the way from Horsens – a wagonette full. They were all sisters and brothers and they all said alleluia and thanks and praise be to Him.

Theirs was a cheerful religion. It didn't require them to talk quietly and look worried. It didn't require anything.

'From the beginning of eternity God ordained all things in His mind,' said Ullnes, 'and we cannot alter them by a hair's breadth.'

'Alleluia,' they all said in chorus. 'Thanks and praise be to Him.'

'God ordained that at this moment a cloud should pass before the sun,' said Staff, 'that Sister Nielsen should be wearing a brown hat, and that Brother Kreutz should be so tired that he has to take a little nap.'

'Alleluia,' they said, and laughed.

The talking didn't go on for long, but long enough for the men to get heavy with Sunday drowsiness. They sat with bent heads and broad shoulders and big helpless-looking hands. Heavy hands. Working hands. Their eyelids were like slack blinds that kept wanting to fall down. Most of them would rather have stayed at home, but they had wives who needed to get out and to mix with other people. Old wives, with wrinkled faces. Big, blown-up wives and little bony ones with thin lips and quick hands.

There was singing and testifying and more singing. And all the time a sort of cloud of sleepiness floated under the ceiling. It sank when people spoke and rose again when we sang, and vanished during the intervals, when people could chat together – chat about ordinary things, earthly things, things of the world. About illness and death. About who was getting married and who was expecting a child. There were always short breaks even in the jubilee-meetings, until suddenly Staff stood up behind the little table with its flowery cloth and its tin tray bearing a carafe of water and a glass; until all at once Staff stood up and said that now it was time for another song.

'Alleluia,' they all said to that, or 'Amen.'

The music was Abeline and I, but sometimes there were more: Sister Thora, for instance. She touched her guitar with a hand as delicate and white as the petal of a water-lily. And she had a daughter called Nina; a girl with thin lips and little slits of eyes. Nina came to the jubilee-meetings, and I played to her, though she had no idea of this. She just came, for unlike me she had nothing whatever to be thankful for. Not the least scrap of miracle had happened to her. She sat there because her mother said she must, and that was exactly how she looked. She never dreamed that I was playing to her.

Valborg was there too. She came with her mother and helped her upstairs and downstairs and over to the chair she was to sit on. But Valborg was a grown-up person; she was a serious person. People talked to her as they talked to grown-up, serious people. And she listened, and sat looking at Staff, with his curly hair and small moustache and big white teeth. She watched him when he spoke and bore witness, and when he sat meditating and waiting for the Spirit to come.

'If I might suggest number 122,' said the chemist whose name was Ludvigs, and he gave an embarrassed little laugh. He sat right up in front with gold-rimmed glasses and a bald patch.

Abeline whispered the 'air' into my ear.

'O, gillyflower,' she said, or 'His life is like a sunrise,' or 'God's little butterfly.'

They called it air, not tune. And then we began to play. First Ullnes and Staff sang alone:

'*Never can we weary of the new and glorious song,*'

And the rest of us answered:

'*Praise be to God, alleluia!*'

'*Played by a myriad golden harps amid the heavenly throng,*'

And we answered:

'*Praise be to God, alleluia!*'

Then we all went on together:

'*For as children of the Kingdom we have received this grace:*
The old law is swept away, the new song takes its place.
'*Tis the new song of the Lamb we sing, in joy and thankfulness,*
Praise be to God, alleluia!'

The men's jackets strained at the armholes; you could see from their faces that their jackets were tight and that their collars chafed their necks, but they sang. Their eye-blinds rolled up and their drowsiness departed. They sat singing with open mouths. And my father sang and rolled his r's. I could hear him and distinguish him from all the rest, because he rolled them so tremendously. It embarrassed me. It embarrassed me on account of Nina, whom I was playing to although she had no inkling of it and didn't want to have inklings of any kind.

'Perhaps Brother Ludvigs would say a word now,' proposed Wedell, 'and share his thoughts with us.'

But Ludvigs the chemist would not testify.

'No,' he said, with his embarrassed laugh. 'I'll mix a good, bland ointment for you, or spread a plaster or handle a pestle. But testify . . .!'

'But is that not a great deal?' said Wedell. 'Not everyone has received such great gifts from God. Brother Laursen, then . . .'

But no; builder Laursen was a modest man. He knew his place – his modest place. He did not belong among the great evangelists.

They laughed and said alleluia and clapped each other on the shoulder. And Wedell wanted us to sing again.

The songs in *Joy of Salvation* had been written by Staff. He was a poet. I didn't know what poets looked like. I knew a professor, I knew specialists and clergymen and schoolmasters and an organist. I knew what lots of people looked like, but I'd never seen a poet until Valborg told me that Staff was one.

'See for yourself,' she said. 'Here it is on the first page of *Joy of Salvation*: Published by Knut Røhr-Staff . . . He's a poet,' she said. 'That's how a poet ought to look.'

Now she said it, I could see it was so. I could see it from his curly hair and his teeth and from the little moustache that moved up and down when he sang and spoke. You could see that Staff was a poet, but I hadn't imagined that a poet would look quite like that.

'You can hear he's a poet too,' said Valborg. 'You can hear it, because it's like roses and lilies and stars falling from his lips.'

'It's the Spirit moving him,' said her mother, whom they called Sister Thomsen. 'It's the Spirit,' she said.

Wedell came up and told me I played the guitar very well now.

'You must have a better one soon,' he said, 'now you play so well.'

'I don't want a better one,' I said. 'I'd rather have a fiddle or a chamber-organ.'

'I thought as much,' he said. 'One day you'll be a great musician. God has His plans for you; I said so at the beginning.'

'Hasn't He for everybody – for each and every one of us?' asked Sister Thora, who sat close by and could hear. She seemed almost hurt because God had special plans for me. Yes, it sounded as if she didn't think I deserved any plans at all.

'I see you aren't wearing your glasses today,' she said.

She said it in a friendly way – indeed very friendly – but she said it so that Nina could hear, and I didn't want Nina of all people to hear it. But she sat with her narrow slits of eyes and her thin lips and didn't hear anything. She sat there simply because she had to sit there. But she sat in an enchanting way; she sat there so enchantingly that I couldn't help playing to her. I had to, even though she didn't know and wouldn't notice.

'We'll talk about that violin,' said Wedell. 'We'll talk about it later.'

His eyes were like the butcher's dead dog's eyes. I don't know how I came to think of the butcher's dead dog. I liked it very much. It often came with me. But it was a dead dog with dead eyes.

'I'll talk to your father and mother about the violin,' said Wedell. 'And why didn't you come and see me when you were in Copenhagen?'

'We went there because of a miracle mostly,' I said. 'And I don't know where you live.'

'Well, when you go there seriously –' he said, but he was interrupted by Ludvigs the chemist, who wanted to ask him a purely scientific question.

136

'Now, during the interval,' he said. 'A purely mathematical and scientific question concerning the possibility of proving the existence of God . . .'

I thought it had been serious enough when we had been in Copenhagen. I didn't want it to be any more serious than that.

His life is like a sunrise
Of majesty and power,

sang somebody, without asking or telling us the number or anything. It didn't matter to me; I knew it. It was harder for Abeline.

Beneath whose growing radiance
The world breaks into flower.
Wonderful life! Wonderful life!

The afternoon sun slanted in. Over in the market-place there was a circus; one could see the top of the white tent above the green trees in the gardens. One could see the sky – a blue, summery sky. But here it smelt of old glue and stain and many people.

Ludvigs the chemist stood and talked out loud to Wedell while the rest were singing and we were playing. He talked and didn't care at all. Valborg had taught me that one should never talk when somebody was playing.

'Only unmusical and badly-brought-up people talk when somebody's playing,' she said. 'And I know you're musical. I know you don't want to be badly-brought-up. That's why I'm telling you.'

Ludvigs the chemist couldn't be either musical or well-brought-up, I thought, since he was talking out loud to Wedell and calling him doctor and asking him about numbers he had come upon in Revelations, which had given him food for thought. Ludvigs was smiling. He smiled with his eyes behind the gold-rimmed glasses and with his hand-movements and with the white edge of his slip-on cuffs. He must have been the only man with cuffs. They all had collars and made-up ties. But cuffs . . .

An interval followed, because they were going to clear the hall and make room for the coffee-tables. I went into the yard and out into the street. I stood and looked into the window of Sister Thora's sewing-room. There were a couple of ladies' hats that looked like startled birds, and a lay figure to hang frocks on.

'Are you allowed to be out here?' asked Nina. She was suddenly beside me. She was with a boy called Carl-Ole.

'Do you think I have to ask?' I said.

'But you did tell them you were going into the yard?'

'I'm old enough not to tell my mother when I'm going into the yard and when I'm not, aren't I?'

'You're not old enough for anything – not to leave your mother's apron-strings, anyhow.'

She said this with her thin lips and looked out of the slits of her eyes, and she was very pretty. She was so irresistibly pretty that I had to go away.

'A silly girl, that's what you are,' I said. 'Nothing but a silly girl.'

'You swallow everything Wedell tells you,' she said. 'But you needn't think you're anything so special – and if you knew what Wedell's really like!'

'He's a baron and he's a doctor,' I said. 'And what are you, may I ask?'

'Doctor,' she repeated. 'Doctor! He gave himself that title, if you want to know.'

I didn't want to know. I didn't care. I liked Wedell as I liked the butcher's dead dog. I couldn't help it if I liked them both in the same way, and there was nothing wrong in it. It was good, because it didn't make one feel uneasy.

'You're a silly girl,' I said, thinking that I would play to her again and go on playing to her. I would come to the meeting in the hall every single Sunday and sit and play with Abeline and

138

be thankful from head to foot, if only Nina would be there too.

'You're a damned silly girl,' I said.

'So you swear too, do you? What would your mother say if she knew?'

'D'you think I don't swear at home? My uncle Anton taught me. And he can swear better than anyone in the whole world.'

'Oh, of course,' she said, and she laughed scornfully out of the slits of her eyes. 'Everything about you is better than anything else in the whole world.'

'Yes, it is,' I said, and went in.

'Where have you been?' asked my mother.

'Outside.'

'You haven't got foggy vision, have you?'

'No,' I answered.

'You look as if you had.'

Outside was the slanting sunshine and the green tree-tops and the top of the circus-tent away in the market-place.

'Wedell says we ought to buy you a violin.'

'I told you that a long time ago.'

'You must be grateful,' said my mother. 'And you must put on your glasses.'

So I put on my glasses and people came and talked about how I was. There was no alleluia when they asked after me, and no joy of salvation in their voices. There was only concern.

'Perhaps I should have a word with the professor,' said Wedell. 'I know him.'

'Surely there's no need for that,' said my father. 'The professor said the boy wouldn't go blind. We must be content with that. You could call it a miracle, really.'

'But he wants to see him again,' said my mother. 'I'm to keep an eye on him, and he wants to see him again.'

'I think he should have a violin,' said Wedell. 'He'll soon learn to play it, and then you'll forget all your anxieties.'

'Well, Brother Wedell, if you really think so –' said my father.

'You can get one for ten crowns,' I said. 'Without case.'

I saw that at last they had decided to give me a fiddle.

Staff had written a new song-book. It was brought out now for people to buy. Every brother and sister had to have Staff's new song-book. He's written it for us, they said. It is a gift sent to us from God through Brother Staff.

'But it costs two crowns,' said my mother.

'Well, I don't think the old songs are worn out yet,' said my father. 'I like the old songs best, and I don't want any more.'

'But you must have the new book,' said Brother Høyer. 'You'll have to have it, so that you can join in.'

So we bought the new book. We bought it partly for my sake, so that I could have it to play from. But I meant to play from quite different things in future. I meant to play from proper music on a music-stand. I wasn't going to come to any jubilee-meetings, unless I was certain Nina would be there so that I could have someone to play to. I was too old to sit twanging beside Abeline. In fact I would have liked to float out of the window then and there, over the tree-tops and down through the roof of the circus-tent, and stand in the middle with my violin and my music-stand. The people there didn't say alleluia and praise and thanks be – they clapped. They clapped their hands and shouted, so that it sounded like roaring surf. I would rather stand there and sink in a stormy sea of applause than sit here and sicken from the smell of glue and stain, or be smothered in worries and alleluias.

Nina came. She said,

'You've gone quite pale with conceit.'

But at that moment I wasn't conceited. I was thinking that I was going to have a fiddle. I was thinking that I should go out into the world with my fiddle and my bow, and the girls would be waiting for me with flowers in their hair, as Stougård had said. They would be wanting to dance so much that they couldn't stand still, and waiting there with flowers in their hair, and perhaps Nina would be one of them. Then people could talk about glandular disease and the inscrutable ways of

God as much as they liked. They could talk about me with sadness and hoar-frost in their voices, and sour mildew and worry. I didn't care. But I wasn't conceited.

'He does well at school,' said my mother. 'The teachers say he's one of the best at everything except writing. And he's good at music. Abeline says she don't feel she can teach him any more.'

'Ah, but what's the good of it all?' said Sister Nielsen from Cross Street. 'If he can't have his sight, what good is it?'

'What good –' said my father. 'Well, as to that, strictly speaking, we ought to give thanks and praise for this and for all the things we don't understand. Anyhow, Wedell thinks there's some purpose in it.'

'Yes, Wedell,' said Sister Nielsen, with a pale smile. You could hear she was smiling, and that the smile was pale and patronizing. 'Wedell,' she said.

I determined not to die. Not ever.

I had known a boy at school called August. He was dead. We went to his funeral, my mother and I. We stood in the chapel and saw him lying in the coffin looking beautiful, before the lid was screwed down.

'August is happy now,' said my mother.

We stood looking at his smooth, black hair and his closed eyes and his mouth, and his folded hands.

'August is happy,' said my mother. 'I wonder whether perhaps you wish it was you . . .'

'No,' I said, and got away from the coffin. 'No,' I said, and decided I would never die. I would *not*.

They talked about me as if there had never been any miracle, and as if Wedell had never said that God had plans for me, and as if I weren't there at all. That was why I stood and made up my mind not to die. Never. And I hated them all, and I would remember to go on hating them. And one day I would be a musician like the one in the story who came to Erik Ejegod's yard and played them all out of their wits. He could play them happy and play them sad and play them angry, so that they fell upon each other and killed each other. I would play every last alleluia out of them; I would play them into wild beasts.

And of course I could become a great murderer too. People would read about me in the papers. I would make their flesh creep so that they never dared to be alone, or walk along a dark passage, because I might be lurking behind a door with my knife.

'You're pale with conceit,' said Nina. 'You'd be better looking if you weren't so horribly conceited.'

They drank coffee and they sang and they spoke and they sang again; there was no end to it. I sat beside Abeline, pretending to play, but I didn't play. But nobody noticed, and I was glad that nobody noticed me. Ullnes spoke and Staff spoke, and to me they seemed to be saying the same thing each time. I couldn't hear that Staff was a poet and I couldn't see that he was a poet, and no roses or lilies or stars came out of his mouth. Perhaps that was because I had put on my dark glasses and saw the world in a blue light – a light that had no golden splashes of sunlight and pure, bright colours; a light that flattened out the distance and washed out lights and shades and made everything look the same. The cloud of drowsiness that hung up there under the ceiling grew heavier and heavier. Nina had gone out again with Carl-Ole. Valborg was a grown-up, serious person, listening for roses and lilies and stars from Staff's poetical mouth. I had nobody to play to. And the cloud sank lower; one could see it now. It became something grey and impenetrable. Grey, dirty wool, veiling everything, wiping everything out and becoming nausea and headache and more nausea and more headache; a tightness round the right eye and in the right eye, as if it was going to burst out of its socket. And every time they said alleluia and every time they said thanks and praise be to Him I felt I was going to be sick. And it wasn't the pain or the foggy vision that was making me sick, but the alleluias and the thanks and praise be that I could no longer keep down. I thought that perhaps after all it would be best if I went and died like August, so that my father and mother needn't go on being sad about me, since I was never going to be like other people. My mother and Sister Thora laid me on some chairs and I wished it had been Nina, but she had gone out with Carl-Ole. They laid me on some chairs and said it must have been the coffee that upset me.

'Alleluia,' said Ullnes. 'Everything comes to pass as it was ordained in the beginning of all eternities in the mind of God.'

'I'll go up and talk to the professor,' said Wedell.

'Don't you fret,' Sister Thora said to me consolingly. 'It's just the coffee. Nina never drinks it.'

I thought I might just as well die, since there was always so much fuss about me, and since I couldn't manage to be like Nina and Carl-Ole and other people.

13

WE had a garden that spring and summer. A sensible garden for potatoes and cabbage and carrots, not for flowers and finery. There was talk of red cabbage too, and cauliflowers, but my father had no knowledge of these rarities. He had seen them, of course. He had seen them at the greengrocer's and in other gardens.

'Back home in Sweden they hadn't been invented,' he thought. 'I don't remember hearing about anything in that line. Parsley, though – we had that.'

My mother shook her head. But what did she really know of such things?

'I could write and ask my aunt Emma,' said my father. 'She knows a lot about plants and that.'

'We can manage,' my mother said.

'I was only thinking it would give me something to write about,' said my father.

We planted potatoes and we made beds for carrots and parsley and a patch of green peas for me. And other people round us hoed and sowed.

The long evenings had come and there were lots of people in Nørremarken; people born and bred in the country who had moved into the town to get regular work and earn more money than they could where they had come from. Now they turned again to the tiny plots of land they could go and cultivate when the day was over. They dug, they raked, they picked up the soil and crumbled it in their fingers. Some of them enclosed their gardens. They put a wooden fence round them or planted a hedge. Some built summer-houses: a framework of slats that would be covered with flowers and greenery when the time came. But there were real houses too: closed-up ones with doors and verandahs and coloured glass in the windows, red and yellow and green and blue. Some had a bench to sit on. A private bench. People worked in their gardens. They sawed and hammered; they straightened their backs and bent over their spades again, and straightened up and looked about. They saw all the others working, and they saw the trees along the roads, the pollarded trees that marched away to Horsens and to Viborg. An endless regiment of trees that were all shaped alike and all the same distance apart. They looked alike and marched to Viborg or Horsens and never stirred from the spot. People straightened themselves and looked over wide fields and perhaps caught the flash of sunlight on the edge of a lifted spade. And there were the edges of the woods – far woods and near.

We had got a garden and we were there almost every evening. There was always something to be done in it. Weeds that oozed up and had to be kept down. Rhubarb that we could already begin to use.

'And what about strawberries?' asked my father. 'We might have a bed of them next year.'

'They'd be good to sell,' said my mother.

'To sell – well, maybe – but I was thinking . . .'

'If we could just keep half a pound for the boy,' said my mother.

'Yes, of course,' my father said. 'I was just thinking . . .'

My mother couldn't always come with us. She had her bags to do, and the lawyer's to do. But my father and I went. We went up the steep path through the woods.

'Yes,' said my father. 'For instance, there's the tree the cooper hanged himself on when there was no more work for him.'

It was a beech. It stood a little to the left of the path. It seemed a perfectly ordinary beech, among other beeches. But when we were going home and it was dark among the tree-trunks, it was not an easy tree to pass.

'And they say it was here that Jacob Hedehus assaulted the girl, so they put him in prison,' said my father, when we came to a narrow track leading into a blackberry thicket and disappearing among young trees.'I heard it happened in a clearing back there. Though what she was doing there, if she wasn't waiting to be assaulted by Jacob Hedehus –' said my father.

We took our time both when we were going to the garden and when we were coming home again. Sometimes we took too long. We sat on the benches along the path. We sat there for the birdsong. And for the silence.

' 'Cause we don't know the names of all the birds,' said my father, 'and even if we found out it would be different from what it was in Sweden. There's such a lot that's different,' he said.

He sat and smoked his pipe. He smoked hard because of the midges.

'And the forester hasn't got any curtains to keep you guessing,' he said. 'But over there there's a tree they call King Hans' Oak, I don't know why. And there's other trees in the wood that's each got a name.'

We sat there with a bucket of early potatoes and thin carrots: our first real harvest.

'They're lovely potatoes,' said my father. 'Really lovely. I don't know that I ever saw any finer ones.'

Sometimes people came and asked what he was hoeing, or what we were taking home in the bucket. They only did this to hear my father call them *potatis*.[1] They laughed at him rather. They thought it was queer he should know no better.

'You needn't answer them,' I said. 'You can pretend you don't hear. Or else tell them you're not sure.'

'Oh, well,' said my father. 'Well, so far as that goes –'

It was growing dusk and the dew had begun to fall. The

[1] The Swedish word, instead of the Danish *kartofler*.

floor of the woods had a spicy smell of sorrel and grasses and flowers, and away across the tree-tops, through a gap, one had a view of the fjord. A ship sailing in had lit her lanterns – her red and green lanterns. Midges sang metallically in our ears, and there were bats.

'That one singing in there in the undergrowth – I should think he's a thrush,' said my father. 'Back in Sweden I'm sure we should have called him that, but maybe they've got a better name for him.'

My father sat listening to the song-thrush and the quietness. I was thinking that presently we should have to go through the dark wood and past the dead cooper's tree. When its leaves rustled you thought it was the dead cooper sighing. And when a branch creaked you thought that was him too. You'd rather have turned your head another way, but something about the place itself drew you. You had to look towards it.

'Yes, there's the tree where the cooper hanged himself,' said my father.

He said it every time we went past, and peered at it as if one might be lucky enough to see the dead cooper dangling up there in the branches.

'And it was in the winter,' said my father, 'so whether he hanged himself to death or froze to death . . .' he said. 'But he had no work. That was why.'

In the dark part of the woods too there was a bench. It was for sweethearts or for old people who had to rest on the way up.

Down on the sportsground they were playing football. Marentcius and Rudolf were there.

I would have liked to be there. I thought it was fun playing football. It was fun when one kicked it right – fun to run after the ball and reach it first.

'Well then, take off those glasses,' said Rudolf. 'We don't want you if you wear dark glasses.'

'You can be linesman,' said Marentcius.

So I was linesman. There was no fun in that, and I couldn't get my eye on the ball. Once Valborg had stood watching.

'You'd much better come home with me,' she said. 'We can play on the chamber-organ.'

After that they used to tell me to go home with some girl or other and play on her chamber-organ.

It wasn't very different at school. When the rest were going to do something dangerous the gym-instructor set me to do something dull.

'Fetch a mattress and turn somersaults,' he said. 'Or play on the ribstalls for a bit. Carry on as long as you like.'

But I didn't like. I wanted to do something dangerous – something very dangerous. More dangerous than anything the others did.

'You can carry on as long as you like,' he said, 'or go for a walk if you'd rather.'

They played football on the sportsground in the evenings. But I walked past with my father as if I didn't notice. We had a bucket of new potatoes and carrots and we were coming out of the dark woods. And there was a café where a concert was going on. We put down our bucket and stood to listen to the music.

'If you could learn to play the violin like that,' said my father, 'I'd get you one.'

There was a balcony with lamps on the tables, and there were lanterns in the trees in the garden – coloured lanterns among the trees.

'I'd get you one right away,' my father said.

There was to be an auction, and somebody told us that among a lot of old junk there was a violin. It had belonged to somebody who was dead. Børresen, in hospital. He must have forgotten it, they said, or he'd have drunk it up while he was alive. Perhaps it would go cheap, being second-hand.

My mother and I went. We looked at bird-cages and chipped cups and bedside mats and an old chest of drawers and greased leather boots. When the fiddle came my mother bid two crowns. She started at two, but was outbid by a man they called Red Martin. He was a carter and Børresen had been his uncle.

'If you want your uncle's violin,' said my mother, 'there's no sense in our bidding against each other.'

'It's worth more,' said Red Martin. 'It's worth much more.'

'And when did *you* learn to play the fiddle?' asked somebody.

'It's worth at least twenty-five crowns,' said Red Martin. My mother bid again. She was willing to go as high as ten crowns, the price of a new one. But Red Martin went higher. He went to twelve and fourteen.

'Pushing up the price for yourself – that's what you're doing,' shouted somebody.

It was a lovely fiddle. The wood was light, almost golden, with a fine grain. I was allowed to hold it in my hands. It was the first time I had ever touched a violin; it made me tremble. My hands trembled and I trembled all over.

'Well, I don't know what a carter like that knows about violins,' said my mother, but she went on bidding.

'Sixteen and a half, sixteen and a half!' shouted the auctioneer.

'Seventeen,' said Red Martin.

'Seventeen twenty-five,' said my mother. Her hands were shaking too. 'It's crazy,' she said. 'You can buy a brand-new one for ten crowns in the shops. It's crazy.'

'No bids under fifty øre,' said the auctioneer.

'Seventeen and a half,' shouted Red Martin.

It was knocked down to my mother at eighteen crowns. It was because the auctioneer asked if it was for me, and quickly said 'Going, going, gone!' The hammer fell. 'Sold to the highest bidder for eighteen crowns.'

I heard the hammer fall, but I still didn't realize that the fiddle was mine. I went on trembling with suspense. People were shouting at Red Martin.

'Look at him!' they said. 'Coming here stinking of old horse-piss so you can't go near him, and he don't want to let a poor half-blind boy have his uncle's violin. It ought to have been sold in a job lot with the other rubbish – that's all it's worth.'

'He'll earn money with it, won't he?' grumbled Red Martin. 'He'll go about and play at markets, or stand at street corners with a tin bowl strapped to his knee for folk to drop pennies in.' But he slouched out of the place, and they made way for him.

'It would have been a bargain at twenty-five,' he said in the doorway. 'It's got a label inside with Stradivarius on it,' he said. 'It would have been cheap at twenty-five. They'll soon earn that, travelling round with the boy to markets, or setting him to play at street corners.'

'Get out, can't you?' somebody shouted after him, and he got out.

'Maybe he was right,' said my mother as we went home. 'I'd like to think he was. I don't want anybody to say we got a bad bargain. Eighteen crowns is a lot of money,' she said, 'and then there'll be the fees . . .'

But I had a fiddle now. It had only two strings, certainly, but one could go for walks with it in its case. One could take it to school and show it to cantor Petersen for him to say what he thought of it.

'It's rather big for you,' he said.

None of us had thought people had fiddles made to measure, like a suit of clothes.

'You ought to have begun with a three-quarter one,' he said. 'But come and see me at home,' he said, 'and I'll help you.'

I could let myself be seen with a fiddle anywhere: at school, on the sportsground, in the yard. I didn't mind anyone knowing that I played the violin.

'Is there a future in it?' asked Lydia, and didn't stop playing with her ball. She threw it up behind her back and under her knee, and bounced it on her forehead. 'Rudolf says he wants to be a post-office clerk. There's a future in that,' she said. 'But a violin . . .'

'I want to be in the theatre,' I said.

I had once looked through an open window and seen a man standing on the stage of a theatre playing the violin.

'I've never heard of anybody playing the violin in a theatre,' said Lydia. 'And besides, your family's religious.'

'I've seen it and heard it,' I said. 'And there are things you and Rudolf don't understand. Things it would be all wrong if you did understand,' I said.

Let her go home now, I thought, and tell that to her father or to her drunken mother.

'Who strung it?' cantor Petersen asked.

'My father.'

'Not exactly a trained violin-maker, is he?'

It was unbearable, the amount of preparation before one could get going properly. Then one had to play on open strings. Long strokes; upstrokes and downstrokes; downstrokes and upstrokes. The whole length of the bow.

At home my father sat and watched me practising, and my mother looked up from her paper bags and watched me. And Oluf came and sat on a chair and said,

'You play just as well as Mr Herskind already.' But Oluf was a growler and knew nothing about music, let alone violin-playing. He was a growler in a different way from me – a more real way. I only couldn't help making up second parts.

'I say you play better than Mr Herskind,' said Oluf, and I didn't mind him saying that; I liked it.

'Some people say he's the best violin-player in the whole of Denmark,' said Oluf.

But that wasn't so, for even cantor Petersen played better than he did, and with my own eyes I'd seen a man in the theatre.

It was a different thing when one began to be able to put a finger on the string, and two, and three and four.

'Yes,' said my father. 'Sounds very different from the guitar, there's no denying. I wonder what they'll say when you come along and play it with Abeline in the hall.'

I didn't wonder at all, for I had no intention of coming along and playing with Abeline in the hall. I wanted to come along and play to a girl called Nina. But this was to be at the theatre, on the stage – I would stand in the very middle of the stage, and play to her from there.

'It comes naturally to him,' cantor Petersen told my mother. 'He's got a good sense of tone,' he said. Whatever that might be.

'Sense of tone,' my mother repeated.

'Yes, he has a quite extraordinary sense of tone – I can see that already. He ought to be a musician, but he doesn't see well enough. He cheats, and learns the music by heart.'

'Cheats!' said my mother.

'He cheats in the sense that he can't read the notes, while he plays. Have you ever spoken to the organist about him?'

We had never spoken to the organist. We just knew him. We knew what he looked like because he lived in the same street and I used to loiter under the open windows when there was music being played there.

'I was thinking you ought to have a word with him. That would be easier than playing in an orchestra, where you've got to keep an eye on each finger and on the music and on the conductor, all at the same time.'

But this was not at all what my mother had in mind. If I could just learn to play some of the tunes they sang on Sundays. If I could just get as far as playing with Abeline . . . All those other things the cantor was talking about: orchestras, conductors, church organs – that is, if she'd understood him – had never entered her head.

'He's not twelve yet,' said my mother. 'And that's an expensive road to travel, and a dangerous road,' she said.

'Dangerous . . .?'

'Don't most of them drink a lot?'

'I don't drink, so far as I know. And neither does the organist.'

My mother got nervous thumbs. She didn't know what to

say. She knew what she meant, but she couldn't say it in a way to be understood.

'It'll be time enough to think of all that when he's been confirmed,' she said, 'and we see how things go.'

My mother was thoughtful when we went home again. She was thoughtful and silent, as she was when there had been bother over me at school or when we'd been to the specialist.

'I can't help it,' I said. 'I don't know what to do, but I can't help it.'

'No,' said my mother.

She didn't say anything more than this one No.

We walked along Nørrebro Street past the shoemaker's window and a window full of old copper things, and the home bakery where there was a hanging lamp, and the photographer's, where Lydia's portrait had been on show. And my mother said nothing. She thought and was silent, as she was when they were unhappy about me.

'If one only knew where he gets it from,' said my father that evening. 'If one could only think how a child gets that sort of thing . . .'

They talked about it as if I'd caught a disease. They talked about it as if it was a misfortune, a new misfortune.

'It must be from God,' said my mother.

'From God . . . I wonder whether he takes after somebody,' said my father. 'But there's no knowing.'

'I don't know anyone he could have got it from,' said my mother, and she started on her paper bags.

I began to write to my sister. I settled down to tell her about the fiddle, and about how one day I would play in a theatre, and about how I helped Big-Peter to sell newspapers for a crown a month, and how I wanted to come and see her and bring my violin.

'Your writing isn't good,' said my father. 'I don't believe Kirstine will be able to read a word of it, clever as she is and second place in Dronningborg School and all.'

'I met Lieutenant Christensen as they call him the other

day,' said my mother. 'He thought we should go and see the blind girls at Pode's Home. He thought it would be a good idea if the boy learned braille – you know, that blind writing.'

'I thought he was keeping up all right now,' said my father.

'He's keeping up so well that Lieutenant Christensen wants him to go to another school. It's only the reading and writing.'

'And isn't reading and writing the most important thing of all? Anyone who can do that can learn about everything,' said my father. 'And if he's going to learn braille, what's the good of going to this professor in Copenhagen?'

'Well, that's a question,' said my mother. 'But ever since we've done the drops like the professor told us, he hasn't had foggy vision. He hasn't complained of headaches or been sick. And that's something.'

I tore up the letter to my sister. I knew they'd never send it. I knew they wouldn't waste money on a letter that Kirstine couldn't read. Then I took my fiddle and went into the bedroom and sat down on the bed and played.

All the same, it was a time of happiness. Happiness swept down upon us with every wind. From north and south and east and west came a warm breeze of happiness. One day my sister swept upon us. She came down the Horsens road on a bicycle, with wind in her skirts and wind in her hair. She brought a school friend with her, and was shy and strange when she was actually there. But she had her brown eyes and her bare arms with the dimples in her elbows. I hadn't remembered that. My sister had dimples in her elbows. But we stood not knowing what to say to each other.

'Your face looks just the same,' she said, 'and so do your eyes.'

'Yes,' I said, without thinking about what she meant.

But Kirstine had grown taller and even prettier. They all said so:

'How tall you are, Kirstine, and how pretty you've grown,' they said. 'You're almost grown-up.'

She had brought this girl with her who was called Jenny and was fifth in Dronningborg School, to show her that she really had a brother, and that he played the violin.

'Only very little yet,' said my mother. 'Nothing really to speak of.'

'But he's got a turn for it,' said my father. 'They say he's got a rare turn for it, wherever it is he gets it from, or who he gets it from . . .'

We were allowed to go out. We were allowed to do what we liked. Nobody bothered to tell us what we must do or mustn't do. We showed ourselves in the yard. We went to see Stougård in his house, and ate baked potatoes dipped in salt, and looked at the ice-ponds. The rushes rustled like silk, and there were dragonflies that caught the flash of the sun on their wings. And my sister was polite, and looked at the ice-ponds as if they were oceans – vast, bottomless oceans.

'And what a rustling in those rushes. A silky rustle,' she said. My sister was like that; she could think such things and say them. 'A silky rustle,' she said.

Stougård nodded contentedly. And behind, the woods were filled with a different rustling – a deeper, more serious rustle. But they rustled with happiness. Everything did. If only the strange girl called Jenny hadn't been there beside us, never leaving us for a moment . . . And if only Kirstine would stay with us for ever, or for a month or a week. But they were going further. They were going to rustle away somewhere else, with their bare arms and shiny handlebars. If I'd had a bicycle I could have gone with them. Kirstine liked me with her now, always and everywhere. And away they swept one morning, towards the west. The girl called Jenny had an uncle over Henning way.

'What was there so important about that uncle, now?' said my father.

'Yes, I'd have been glad for her to have worn down our stairs a bit longer,' said my mother. 'But there, we've got no right.'

I stood in the best room playing my fiddle. I was playing about my sister.

'Is that something you're learning for cantor Petersen?' asked my mother. 'It sounds different.'

'Yes,' I said. 'It's something I'm learning.'

Afterwards I went up the Jelling road. It was as steep as a mountain-road. I thought how my sister had ridden this way only a few hours before. But I could find no trace of her, no scent of her hair or of the wind about her. She had been at home with us in our rooms, and she had been along this road, and it was only a few hours ago, but now she was gone, vanished, leaving a sinking emptiness behind her. An emptiness that might perhaps be filled by a girl who answered to the name of Nina, but by nobody else. A girl with narrow slits of eyes and thin lips and hands thrust into the pockets of a pea-jacket, or whatever the garment was called. And yet . . . That empty sinking that Kirstine left behind her couldn't really be filled by anyone or anything. It could be forgotten, forgotten for a while when one's attention was caught by something, but it came back. It was waiting when the hour of forgetfulness – that brief hour – was past. It was waiting, and remained in the soul. At first it was longing – loneliness and pain and longing. Later it would change and become a scar.

I walked the paths and the roads that I had walked with my sister Kirstine, and it happened that I met the girl called Nina. I didn't know what she was doing there, and I didn't ask. We knew each other from the meeting-hall in Tønnes Street. It felt as if we knew something about each other – as if we shared a secret. I went with her for a bit – not very far. She made me understand that she hadn't come here on my account.

'And you needn't touch me,' she said.

I had taken her by the wrist, as my sister used to take me. I held her wrist, but she didn't take her hand out of her pocket for that.

'You don't have to touch me,' she said. 'And anyhow I'm going to meet another girl here on the bridge.'

I turned grey with shame. I felt myself turning ashen grey with shame and humiliation. I was walking here to think about my sister Kirstine. I walked defenceless, with an all too vulnerable heart, and I had caught at a hand. And Nina had spoken to me as if I were a leper. Could I do other than love her – and love her . . .

Happiness and torment, longing and sweetness – nothing was as simple as before. The world was turning to chaos.

One day Uncle Anton came swinging round the corner. He came entirely unannounced. He came with what he stood up in.

'Good heavens above, what a tramp!' said Lydia. 'So that's your uncle. I believe he was drunk, too.'

'Well, you should know,' I said, 'if he really was. But he was no funnier than he always is,' I said.

He came with his shirt open at the neck and fringes at his cuffs and at the bottoms of his trousers.

'And your shoes!' said my mother.

'What do you expect shoes to look like after walking half the way from Copenhagen?'

'You smell of *braendevin*,' said my mother.

'Not nearly enough. I've had more than you can smell – more than both you and Jane could smell if you both went at it together,' he said. 'Have you got anything to eat?'

My mother was anxious, and she did everything in her power to maintain her anxiety. But Uncle Anton behaved with a flourish of festiveness and irresponsibility. It felt as if he were turning everything upside down and playing ball with the law of gravity itself.

'Leaving a good, steady job like that,' said my mother, 'just because they wouldn't give you a fortnight off for idling and worse.'

'No, better,' Uncle Anton corrected her. 'Now I'll have a whole month to take the road. I want to look about me and get wiser. So long as I don't go and get so wise I never go back.'

But later, when my mother had gone to the lawyer's

house, his manner altered and he suddenly became tired and serious.

'Well, now, and how are you?' he asked. 'Come here and let's have a look at you.'

He looked right into my face and into my eyes as if I were a photograph. You felt he was really playing a little at being a specialist.

'I'd like to take you with me on a journey,' he said. 'A long, long journey. So you could see mountains, high mountains with snow on them, and the pyramids in Egypt, and hippopotamuses and elephants and zebras and leopards; and we'd talk to negroes and Malays and Chinese. How would you like to sail right round the world and land on a coral island with palms on it and volcanoes and everything . . .?'

'Oo yes,' I said. 'That would be fun. Have you seen all those things, Uncle Anton – mountains and all that?'

'Since you ask me I must admit I haven't,' he said. 'But as far as I'm concerned there's plenty of time. I don't mean to die yet awhile.'

'Nor do I,' I said. 'I've made up my mind I won't ever die. Never.'

'Good,' said Uncle Anton. 'All the same I'd like you to see all the wonders of the world before very long. Why, we could walk out right away, for that matter.'

The tiresome thing about him was that you never knew for certain whether he meant what he said; whether he was in earnest now, for instance, or just fooling. He sat on the platform looking out at the houses in Freden Street and at the trains running past. And we heard the bell at the level-crossing.

'I met your father on the road,' he said. 'It's wonderful how you're all getting on in the world. He's actually become a horse now.'

What could he mean by that?

'Yes, he'd had himself harnessed to a cart full of timber and cement and lime. It was so heavy there ought to have been a horse in front of it, if not two. And I suppose your mother thinks that's a step forward.'

'My father's got a steady job,' I said.

That was another bit of happiness that came upon us one day; my father got regular work at the lime-kiln and the timber-yard, and went about the town carting planks and cement and anything else that was to be brought in. A steady wage to bring home every single Saturday. Eighteen crowns in the summer, fifteen in the winter.

But now Uncle Anton said he'd become a horse, a draught-animal.

'Once and for all, will you keep your jokes and your socialism to yourself,' said my mother. 'We're satisfied with what we've got.'

'That's the damnable thing,' said Uncle Anton. 'People are satisfied the moment starvation isn't actually knocking at the door. If they can just push the spectre downstairs a flight or two they're quite content.'

'I won't have you swearing here,' said my mother, 'and sowing discontent and ingratitude. A fine place the world would be if we were all like you. I've got a husband who don't drink and wouldn't ever dream of taking to the road.'

'He'll never get a chance to do either. You're the slaves of plush chairs and silver teaspoons and a heap of cheap finery. I owe no one anything. I'm a free man. No one's going to turn me into a horse.'

'You owe yourself a new pair of shoes and some decent clothes, so we wouldn't have to feel so ashamed of you,' said my mother.

But Uncle Anton just laughed. He laughed and said my mother didn't understand, and that she could go off and clean the lawyer's place with an easy mind, because he was going to take me into the town.

But my mother wouldn't let me go into the town with Uncle Anton.

'You can do what you like with *yourself*,' she said. 'You can turn everything upside down, call black white and evil good if you like.'

Uncle Anton laughed, but all at once he was grave again.

'So I'm not worthy to take a child into the town,' he said. 'I can assure you I'd have done him no harm. But if I'm so worthless I'd better go where I belong.'

Did he mean what he said? Was he joking or was he serious? Sometimes he said something deadly serious, and then he'd laugh. At other times he could joke with words that nobody else dared to joke with. But this time his seriousness was serious. He pocketed a packet of cigarettes that had lain on the table, tied up one shoelace and picked up his cap.

'Well, goodbye, then,' he said. To me he said, 'We'll meet again sometime. But you, sister Lisbeth . . . To you I'll just say goodbye.'

We heard him go downstairs, but his steps soon died away. We didn't hear him go out of the gate, for he wore leather shoes, even if they had got holes in them.

In his wake was silence. It began in the living-room and went on down the stairs and out through the gateway. I wondered where he was going. Whether he was walking away to Horsens. Or westward. Or back towards Copenhagen. Or whether he wanted to go out into the world and see mountains – high mountains with snow on them, and the pyramids of Egypt and all the other things he had talked about. Always supposing one could appear before the pyramids of Egypt in a dirty shirt open at the neck and a jacket that was frayed at the wrists.

'He'll come back, won't he?' I asked.

'No,' said my mother. And a little later, 'No, I'm afraid not.'

'Where will he get anything to eat?' I asked. 'And where will he sleep tonight?'

My mother didn't answer.

'You oughtn't to have driven him out,' I said.

'I didn't drive him out. But he mustn't come here and turn everything upside down and turn wrong into right and sow discontent. "If any would not work, neither should he eat," ' she said. 'It is written.'

I imagined him walking along the highway and falling down from hunger and thirst and lying there with an exhausted smile, unable to get to his feet again. He might lie there and die, turn into a skeleton, a row of bones whitening in the sun and wind, as they said happened in the Sahara Desert. 'If any would not work, neither should he eat,' as it is written.

My mother took off her apron. She didn't say what she meant to do, but I knew she wanted to go after Uncle Anton, try to find him and bring him back again. So she's repented, I thought. She must be repenting that she, who belonged to those who were 'set free', to those who sang aloud from Staff's *Joy of Salvation*, had nevertheless stood with the law and the prophets in her hand and condemned her own brother; although when all was said and done, he could only be acting as it had been ordained he should, in the mind of God, from everlasting to everlasting.

My mother went to look for Uncle Anton, and she was away for a long time, but she came home again without having found him. She had been into all the inns – first those nearest, and then those that were further away.

'I felt so thankful that I never had to look for your father like that,' she said. 'We've never had to fetch father home from the tavern or wait for him on a Saturday evening.'

'But where's Uncle Anton?'

'Someone saw him going up Horsens hill,' she said. 'That means he's going home – home to grandfather and grandmother and the rest. That's what he's doing today,' she said. 'Tomorrow or next day it'll be something else.'

So he was strolling away now in his broken shoes, with no companions but the pollarded trees, who always and for ever were on their way to Horsens. But he left an emptiness, a void in existence itself.

'At least I could have trimmed his sleeves and trousers with the scissors,' said my mother. 'I could have given him something to eat and some coffee and mended his clothes,' she said. 'Then I wouldn't have had it on my mind – no regrets.'

14

ONE day we went to L. Pode's Home for Blind Women. We stood at the corner and saw the faces behind the window-panes. My heart was thumping. I don't know why it was thumping. I wasn't afraid of anything. I knew the faces behind the window, and the corner where we were standing. I knew it all better than my mother guessed. Then we went up and rang the bell. Presently we should hear footsteps. Presently we should hear a hand fumbling at the door-handle. Presently the stringed instrument would ring. Today it would ring for me. I wished the door might be opened slowly, so that I had time to hear each separate string.

There were the footsteps. Now came the fumbling round the key and the door-handle, and now the door opened.

'Good day. Here you are, then.'

She said it before she had quite opened the door. She said it before she could have been able to see us, and she thought it was somebody else. She didn't expect strangers.

'Yes, Sofie's at home,' she said, 'but I don't think she's expecting visitors.'

Her eyes were closed, and you could hear that she talked with closed eyes. It sounded as if there were a wall in front of her face.

'Visitors for Sofie,' she called into the dark room.

'Good day,' they all said. They said it very loud and in chorus. It sounded as if they were glad. 'Good day, and welcome.'

'Sofie's upstairs, but I'll go and fetch her,' said one of them. 'I'll hurry and fetch her.'

She hurried slowly. You could see that she was hurrying, but it happened slowly. She held one hand a little way in front of her. With the other she felt the wall. It wasn't as dark in the rooms as one would have thought from outside. They weren't as empty, either. In each of them there was a big table: a big, dark table with many chairs round it. There was also a little shelf of books – thick books – and a cupboard. But there wasn't a single picture on the walls and no texts over the doors. There were only the bare tables, the bare floors and the bare walls.

'Won't you sit down while you're waiting for Sofie?'

'Yes, won't you sit down?' they all said in chorus.

They remained sitting on their chairs. They didn't get up. They didn't even turn their faces. Some were knitting and they went on knitting. Some just sat still with their hands in their laps. They went on sitting still. They brooded and kept watch over what they had – their knitting, their empty hands, their blindness – fearfully, as if afraid that someone would come and steal away their happiness.

It was Lieutenant Christensen's idea that we should come here.

'Why don't you learn braille?' he said. 'If you did, you wouldn't have to strain yourself trying to see. Perhaps you could get braille books. Anyhow, you could write your compositions in it. If you'll learn it,' he said, 'I will too. Your mother shall take you to Pode's Home; there's a girl there called Sofie; she can teach you. Remember to ask for Sofie. She's clever . . . They all are, but she's the best. She'll teach you to read braille and write it.'

The blind girls began talking to each other. They seemed gradually to forget that we were there.

'I wonder what the time is,' they said. 'I wonder what the weather's like.'

Some had ordinary voices, but others had children's voices.

They sounded as if they were ten years old. It was strange, I thought, that they didn't know the time, and even stranger that they didn't know what the weather was like. My mother and I could have told them. We could have told them that it was three o'clock and that it was cloudy, but that with this wind it wasn't likely to rain. It would have been easy to do this, but they weren't talking to us. They had forgotten we were there. We somehow didn't exist. A little while ago we came into the room, and then existed. We existed as two unknown people who came into their room suddenly and unexpectedly, and into their world. But immediately afterwards they lost sight of us. We sat down and were quiet, and then were forgotten.

'I wonder what the time is,' they said. 'I wonder what the weather's like . . . Has anyone heard the clock strike?'

Nobody had, but at that moment a clock struck three somewhere in the house. One heard it clearly, because at the same moment the door opened. It was the girl coming back with Sofie.

I'd thought she would be young. I'd thought she would be about my age. Lieutenant Christensen had called her Sofie. She had no surname. It was usually only children who had no surname, but this was true of blind girls too, it seemed. Sofie had no age. She might not have been old, but again she might have been. Her face was different from the others'. There were lines in it. It had been written on, and one could read the writing. It was a careworn face. Her eyes were white and the pupils were misty; you could only just see them, behind a whitish film. And she never blinked.

'So this is Sofie,' said my mother, and she began explaining what we had come for.

The other girls stopped knitting. They all sat with their hands in their laps, listening. They heard about the professor in Copenhagen who had said that I would never go blind. And about Lieutenant Christensen who had had this idea about braille, so that I could save my eyes and my sight.

'Well!' they all said. 'How exciting. And then perhaps he'll go to the 'Tute.'

'We'll pay you, of course,' said my mother to Sofie.

'I shall be glad to teach him to read and write, but I won't take money for it,' she said. 'I didn't pay for my teaching, and I won't take anything for teaching it to someone else. We blind people help each other,' she said.

'But he's not blind,' said my mother. 'Not a bit blind.'

It seemed to me not very polite to make me so very unblind here, among all the girls. I was ashamed. I said that when I wore my dark glasses as I was supposed to, I really couldn't see very much.

'Yes, he's for ever taking them off,' said my mother.

'Well, fancy,' they all said. 'But sometimes it passes off,' they said. 'It may pass off altogether,' they said, with an invisible light in their voices.

'We've so often heard of that happening,' said one of them, who was sitting by the window. She said it like the leader of a choir; and the rest joined in:

'Yes indeed, we've so often heard of that happening.'

They sat in their places, in caps that were all alike and aprons that were all alike. They looked like birds. Peculiar birds. Night birds.

'I'll soon teach you to read,' said Sofie. 'But first you must practise feeling with your fingers. You must practise never using your eyes.'

'Yes,' I said.

'It's not so easy as you might think.'

'No,' said the others. 'No, it's not easy.'

'We've got a story by Hans Andersen. It's printed with ordinary letters in relief. *The Nightingale* it's called. Do you know it?'

'Yes, do you know the nightingale?'

'No,' said my mother. 'I don't think he's ever seen one.'

'It's red and green, with gold on its breast and wings,' I said. 'I've often seen them.'

'Hans Andersen's nightingale isn't like that,' said Sofie. 'His is a modest little grey bird. But perhaps he made a mistake about that. I'd like to think so, because I once heard a nightingale sing, and it has a golden throat. When I think about it, I'd like to think you were right.'

'It has a golden throat, anyway,' said the girls, nodding. 'You can hear it,' they said.

'If we could borrow that book,' said my mother, 'he could begin. I don't know whether it'll be any use to him, but his teacher thinks so.'

Sofie went over to the little shelf. She walked more surely than the others. She didn't grope and she didn't hold one hand out in front. She went over to the shelf and let her fingers run over the backs of the books.

'Here it is,' she said.

Her hand stopped and she pulled out a big, thick book.

'We can spare it, can't we?' she asked the others. 'Nobody's reading it.'

'No, we can quite well spare it,' they answered in chorus. 'We're not reading it.'

It was a big book and a thick book, but it weighed nothing in the hand. It was quite light.

'They're ordinary letters,' said Sofie, 'just like the ones in your other books. But you mustn't cheat. You mustn't use your eyes,' she said.

She opened the book. When I bent over the table where it lay I could see it said *The Nightingale:* A Story by H. C. Andersen.'

'Give me your hand,' she said.

I held it out, and thought it was funny she didn't take it.

'Give me your hand,' she said again, and groped for it.

When she caught hold of it she guided my fingers along the lines. I couldn't distinguish one word from another, let alone the letters. I could only feel that the paper wasn't quite smooth.

'But he must have an alphabet and a frame and a stylus,' said Sofie. She talked like an ordinary person in spite of having no pupils and in spite of the whitish film over her eyes. 'Next time you go to Copenhagen you must go to the Blind Institute and buy an alphabet and a frame and a stylus.'

'Very well,' said my mother. 'If he must,' she said.

'Yes, he must.'

'Yes, he must,' they all repeated. 'He must have an alphabet and a frame and a stylus. Everybody has to have them.'

A lady came into the room. She came in from the passage where the staircase went up to L. Pode. She had dark glasses and a delicate white face.

'Good day,' she said, in a high clear voice.

'Good day, little mother,' they all said in chorus.

'It's half-past three, so we'll have our singing, shall we?'

'Sofie has visitors,' said somebody, in the silence.

'Oh, are there visitors here? I didn't know.'

We didn't know how to manage a greeting.

'Good day,' she said, and put her hand out where she was standing. My mother got up, went over and took it.

'It's a boy who may go blind, and go to the 'Tute,' said one of them.

'Oh, but how nice,' said the lady. 'How very nice. But we must have our afternoon song all the same. What shall we have today?' she asked, loudly and clearly.

'It's Ingeborg's turn to choose,' said somebody.

'Yes, it's Ingeborg's turn,' the others repeated.

There was stillness, but in the stillness the one called Ingeborg said,

'Yes, it's my turn. But I want to give it to Alma. She's been waiting for a letter from her father and sister, and today it's exactly six months since they last wrote, so I'd like Alma to have my turn.'

'Thank you, Ingeborg,' said Alma. She was one of the ones sitting by the window. 'Thank you, Ingeborg. You're always so kind. You're always ready to make other people happy – you always have something to give away.'

Then they began to sing. It was a song I didn't know: a slow

168

and sorrowful song. I thought it had to be slow, so that they could grope their way from note to note. There was a leader, as there was when they walked in the street; one who sang out and carried the rest with her. It was as if she was saying all the time she sang, 'Come along now, don't be afraid. Here come three notes following one after the other like three steps on a staircase – one, two, three – and then a little jump – so!' She sang and the rest followed her with pure, clear voices. Not for a moment did they sound like grown-up, tired, sad people. Worried people. In each verse there were two places where they divided into three parts; they stepped away from each other and answered each other and then joined into one again.

I had never heard so beautiful a song. I had never heard anybody sing in that way. It brought longing, a great, nameless longing. 'It must be for my sister,' I thought; for who else was there to long for? But it wasn't Kirstine. Or it was both her and something else, something that had no name?

The blind girls sat in their places. They had put down their knitting, those who had any. They sat with their eyes shut and swayed from side to side. They forgot everything in their singing – themselves and us. They forgot that they were at L. Pode's Home for the Blind. Perhaps they weren't at L. Pode's Home for the Blind just at this moment. They were in another world, and they sang to us from this other world, and about it. A slow and sorrowful song.

'Thank you, Alma,' said Mrs Pode, when they had finished. 'That was a good choice. I don't know anyone who's better than you at choosing the right songs.'

'Thank *you*, little mother,' said Alma, and she smiled one of the faded smiles that someone had forgotten to brush off and bury.

'We learned to sing at the 'Tute,' said Sofie. 'You can learn lots of songs there.'

My mother and I went home with the big, thick book. The paper in it was blue. I got the idea that everything to do with blind people was blue. Their spectacles. Their paper. It was blind-blue and marked with many fingers.

I sat at home and tried to read *The Nightingale* with my fingers, but it wouldn't work. I could just feel that the paper wasn't smooth, as paper in a book ought to be, but I couldn't make out any of the words and letters.

'He just hasn't the gift for being properly blind, then,' said my father. 'They say when people lose their sight they can hear and feel better.'

But with a light across the blue pages in the book I could see what was written there, and afterwards it was possible to recognize some character or other: nothing connected, only a round O for instance, or a full stop. And what good was that? I should never get any meaning out of it like this. It was much better with an ordinary book, and best of all when my mother read aloud. She often did that. We had got into the habit in Copenhagen. After that time she read almost every day. She took ten or fifteen minutes off a couple of times during the afternoon. She sat up on the platform.

'Makes you feel almost like a lady,' she said, looking for the place where we'd left off. 'Sitting here reading novels in the middle of the day, while other people work,' she said. 'But I'm not doing it on my own account. I only do it because you've got so mad about reading and can't do it for yourself.'

She felt ashamed about it. If we heard anybody coming up-stairs she quickly shut the book and hid it behind the curtain, and sat down at the table with her paper bags. People mustn't find out that we read.

'You must practise, too,' she said. 'You mustn't sit here listening all the time. Or go for a brisk walk,' she said, 'and find someone to keep you company, and get some rosy cheeks.'

'But it's braille you're supposed to be learning,' said Lieutenant Christensen, 'not that stuff. I read somewhere that they gave that up more than fifty years ago. I'll send for the alphabet and the frame and all the rest of it, for both you and me.'

And so at last I had what everybody had to have: an alphabet, a frame and a stylus. I began learning proper blind writing with Sofie, at L. Pode's Home for Blind Women.

'A is a dot at the top on the right,' said Sofie. 'A little tiny dot, like that. It's quite easy,' she said. 'Easy to write and easy to feel.'

'Yes, A's easy,' said the others. 'You can feel that all right. People say it's like a full stop.'

So I wrote a whole line of A's. We took the paper off the frame and Sofie let her fingers glide along over the dots. Her hand moved like a little animal. She had fine, sensitive skin at her finger-tips, like the muzzle of a horse.

She sat there with her white eyeballs, not blinking, not seeing. But her hands moved like little live animals over the paper.

I went on to B's and C's.

'Now it gets more difficult,' said Sofie. 'It's more difficult until you've learnt the first ten letters, and after that it's easy.'

'Yes, after that it's easy again,' said the others. 'When you get as far as J it's easy.'

They sat knitting, each in her place. Now and then one of them got up and went out. She followed the wall with one hand, and held the other one out in front. Now and then one of them came in. But most of them stayed where they were and knitted their long, grey knitting.

We had an A B C too, which I had to try and read from. I did much better with this than I had done with *The Nightingale*. I could feel the dots and recognize them as letters.

'Who's taken my knitting-bag?' asked somebody in a complaining voice. 'Who can have taken my knitting-bag?' she asked, and she sounded as mournful as if someone had stolen her happiness.

I thought it was odd, for it was almost exactly in front of her. I had only moved it the slightest bit to make room for my elbow. Surely she can see it, I thought, because I hadn't pushed it far.

'Who's taken my knitting-bag?' she mourned. 'Was it you, Sofie?'

No, it wasn't Sofie. It wasn't anybody. I just sat wondering, and was too stupid to understand. A whole flock of hands, a flock of little live animals raced out over the dark surface of the table and sought blindly in all directions with their sensitive horse-muzzle skin.

'Why, here it is,' said someone. 'It's almost straight in front of you.'

'Who put it there?' she asked, still complaining. 'Who was it who hid it from me?'

A sudden hush fell over the room. All the knitting-needles stopped. Hands lay down to rest in their laps. Complete and disturbing stillness.

'Did you move Betty's knitting-bag?' asked Sofie sternly, turning her white eyeballs on me. One got only a hint of the long, blurred pupils behind the film.

'I didn't move it,' I said. 'I just shoved it a little. I . . .'

I wanted to offer some sort of explanation; an explanation of something I didn't understand – of something utterly incomprehensible. But I found none.

'If you do that sort of thing we won't have you here,' said Sofie, not blinking. 'You can tell your mother that if you're going to amuse yourself by hiding our things you shan't come here again.'

'No,' said the rest in chorus. 'He shan't ever come here again.'

'Yes, but –' I stammered at last, 'I didn't try to hide anything.'

'You could have told Betty where her knitting-bag was,' said Sofie.

'Yes, he could have told Betty,' the others joined in.

'You'll be blind yourself some day,' said Sofie.

'No, I shan't,' I said, and I said it very firmly. 'I don't want to. The other day when we had *The Nightingale* I wanted to, but not now.'

'Why have you come here to learn, then?' asked Sofie. 'And anyway, it's not for you to decide.'

'The professor in Copenhagen said so.'

'It's not a thing he can decide, either,' said the others.

They sat in their places like birds – birds of ill-omen – and said it.

'I want to help you, and you're welcome to come here,' said Sofie. 'But you must be good.'

'Yes, he must be good,' the others repeated.

We read some more and we wrote some more, and in between-whiles I reflected that it wasn't just that they were blind: I knew that the girls in L. Pode's Home for Blind Women were blind. It was that they couldn't see anything. This had never struck me before. I hadn't understood that they couldn't spot a knitting-bag when it was right in front of them. I hadn't thought it was so absolute and impenetrable. I'd imagined, in spite of everything, that they were more or less like me. But a sudden cold breath had passed through the room and made me see and understand. See everything and understand completely.

I wrote F's and G's and learned to read with my fingers. And the others knitted. The grey strands of wool wound from the ball in their baskets up through their soft fingers and were knitted into the grey infinity, which had no pattern at all. Just a long trail of unbroken grey.

'I'm certain you're going to be good at reading,' said Sofie. 'And quite soon, too.'

15

In a house on the Embankment there was a man who played
the fiddle. I had heard him one day when I went past. I had
stood outside listening and I had seen him walk up and
down the room playing. Sometimes he put the mute on, so that
one couldn't hear anything, but one could see his arm, his right
arm, moving up and down, and the fingers of his left hand on
the strings, and one could see a tense look on his face. Then he
took off the little thing he had put on the bridge and the strings,
and the sound came – a shiny, quivering violin sound. It
seemed to shine like light, and there was a nightingale sob in
it.

'You can go in if you like,' said a strange man. 'If you like
listening, just walk in. The door's open.'

It was a shop door.

I lingered on the step and hesitated and couldn't bring myself
to go in. Then the strange man came straight up and pushed
the door open.

'Jacob,' he said. 'There's a little chap here who'd like to hear
you practise. I don't know who he is, but he's been standing
here quite quiet and listening.'

'I can't have anybody here when I'm practising,' said the
man with the fiddle.

'Well then, give him a ticket for your recital.'

'Why should I? Are you poor?' he asked me.

'I don't think so,' I said. 'But I wish I was.'

'Why?'

'Because then I might get a ticket.'

'Go on, give him one,' said the strange man. 'Or give him your card. He can get in on that.'

He took his wallet from his pocket and found a card. On it was written Jacob Gade.

'Just show that and they'll let you in without a ticket,' said the strange man.

But Jacob Gade had begun playing again. He was walking up and down the room and his bow danced over the strings and notes flew from the violin. I had never heard anything like it in my life. His arm was still, but he moved his right wrist until his hand was a little white patch of mist.

I arrived before anybody else that evening. I showed the card and went in and sat right in front with a crowd of empty chairs behind me. I wanted to sit where I could see. The organist came in and struck a note on the grand piano up there. Behind, Jacob Gade was tuning his violin. The organist, whose name was Brieghel-Müller, went on striking the same note. And there was a great empty space between him and me. A space so big and so empty that I never imagined the possibility of talking across it. I was surprised that one could say anything at all where he was standing; I somehow imagined one would have to express oneself in music.

'Hullo, have you come to the recital, then?' he said. 'And you're the very first, too.'

If a monument, a divine image, had opened its mouth and spoken to me I couldn't have been more astounded. I couldn't utter a sound. Wonder had struck me dumb.

'Do you think you'll make anything of it?' he asked.

But I still didn't say anything, and since I was so completely silent he could find nothing more to say either. He went away again, and I heard them talking and laughing behind a closed door.

Then people came. Little by little the hall was filled with people. Ladies and gentlemen of whose existence I had been quite unaware. It was like being in quite a different, unknown town. I thought I knew everybody. Here I knew no one, not a single face in all that throng. I was as lost and forlorn as I had been at the professor's clinic in Copenhagen. Nobody came and sat beside me or near me. But at last something happened. At last they came in, to play.

I sat and watched them. I saw them arranging their music and exchanging glances. And then came a deathly hush. Jacob Gade stood up there with his violin under his chin, looking down into the hall as if he wanted to find somebody to play to. And again he exchanged looks with the organist. There was a kind of tension that rose and rose. It was as if one couldn't be sure what was going to happen: whether Jacob Gade would make up his mind to play, or whether he would suddenly send his bow flying like a sharp arrow at one of the white shirt-fronts in the hall. It was a suspense so great and so acute that nobody dared breathe. It was resolved at last in a chord, a sound from the piano, and a violin note that spun itself out of that sound – thin and glittering like a gold thread in sunlight – a quivering golden thread. The sound that lingered after it, the echo, felt like a kind of weeping in one's chest. A weeping that could not be wept. Something altogether marvellous and dazzling. A golden thread that spun itself out of the violin and hung shining in the room, then faded and was gone, but returned again and was gone. As the organist had said, I probably didn't make much of it. But here I sat, hearing and seeing and living it, growing tired, and then living it again.

In the interval cantor Petersen appeared and was surprised to find me here. He praised me. He said that this was exactly where I ought to be and that he had thought of it, but that it was far better that I should have thought of it for myself.

'Notice now how he plays his Mendelssohn,' he said. 'That should be interesting.'

He spoke to me as one speaks to a sensible grown-up person. And I'd learnt enough to take his cue and agree that it would be interesting, though I had no idea what 'his Mendelssohn' might be.

Jacob Gade and the organist came in again, and the recital went on exactly as before. Notes flew like sparks of fire from his violin. And he did that trick of letting his right hand rotate until it was transformed into a little white patch of mist, and the bow danced over the strings. I sat dreaming that it was I up there, and that a certain person was to be found somewhere or other in the assembly of chairs. I felt like a victor, a great conqueror, a magician who, with such slight and simple means as a violin and a bow, was able to subjugate worlds, and perhaps even cause a pair of girl's eyes to widen in amazement and admiration. Perhaps she would go so far as to take her hands out of her jacket pockets and no longer refuse to let me touch her, just a little.

I made the concert go on in my own way. I didn't understand much about it and couldn't notice everything. Perhaps I couldn't truthfully claim to have listened. Time after time the golden thread was lost to me, and at last I could not find it again. But I sat there with a feeling of being carried up and up – of floating over an unknown land, a land of marvels where anything could happen. Where nothing was impossible.

When I came home my father was sitting with his Bible and my mother was pasting paper bags.

'You must have your drops,' she said, 'and go to bed.'

I would rather not have had my drops. It was like giving myself foggy vision of my own free will.

'And you look feverish,' she said.

'It's all this worldliness, and these music-halls,' said my father. 'If this is what comes of it, it would have been better if he'd never had that violin,' he said.

The lamp with its green container and brass shade shone and looked poor. My mother pasted paper bags and my father read his Bible, and there was no radiance in life any more. Nothing to dream about. There was a dearth of words – almost silence – and no golden thread that could turn into a golden web. It was everyday and dullness and bleak penury.

16

THE time had come when the professor wanted to see me again. We had to set off for Copenhagen.

'Let's hope it's for the last time,' said my father.

There was no answer. My mother was silent. She was silent, so one could see she didn't really believe that it could be the last time. But we went. My father stood alone on that nocturnal platform to see us off.

'Let's hope this is the last time,' he said as the train began to move.

He was left behind alone and we slid out into the darkness. The darkness of Sønder Woods. Into autumn and the wet. People slept in the corners of the carriage.

Raw sleet crossing the Belts.

Speech that altered. Newspaper boys in Korsør. A different kind of people – quicker, more talkative. They wanted to know so much – and were told so much. In between-whiles one slept. Slept sitting up, and woke now and again to hear the same story being told in the same mournful voice to new people. My story.

Copenhagen. A cold, grey morning. Trams and horse-drawn cabs. Busy people who hurried along and didn't mind bumping into you. The road to the clinic.

'I can see them up there in the windows with bandages over their eyes,' said my mother.

Then we were with the professor with the white head and the white hands. The same purgatory as before.

'Look up. Down. To one side. Look at the card. Look at my hands. How many fingers?'

The professor was not satisfied with me. He was not at all satisfied. He had to have me in his clinic again. It all happened exactly as before. Right from the beginning, all over again, just like last time. But no cheerful and comforting message from the operating-theatre. Only a hope. A frail hope, but still a hope.

'It may be years,' said the professor. 'Many years. It may never happen. There's always hope. What's he going to be?'

'I don't know,' said my mother. 'We haven't thought. Could he be a gardener?' she asked. 'He likes being in the garden. We've got a garden,' she said.

'A gardener must be able to tell the difference between weeds and other plants,' said the professor.

'But he can.'

'Yes, he can now; but will he be able to in two years' time, or five, or ten . . .? There's always this problem with the ones who can't see well enough to learn anything properly,' said the professor, 'and aren't yet blind enough to go into the Institute. Not blind enough yet . . .'

My mother thought and thought herself into dumbness.

'Wedell,' said the professor. 'You know Doctor Wedell? He told me the boy was musical.'

'Yes, but it's nothing,' my mother said. 'He amuses himself by playing a little. He passes the time like that when he can't play with the other children, and often he doesn't want to. He'd rather be with the others and do what they do. It isn't anything at all, really,' she said.

'I don't know,' said the professor. 'It's a subject I know nothing about. Have a word with Wedell,' he said. 'Perhaps you could call at the Institute now you're here. Look straight at me,' he said. 'Look at my forehead. Don't move your eyes. Tell me when you can see my hands . . .'

'The Institute,' said my mother. 'Do you really think so, professor? The Institute,' she said.

She stood there waiting, unable to do anything, superfluous and left over. Now and again she found a chance to slip in a question, and wait for the professor to let drop some kind of answer between two pipettes. Now and again she ventured to express a hint of doubt and anxiety. But it won her no comfort, far less any reassurance. She felt it was somehow her fault. Not all of it, perhaps, but some of it – a great deal of it. If we had come earlier, both this time and last. Especially last.

The professor didn't answer. He was utterly absorbed.

'I really think you should talk to Wedell,' he said once, absently. 'He's a remarkable man,' he said. 'A peculiar man. But talk to him. And go out to the Institute. I'll make you out a certificate to take,' he said.

It didn't seem to me so bad. Nothing to be cross about. Nothing to shrink and get narrow-faced about. I was doing perfectly all right. I knew the nurse. I knew the other patients. I talked to them. I stood by the window in the mornings looking to see if I could spy my mother when she came. Sometimes I could. Sometimes I spotted her. It was no worse than it was for lots of other people. In fact it was better. I didn't have to go about with a black patch or two black patches. Of course I ran into things; but I was used to running into things and grazing my nose and having bumps on my forehead. One could get used to that too.

'And you could be more careful,' said my mother. 'You could walk carefully, like the girls in the Blind Home.'

But I wasn't the careful kind. I hadn't the gift for being blind, as my father had said. He didn't say it as a reproach. He said it because he believed that nature was kind – or God. He was quite certain that if a person was fated to lose his sight, one of the signs would be that his other senses would grow keener before it happened. It wasn't like that with me. I didn't learn caution. I ran into things. I neither heard nor felt anything more than usual. So it was not nature's – or God's – intention that anything unusual should happen to me. My father believed that everything was connected and consistent. He was certain of it. My mother was not. She felt she had learnt differently. She was sceptical. Sceptical of good fortune and bad, but less sceptical of bad.

'We'll go and see the people at the Institute,' she said, 'and we'll call on Wedell.'

Yet at the same time she could see how unreasonable it was always to look on the dark side. Certainly there had been no miracle, but that was not to say there might not be an improvement. Might one not venture – without forsaking one's humility – to hope for just the tiniest improvement? Not that she didn't appreciate the cleverness of such a famous professor, and it wasn't that she doubted his word. But in the old days there used to be something called 'growing out of it'.

'No,' said the professor. He said it in an absolute and decisive manner. He said No so that it sounded like a sabre-stroke. 'What's lost is lost,' he said. 'It can never return.'

My mother had nervous thumbs again. She stood there tense with the questions she had thought about in the course of the night at the mission-hostel. But she never got them out. They must have shrunk inside her, as she herself shrank. Faded in her mouth, as she herself was fading. And all at once the professor must have noticed that she was shrunken and faded, and that she mourned day and night.

'It's bad,' he said. 'But think how much worse it would have been if your boy had died.'

'No,' said my mother. 'We know what death is.'

'And what is it?'

'It's the door into a new life.'

'H'm,' said the professor, shaking his white head. 'H'm,' he said. 'Perhaps this too may be a door into a new life, as you call it. Another life,' he said. 'A life different from the one you expected. Perhaps better . . .'

We went to Wedell at Dosseringen. He lived in a perfectly ordinary house. A fine house, certainly, with a garden in front

181

and a porter. One had to ring a bell before one could get in and walk upstairs. But I'd never thought that Wedell would live exactly as other people did. He had a favourite song which told of the new Jerusalem, the heavenly city with streets of gold. I think I had imagined that Wedell belonged to this new Jerusalem, and he would be surrounded by at least some reflection of its splendour and glory. But he wasn't. He just had a couple of rooms at the end of the baroness's flat. A big, light room with windows overlooking the garden and the lake, and a smaller, dark room behind.

There was a chamber-organ, partly in pieces. The front was unscrewed and some of the keys had been removed. It looked like gaps in a row of teeth. There were books on the table: big books. One or two of them were open, the rest were stacked up. There were little metal reeds from the inside of the organ. There were files. There was also a little bellows in which the reeds could be fixed when he filed them and altered their notes. Above, on a little white cupboard with gold on it, lay a guitar without strings. He was walking about in a long coat with an unlit cigar in his mouth. One could see his thin legs below the coat. But he was not the same here as he was when he travelled about the country holding jubilee-meetings with the Norwegians, with Staff and Ullnes. Here he had no congregation. People didn't flock to him. Nobody said alleluia or thanks and praise be. He was a perfectly ordinary person, occupied in mending guitars and tuning chamber-organs according to his own divine system. He was alone, and his loneliness made him somehow naked – as if he were shivering a little in his long coat. He seemed to have too little fire in him for even his cigar to burn.

'No, I don't smoke,' he said, as if he could look into my mind. 'I don't smoke. I just bite a havana to get its bouquet – the bit of strength that's in it. I don't need to light it,' he said. 'That's just vulgar.'

Here in his own home he talked differently from the way he talked at the meetings. He may have talked to Ludvigs the chemist like that, using unknown, strange words, but not when he wanted to say anything to other people.

'Everybody cuts the end off the cigar and lights it and smokes,' he said. 'It's so dull . . .'

But we hadn't come to talk to him about the best way to enjoy havana tobacco. We'd had no idea that there was anything called that. It was really because he had always taken so much interest in me, first giving me the guitar, and then – what with one thing and another . . .

My mother got rather stuck. And indeed it was all quite different from what she had imagined and expected . . .

'Ye-es,' said Wedell, standing by the window and looking down at the water of the lake. 'Ye-es,' he said.

His back was turned to us and he looked down at the water and over to some leafless trees in Østersø Street. He stood as if awaiting a sign; as if something would be written on the surface of the water, or as if the branches over on the further side would yield and bend and form a word – a word of God . . .

'Ye-es,' he said, and sighed. It sounded as if neither in heaven nor on earth, neither in the water and the clouds nor on my own forehead was there any sign of a divine plan for me. Today Wedell was not as clear-sighted as usual.

'Perhaps it is because I'm rather tired,' he said. 'I'll order some tea. Sit down,' he said. 'And you can touch anything you like,' he told me.

Tea was something we didn't know about. Rich people drank tea. Ordinary people stuck to coffee. But Wedell was no ordinary person, after all. He used unusual words. He drank tea. He had no work. He just busied himself with books and instruments: the things that interested him.

There was a kind of basket-work sofa with cushions on it. It was rather like a big, oblong dog-basket. When he came back he lay down on it.

'I'm rather tired,' he said. 'I'll be better if you'll excuse my lying down. We'll talk over what would be best,' he said. 'And we'll be silent, and listen for God to whisper something to us . . .'

The basket-work creaked and I thought of the butcher's dead dog at home. The dog had a basket too now, so that it didn't have to sleep on the mat any more. It was a good dog. It had taken to coming more with me than with anybody else. It had joined me and Anders; it let Anders tie his red reins to its collar and play with it.

My mother and Wedell talked about the professor and the Institute and the future. I'd heard it all before. My mother said the professor and the Institute and the future in the same anxious and mournful voice as ever. I didn't want to listen. I was tired of the same words and the same anxious voice. It became a weight in one's head, a heavy leaden weight at the back of one's head which was not to be borne.

A maid came in – a grand parlour-maid with a white cap on her head and a tea-service on a silver tray. There was toast and jam, but the baroness wanted to know whether the doctor would like anything else . . .

No, that would do. Wedell was satisfied. 'Thank you,' he said, and the maid bobbed.

A space was cleared on the table. Wedell closed his big books, and pushed tools and metal reeds to one side.

'It was like being with the King,' said my mother afterwards. 'I'm sure it could be no finer at the King's palace.'

The tea revived Wedell. He still had those odd, dead eyes, but he talked more. He seemed able to see and read things on my forehead that he had seen and read before.

'Music,' he said. 'I feel convinced that it should be something to do with music.'

My mother didn't think I had shown any particular fondness for it. I'd liked it for a time, but I had no perseverance. She could not honestly understand why Wedell had that idea.

'There's something called intuition,' he said.

My mother knew nothing about that.

'And there are certain outward signs,' he said.

184

These too were hidden from her. She knew of none.

He asked suddenly whether I was good at mathematics. And I was. Unusually good. Quite remarkably so, my teachers had said. Wedell nodded. He nodded most significantly.

'I hold the belief,' he said, 'that all great musicians were mathematicians in a former existence.'

After that there was silence. A deep silence, full of reflection. Wedell believed in the transmigration of souls. I could see how deeply shaken my mother was by this idea. It made her silent. What faith could one put in a person who believed in that?

'Or rather reincarnation,' said Wedell.

'Oh.'

'I only mention it,' he said, 'because it's a little sign – an arrow pointing in the same direction as other little arrows.'

'Oh!' said my mother again, and she no longer attached much importance to Wedell's words. But I did.

Outside dusk was falling. Early December dusk. The trams along Østerbro Street carried lights in their hats, and the yellow lamps on the other side of the lake were lit.

'I'll go and ring up the Blind Institute,' he said, 'and ask if you can go along there right away. It's no distance.'

My mother would have prevented this. She had been thinking it over for some time, and yet it came upon her rather suddenly. Not enough thought had been given to it; it seemed hardly more than an impulse. But Wedell didn't think so. The dog-sofa creaked under him as he got up. The long coat hung limply over his thin legs. He was going to telephone, and warn them that we were coming.

'I did what I could to prevent it,' said my mother when he was out of the room. 'I didn't want him to do it, but perhaps it's better as it is. If it's best,' she said, 'we'll go, in Jesus' name.'

A dim road with big trees. Tall trees. It was rather windy, and it was drizzling. There was a smell of wet earth, from the old gardens behind the board fences and from the wet trees. A gas-lamp shed yellow light on an empty bench and a few withered leaves. The Deaf-and-Dumb Institute. A post-box. An entrance drive. To the right, in the darkness, an organ growled with deep bass notes. We went through the wicket-gate. The wind and the rain caught hold of the trees – the trees in the garden and the trees outside along the road. In front of us loomed a giant wall laden with darkness. Three or four windows with lights in them. They made the house bigger and heavier and more darkness-laden.

A narrow line of flagstones led from the gate to the main door. One could feel them through one's shoes and follow them. Tinkling on a piano from somewhere – from two places. There were violins too: people practising. We stopped and listened, but it told us nothing.

Ahead of us was a lighted window. A naked window. There were no flowers and no curtains. And inside was a naked room. Even more naked and bare than the rooms in L. Pode's Home for Blind Women. A man was walking round inside. He walked round and round like the second-hand of a clock round its centre. A gas-pipe came down from the ceiling. It bent and ended in a flame. Perhaps there was a circle of light on the floor, and the man was following this circle. He went on going round as if he had been started years ago and would go on going round for years to come. Round and round with his head bent forward. The same tempo. The same beat. A piece of clockwork. Perhaps a perpetual-motion machine. One didn't hear his footsteps and one didn't hear the hiss of the gas-jet. It was just a picture. A mute vision. An image of time . . .

An iron scraper rattled underfoot. Some worn stone steps. A heavy door. We pushed it open. There was no instrument to ring when one went in. This place had nothing in common with L. Pode's Home for Blind Women. Absolutely nothing. Long hospital corridors. Broad staircases to right and left. Above, in the middle, a light with a dull white shade. But people . . . There were no people. A smell of paint – of paint and øllebrød[1] and damp floorcloths. But no people. Music was

[1] A kind of gruel made with beer.

being played, near and far away and right over our heads. And there was a big clock that ticked – a Bornholm clock. It struck the quarters. The dull white shade shone, but the stairs were deserted and the corridors were deserted and nobody appeared. We stood waiting and listened to people playing everywhere and heard the clock strike the quarter and smelt the smell of paint and *øllebrød* and damp floorcloths. We were rather cold.

Then we turned and saw that in a door to the right of the entrance was a little oval window. Behind the window was a forehead. Beneath the forehead a pair of eyes. They stared out at us, hostile. The man dropped a white blind over the little window, and immediately afterwards he came out and asked what we wanted at that time of day. My mother told him. He didn't answer, but went over to another door opposite. He had a big bunch of keys in his hand.

'Come this way,' he said.

A little office – little and narrow. A green-shaded lamp on the writing-table. A man was sitting there writing. He had white hair that grew thick at the back of his head and fell down over his collar. I saw his right hand and the pen and his right ear, a shell full of darkness. He told us that we were to sit down and that he would soon have finished.

The man with the bunch of keys growled crossly and went out, shutting the door hard behind him. I wondered if he was going to lock us in, but he didn't. He just went away snarling something or other.

My mother sat down in an armchair. There was no other. I stood beside her. She held my hand. I didn't know why: there was nothing to watch out for here. But she held it tight and wouldn't let go.

The pen scratched over the paper. Music was being played all about us in that big house. You could hear it, but it sounded far away. One of the deep bass notes of the organ made a door-panel vibrate. Each time that low note came the panel vibrated.

The principal finished writing. He put down his pen and picked up the blotter. He pressed it down and kept it in his hand and cleared his throat. My mother handed him the certificate the professor had given us. He read it and looked at me, looked at the letter again and cleared his throat.

'I see,' he said. 'But would you like to come here?'

'Yes.'

My mother started. A stab. A sudden pain. I felt it in her hand. She hadn't expected me to answer yes. She had probably expected the very opposite. She had thought I would say no. Or that I would be afraid or sulky, and refuse to speak at all. She had thought that she would have to answer for me in one way or another.

He looked again at the doctor's certificate and said,

'According to this your sight's too good. Too good for you to come here, I mean.'

'Oh!' I said, disappointed.

I'd never heard anybody say this before. So my sight was too good.

No, nobody had ever told me that. I was disappointed. A little light had been burning inside me. Perhaps many little lights. They had been extinguished one by one as we came along the dim road and in through the garden; while we stood watching the man walking round and round, and while we were waiting. I don't know what I'd thought or imagined. And now the last little light went out. Instead, his words lit little lights in my mother. She was narrow-faced, but little by little she began to shine. She had nervous thumbs and her face was narrow. But she shone . . .

They began talking about how I did at school. Among other children. In class.

'Well, yes,' said my mother. 'He gets on, you know. He gets on all right, I think. Quite all right,' she said, correcting herself.

But she said nothing about the bother there had been over me. Nothing about my learning braille with Lieutenant Christensen and being a laughing-stock. I still had the 'eyes like a hawk' that the Kolding specialist had talked about. My arithmetic books were mentioned. But I didn't have them because I couldn't see the board; I had them because I was so much better at it than the others. Ahead of them. My mother had forgotten that I used to hide in the lavatories during break. She forgot, because that time had gone past. Nowadays I could stay in the classroom if I liked, or go away. But I remembered it all. I would never forget it. She had suddenly forgotten too that I couldn't play and read music and follow a conductor all at the same time, as cantor Petersen had explained. I was almost a genius at seeing. My mother wanted to believe . . . She wanted to believe that I had no business in an Institute for the Blind.

'Music,' said the principal. 'Everybody thinks of that. That requires talent – very special talent. Not many people have it, and very few get really far. Music,' he repeated, and cleared his throat. 'No, I don't think so. They all want to do that.'

Outside a bell rang. One could hear that someone was pulling a cord and making it ring. And one could hear that it was ringing in the wind – a cold, wet December wind. The music all through the house stopped. The door-panel didn't rattle any more. There was no tinkling on the pianos. Everything stopped. Steps outside along the corridors. Many steps. Quick steps. One couldn't hear that the people out there were blind. The voices didn't sound blind, either. They didn't talk with their eyes shut. They didn't talk inside a wall of blindness. They were ordinary voices. Boys' voices.

But of course, explained the principal, a doctor's certificate wasn't everything. There were complicated cases. Perhaps I was one of them. There were children whose sight was too good for them to come here, but on the other hand not good enough for them to learn a trade outside. Had I, for instance, shown any liking for making brushes? No? Baskets? Not that either. Shoes?

The thing was, my mother had to confess, that I was rather stubborn by nature. I had got it into my head that I wanted to play an instrument, or others had put it there for me.

'Unfortunately we haven't much choice,' said the principal. 'If it becomes necessary for him to come here when he's finished school, he'll almost certainly have to get that sort of thing out of his head again. Brushes,' he said, 'shoes, baskets,' he said, and at every word he gave a little thump on the table with the blotter. 'Or rope-making. I'd almost forgotten rope-making. Would you like that?'

'No,' I said.

'He's not good with his hands,' said my mother anxiously.

'He'd have to use his hands for music, wouldn't he?'

'His handicrafts master says he's one of those who can't saw straight.'

The principal shrugged his shoulders.

Now it was my mother's little lights that one by one were going out.

'Yes, well,' he said. 'We shall have to see about it when he leaves school. Not before. Certainly not before. Unless something happens. It wouldn't be wise, anyway. Write to us,' he said. 'Write to us nearer the time, and we'll see about it.'

He was silent, but remained sitting with the blotter in his hand, looking straight in front of him.

'We can't get any further this time,' he said at last with a thin smile, and held out his hand in farewell. A smile that was not unfriendly and a hand that was not entirely hard. 'Perhaps we shall meet again,' he said. 'If that's how it turns out we shall be glad to see you. But it would be better if it didn't.'

Long, deserted corridors. Stairs. Institute smell. A cold gust of wind and rain through the main door. The lamp hung with its glass clattering with cold. A blind was drawn aside. Carefully. A very little. A forehead. A pair of hostile eyes staring out at us. The blind fell again. The narrow line of paving-stones through the garden. In the big, bare room the same man was steadily walking, circling about his invisible axis. We stood for a moment watching him, as one watches a clock, a second-hand that follows its path round the dial, measuring time.

We went along the row of flagstones. We passed through the wicket-gate. They were beginning to play in there again. On the organ. On the piano. Far away a single violin. Trees stood soughing leaflessly in wet December wind. The big trees in the garden and the ones along the road. A dim road with a deserted bench. The gas-lamp shed its yellow light on some floating, withered leaves.

We went home, and there were only a couple of days to Christmas.

'I was thinking you mightn't come back,' said my father. 'I was just wondering if I should be spending Christmas alone,' he said.

But of course not. Naturally we came home as quickly as we could.

'Maybe it would be better somewhere else,' he said. 'More fun, more celebrations.'

No. No other place was better.

'No improvement?' he asked.

No. No improvement.

'The opposite, then?'

Yes, the opposite, if anything.

'But the principal of the Institute thought his sight was too good,' said my mother. 'Much too good to go there.'

'And will it last?'

'Last . . . Well, I don't –'

'I mean did the professor promise that the boy would have the light of his eyes until next Christmas, say?'

'It's not easy to get anybody to promise anything in this world,' my mother said. 'And I don't know that I put much faith in promises.'

My father nodded to himself. He nodded as if he'd been thinking the same thing, but he didn't speak. He had things to do in the cellar and in the attic too. Nothing special. Nothing at all.

'It's only something I started on when I was alone here,' he said.

But there was a new, mysterious look in his face. A slyness we had never seen there before.

'Have you thought about Christmas at all?'

'No; it seemed . . . There's been so much expense over all this,' said my mother. 'And now we don't know what the future's to be.'

'Nobody's ever been sure about the future so far's I know,' said my father.

An evening passed in this way, and a day and another evening. A little bickering. A little argument, but not un-friendly. Not a bit unfriendly. Silence between-whiles. Naturally. But not an oppressive silence.

'If this is to be the last Christmas the boy has the light of his eyes –' said my father. He used those words: 'the light of his eyes.' '– oughtn't he to have a tree that would go on shining for him year after year? In his memory?'

What could he mean by that . . .

If anyone had asked, the answer was in the cellar and in the attic. It was in the shape of a tree.

'I fetched it from the woods myself,' said my father. 'I went out one evening and chose it out of a hundred others. Nobody could see there's one missing. I cut it down myself. I stood in the starlight and did it. Not that it's important. I just mention it because that's how it was.'

'Isn't that stealing?' asked my mother.

'Yes,' he said. 'But buying seemed too easy, like. The decora-tions – I bought and paid for them. They're in the attic – boxes of them. Every scrap bought and paid for. I thought, if this was to be the last Christmas . . .'

It was a fairy-story he had thought out in his solitude – a tale from the *Arabian Nights*. There were boxes of gold and silver, and tinsel and coloured candles – enough for the tree at a club gathering. He carried it all in and dared not touch it, for the balls were so brittle that they broke if he took them in his fingers. And the tree reached from floor to ceiling with a star at the top and all sorts of rich-man's finery. It was luxury and splendour.

'It's only because I thought this might be the last Christmas he'd have the light of his eyes,' said my father. 'I don't say somebody else shouldn't have thought of it first,' he said, 'but it was me who did think of it. I thought he should have a tree to stand and shine in his memory, year after year,' he said.

The bell at the level-crossing rang, and the trains went by. And my father listened for the trains, to hear whether they were coming from the south or from the north. And he listened for footsteps on the stairs. Something was making him restless, but we didn't know what it was. We didn't discover it until my sister came. We didn't discover it until she was standing in the room; for she ran up the stairs as if she'd never run up any other stairs in the whole world.

This should be remembered, I thought. This should be remembered for a thousand years. But this evening was to be remembered for a reason I didn't then know. For then it was still sheer glory and festival and joy. I stood there full of a billowing sea, unable to speak – unable to utter one word. But my sister had her hands. She had hands full of tenderness. Great tenderness. Involuntary. She needed no words to express herself, to utter the unutterable.

Then it was our father who lit the tree. He stood there in the radiance of the candles – that shimmer of silver and gold and red and blue. He stood quite still and grew out of himself and over himself. He became great. He became the father of lights, from whom all this splendour and glory came. Generous. Almighty.

Even my mother yielded and abandoned herself and allowed the light to shine through her. It was Kirstine who made her slip her moorings from an everyday which perhaps had never seemed to her grey or joyless. It was her nature never to light one festival candle until she had at least two within reach.

We walked round the tree and sang. And I had to get out my violin and show Kirstine how far I'd got. And she was full of admiration.

'It's moving,' she said. 'Really moving . . .' What a word. That must be Dronningborg School. Dronningborg must be a strange town full of unknown people who spoke and said things in a way that sounded strange to our ears.

'Moving,' she said. 'When you play I could almost . . .'

'Come now,' said my father. 'Come now, let's sing Gold and Frankincense and Myrrh.'

The world had gone topsy-turvy. It was fine and warm and safe, but it was impossible to hang on to a grain of common sense. Everything melted away in a quivering fog of light. Yes, the world was topsy-turvy.

But the room grew too cramped. The ceiling too low and the walls too close to each other. We had to get out, my sister and I – out under the open sky. And our father came with us. We walked together along the street. We heard people talking and singing behind lowered blinds. But we met nobody. We went to the woods. They were where they ought to have been. They stood there big and black and windless, breathing into Christmas Night.

'But there'll be frost,' said my father. 'The sky's full of stars. It's freezing already, I expect.'

'Yes,' said my sister, and she wriggled against the cold.

I looked up at the sky too, but for me there were no stars to be seen. They had paled away. Vanished. There was only the sky. A vast, dark night sky without the least glint of light.

'Bright starlight,' said my father. 'The Milky Way,' he said; and for a moment he was elsewhere.

I could see it in my mind: a sky full of stars. I saw it sharply and clearly. It was like a page of braille with golden dots. But if I looked up at it there was nothing but darkness – deep, impenetrable gloom.

I didn't attach much importance to it. I said nothing about it to my father or my sister. I just thought I'd look again some other time and look more carefully, if that would help.

But would there be another time . . .

17

ALITTLE way into the New Year a letter came from my Swedish grandmother in Småland. She was now seventy, and couldn't expect to live much longer. This was a thought that had struck her more and more often as the days went by. 'The earth reminds me,' she wrote.

My father took the letter and carried it about and pondered its contents. He carried it in his jacket-pocket and took it out in the evenings and read it aloud.

'The earth reminds me,' my grandmother wrote. She had felt for a long time that the hour would soon come for her to die. She had put her house in order and talked to the pastor and been to communion, and the schoolmaster had explained to her about the long journey and promised to get her ticket. He was going to arrange it so that she could break her journey at Växjö and say goodbye to Britta Johansson, who lived at the Sandströms' place, and whom she hadn't seen for sixty years, since they had worked together as little girls. Did my father remember Britta Johansson? No, it wasn't likely. She would stay for a few days with Britta at the Sandströms' place and then continue the long journey . . .

All this she wrote, and more, a whole long letter, which my father read aloud from and pondered over.

One day he came home after a conversation with the sexton. 'What's that? With the sexton?' My mother was so startled that she stopped work. 'What about, for goodness' sake?'

What was so queer about that? Didn't it say plainly in the

letter that grandmother had been to communion and all that, and that she was coming here to die . . .?

'She's not coming here on any ordinary visit,' said my father. 'She writes what I've read out to you: "I'm coming to die." '

Well, yes, of course. That was true enough. Nobody could argue with that. But all the same, to go straight to the sexton . . .

'Letter comes with a ten-øre stamp on it,' my mother said, 'and off you go to the sexton to ask about a burial-place! Eh?'

My father nodded; that was how it was.

'Exactly,' he said.

'But couldn't you have thought of fetching her?' said my mother. 'Travelling with her? Helping her when she has to change trains?'

My father sat twiddling the matchbox between his fingers. He took out his Bible and read it for a bit and put it away and sat again with the matchbox and then took out the letter.

'I did it because she says she's got to die now,' he said. 'But of course we wouldn't want her to lose her life on the way . . . If only we could make out when she means to start.'

The letter was examined again from end to end. There was no sign to reckon from – not the least little date. There was a blurred postmark, and that was all.

'But we could write to the schoolmaster and find out,' said my father. 'We could sit down right away and send him a post-card. If we had a postcard.'

We managed the postcard. We stood at the table – my mother and I – tensely and most respectfully and watched my father write to the schoolmaster and ask cleverly about day and hour and request information at his earliest convenience . . . After that we had only to wait.

'But supposing you'd gone so far as to order the coffin and the funeral and everything,' said my mother, joking.

'No. I never thought of doing that. But I thought I might as well have a place ready, so I could show it to my mother when she comes, and say: "Look, this is where I thought you could lie; it's a good place and I've got it cheap." ' Thus my father explained his ideas. 'I know my mother,' he said. 'I know what she'd like. And it's nothing to joke about . . .'

'Well, am I supposed to cry?'

'No,' my father said. 'It's nothing to joke about nor cry about either. It's just as it is.'

The schoolmaster's answer came before we could have expected it. He could only make a guess, since grandmother had already left for Britta Johansson's in Växjö. So of course my father had to get away at once.

'As soon as possible,' he said. 'I must get ready as soon as possible.'

We went to the night train in the frost – sparkling frost and a thin, keen east wind that pricked our skins. But we had thick, warm winter clothes on. And my father was carrying a new brown leather suitcase. We had won prizes in the goods-lottery, and it showed.

'But I think I could have found my way by myself,' said my father. 'I've had to go this way alone quite often, and about this time of night – exactly this time, I should say.'

He meant when he had come with my mother and me to see us off to Copenhagen. Now it was he who was to go.

'I only hope you can coop with it all,' said my mother – and wherever could she have picked up that extraordinary word? 'I only hope you can coop . . . All those people . . . and the traffic . . .'

Once more she described in detail the way my father must take from the station to Aunt Jane's. My mother and I had come to know Copenhagen amazingly well. Sometimes we talked about its streets as if it was there we really belonged, and as if this place were a sort of exile – a purely temporary arrangement.

But my father told us we weren't to fuss. In the old days he had roamed the world, and knew more about it than he had needed to know for many, many years. It was fine to have so long a journey before him and not feel nervous.

The frosty snow creaked under our thick boots, and the cold east wind pricked our skins with little pointed needles. There was fine snow-dust in the air and something reminding one of sulphur – a faint smell of sulphur. But the houses slept and there were no people in the streets. Nobody on the Embankment along the river. Only from behind the dingy yellow curtains of the Trades Association one could hear laughter and song.

'No, you needn't have come with me,' said my father. He was really rather excited. 'You needn't have come all the way to the station.'

He was rather sly and just a little excited. He didn't sound as if he was merely going to meet an old woman who was coming here to die – an old woman who was his own mother. Though of course he was going to prevent her losing her life on the way. And he talked as if one didn't always meet people at the station and see them off when they went.

'It's not like animals,' my mother said. 'They come and go as best they can.'

'Many's the horse I took off the train while I was at the Ground,' my father said. 'And I sent even more of 'em away.'

It was true, every word of it. Who could forget?

We sat and waited on the platform, and it was as it always was. People yawning and stretching. People saying good morning to each other, though it was only an hour past midnight, or not even that. The mail-cart driving up.

My mother went over the route again.

'First you go along Farimag Street, right to the end, and it's a long one. And then . . .'

'Now don't you worry,' said my father. 'If I've never been just that very way I've been plenty of others. I'll get there,' he said. 'I'll get there somehow or other . . .'

Then at last the train came in and we found a carriage and said goodbye again, and my mother told him about the way down to the ferry at Fredericia:

198

'Just follow the crowd,' she said.

But my father was no longer listening. The train was still standing at the platform, but inwardly he had started upon his journey. He remained at the open window and we stood below on the platform, but his journey had already begun.

'Is it nice and warm in there?' asked my mother. 'Shouldn't you take off your overcoat?'

'Eh? No,' he said.

Steam hissed out of some valve or other.

'No,' he said. 'Goodbye till I see you.'

It was a leave-taking without sorrow. A leave-taking with expectancy – happy expectancy. Not like my mother's and mine. The whistle blew and the train began to move. My father stood at the open window, but he was far ahead of the train. He had started on his journey long ago and was hastening on ahead. We watched the red rear-lights on the last coach disappear in the darkness.

We crossed the station square. The thin east wind from the harbour had grown even keener, and it brought more fine snow-dust with it. The dust settled round one's neck and in one's ears and melted there. Voices and laughter and singing still came from behind the dingy yellow curtains of the Trades Association.

'You'd think those people never went to bed,' said my mother.

At that moment a man came out. He came out in a cloud of tobacco-smoke and stuffiness. He halted and waited for a moment, blowing through his lips like a horse at the frosty air and the snow-dust. Then he began walking. He walked and tooted a march between his lips – a monotonous little march: 'Boo-boobooboo-boo-boo . . .' he sang. 'Boo-booboo-boo-boo-boo.' Now he lurched a little to one side and now to the other.

'Hurry,' said my mother, holding me firmly by the hand. 'Why do you keep staring behind you?'

'It's only Valborg's father,' I said.

Sometimes when I was up at Valborg's I could hear her father clattering with bottles and glasses in the next room, behind the closed door. He opened cupboards and clinked glasses and Valborg said it was her father making chemical experiments for next day's classes. But if one stayed long enough it always ended by him walking up and down in there, or round the table, tooting. He tooted the same monotonous little march as he was tooting now, on the Embankment that was like a street in Amsterdam.

'Nonsense,' said my mother. 'Hurry up now, and stop turning round.'

'Boo-boobooboo-boo-boo,' he tooted close behind us.

At the hospital corner we turned off. But he put a hand to his hat as he walked by, and he said good night.

'Did you ever see anything like it!' said my mother. 'Touching his hat and saying good night. I wonder he's not ashamed...'

'Boo-boobooboo-boo-boo,' he tooted, marching on down West Street. He was marching home.

By now my father was half-way to Fredericia.

There was a grand piano in the corner room. And a chamber-organ too, only it was called a harmonium.

'So you haven't even got a harmonium,' said the organist.

'No, I haven't. But we've thought about it,' I said.

I didn't know whether anybody but myself had thought about it.

'H'm,' he said, rubbing his hands. He walked up and down and into the next room where there was a porcelain stove, and back again, rubbing his hands. 'H'm,' he said. 'You really ought to have one . . .'

I'd been standing in our gateway, not wanting to go out because it was blowing and snowing and there was no one to play with but Anders. And I just didn't want to. I'd been sent out for a breath of fresh air, and was standing there in the gateway when the organist came past and asked whether I'd like to go home with him. I thought I might just as well get a breath of fresh air there as here.

'Cantor Peterson tells me you've got a good ear.'

I had nothing to say to that. The organist struck a couple of notes and asked me what they were. I could tell him that all right; I used to play that game with Valborg. It amused her. It didn't amuse the organist. He simply said,

'Absolute pitch. Try again,' and chose one low note and one high one. 'Absolute pitch,' he said again, like the professor in Copenhagen when he examined me and found out something and said what was to be written down in his case-book. 'Harmonies?' he asked. 'Can you hear harmonies too?'

'N-no, I can't,' I said. 'What are harmonies?'

'A number of notes played together.' He struck a chord.

'Does one have to know that?' I asked.

'No,' he said. 'It doesn't really mean anything at all. Absolute pitch . . . Unless you were going to be a piano-tuner – not otherwise. You can have absolute pitch and still be quite unmusical.'

So it was no good. That was something I didn't understand. When at last I could do something that other people couldn't, it meant nothing. It made no difference. It was unnecessary.

'Imagination,' he said. 'Have you got imagination?'

How should I know that? What did he mean, anyway? He sat down at the piano, rubbed his hands again and began to play, asking me questions at the same time. He asked me all kinds of questions – like a professor on the track of a new disease in me – a new way of being different.

'You go about on your own a good deal. What do you think about?'

'Nothing,' I said. 'I just go about and look at things and notice things and . . .'

'Notice what?' he asked, and stopped playing.

'Oh, nothing . . . I just play or talk to people or . . .'

'Do you day-dream?'

I thought of the story of Joseph and his brethren, and how

they had said, 'Behold, this dreamer cometh. Let us cast him into some pit.' I wasn't going to be cast into any pit. And I thought of the sun and the moon and the eleven stars that made obeisance.

'Do you day-dream?' he asked again.

Outside the snow was like gauze against the window, and the wind swept round the corner. It sounded different from the wind at home. Stronger. Bigger.

A door was slammed open and slammed shut and a lady came into the next room on hard heels; she made up the stove and coughed.

'Oh, that noise!' he said irritably, and with a look of suffering on his face.

'I didn't know you were composing,' said the organist's wife. 'It didn't sound like it.'

So he composed too, I thought. I didn't know that any living people did that. Valborg had told me about Beethoven and she had told me about Mozart, but they were dead. I had got the idea that people who composed were dead – extinct, as it were.

'You ought to put on a red goblin cap when you don't want to be disturbed,' she said, 'and then . . .'

He had that suffering look again and shrugged his shoulders and rubbed his hands.

'Well, go now, anyway,' he said. 'Get finished and go.'

She slammed the door of the porcelain stove and clattered the coal-scuttle, walked on hard heels across the floor and slammed the door.

'What a shame,' he said. 'We were having such a nice talk. What was it we were talking about?'

'Nothing.'

'Nothing? Oh well, perhaps. Shall I play for you . . . shall we find something . . . Haydn?' he said.

I didn't know Haydn.

'What was it I wanted to ask you . . .' He stood looking through the music on the piano. 'What was it . . . I wanted . . .'

He came to a stop and began reading some music, and he read it as one reads an ordinary book. He was far away.

'A sonata,' he said. 'Would you like to hear a little Haydn sonata?'

He began to play properly, and as he played he rocked back and forth and from side to side. He looked as if he were suffering, but he sounded happy. At other times he looked happy and played gravely and gloomily. You didn't know what to make of it.

'Now the andante,' he said. 'Do you understand it at all?'

'I don't know,' I said. 'I don't think so.'

'What do you see when you're listening? Do you see knights on chargers – knights with shields and big swords . . .'

No, such things had never entered my head.

'Don't you ever read?' he asked. 'Don't you know Ingemann's novels?'

I thought that here I could safely reveal what we were usually so careful to hide. Here it wouldn't be necessary to slip the book behind the curtain when anybody came upstairs, so as not to be found out.

'My mother reads me novels,' I said.

'Ingemann's?'

'I don't know.'

'Don't you know who wrote the books you read?'

'No,' I said. I said it quietly and with shame. I realized that this was something really awful. Something . . .

'Well, don't bother about that now. Just be interested. A book is written by an author. It's the author who's telling the story. Don't you always like to know who's talking to you? Of course you do. And a piece of music . . . Well, now I'll play the andante. Here you might think of beautiful ladies – grand ladies watching the tournament, smiling and waving and watching the knights who wear their favours . . .'

He played again. But I couldn't do it. I was so entirely unfamiliar with knights and ladies. I could imagine Nina. But she wasn't the kind to be a lady at a tournament. And

I could easily imagine a man on a horse. Perhaps that would do . . .?

I sat there and forgot to listen, lost the thread and looked at the snow. I looked at the black cross of the window-frame and at the snow which hung like light, white gauze on the arms of it and fell in folds at its foot. And I listened to the wind sweeping round the corner and whistling in some crack or other.

'And now the rondo,' he said. 'It's all gay and cheerful. Everything's over now.'

And the rondo tripped away; it was like beads on a string – fine glass beads that rolled and ran and rolled again. Beads on a string, I thought. Long rows of beads, all alike . . . But then it was over.

'Show me your hand,' he said, coming over to me. He took my hand and pressed it and bent my fingers and spread them out. 'You've got a good hand,' he said. 'That's just as important as having a good ear. Could you get that harmonium . . .? Or better still, a piano? You can learn to play the organ in church, but you really ought to have a piano.'

'No,' I said. 'I haven't heard anything about our getting a piano.'

'You could go over to Berntsen to start with. I'll talk to him about it. And you can play in the church. But a piano . . .'

No, that's going too far, I thought. I was allowed to play at Abeline's and at cantor Petersen's, but I'd never get further than that. Now and again I could go up to Valborg's. But not too often.

'It won't be any good,' I said, and I could hear that it sounded different from the things I usually said. It sounded precocious. 'They all say it's no good, and I can't do anything because my sight's too good to be properly blind and not good enough to . . .'

'If I think you can do something it's not for you to argue. I'll talk to your father and mother,' he said.

I ran home and told my mother about it and rushed at my fiddle and did silly things with the bow, trying to make it jump on the strings and dreaming that I was Jacob Gade. And soon I should be going over to play with the organist in front of lots of people – in front of knights in armour and coats of mail: and in front of grand ladies sitting on their balcony, waving and smiling and . . .

'We ought to have done some bags,' said my mother. 'But that's something you *can* do, so of course you don't want to. But all that other business which nobody knows whether you could do or not and costs a lot of money – you're wild about it.'

I put down my violin and helped my mother with the paper bags and said nothing. I was sulky and stubborn and my usual self.

'Now you're yourself again,' said my mother, 'and I wonder what the organist would say if he could see you. I can't think why Valborg isn't good enough for you any longer.'

I sat and did my work and helped my mother with the bags and said nothing. What difference did it make? I might just as well sit here on the same old chair at the same old table and make bags for the rest of my life. It wasn't that I didn't care. I was just angry – angry with my mother, and with myself because I was no good at anything in the whole world. But I was willing to look as if I had no idea of doing anything but sit here at home with my mother and talk about builder Laursen and Sister Nielsen, and what we could have this evening and for tomorrow's dinner. In other places people talked about sonatas and played bead-necklaces of music, and talked about andantes and rondos and Ingemann's novels. I would pretend I wanted to do what I was doing. But I didn't.

My Swedish grandmother arrived at night and alone. She had seen nothing of my father. She stood outside in the passage looking like a bundle of shawls and head-dresses: broad below and narrow above. There was a policeman with her; he explained how he had found her and brought her all the way here. And there she stood not understanding anything and asking to see my father, to speak to him . . . Didn't he live here? Wasn't this his place – his home? She looked lost – a fugitive overtaken by fate. Ready to go away again if she didn't find the man she was looking for. A carpet-bag, a bundle in a knotted cloth and an oblong object in a grey paper parcel. The policeman helped us to bring the things in. She followed. She followed to see what we were doing with her belongings. She didn't understand what it was all about, but she didn't want to lose sight of what was hers.

She waddled into the room and stood in the middle of the floor, looking helpless and lost and even more at the mercy of fate. Now and again she said something. Just a noise. A broken noise. Like a wild goose that can't follow the skein and lacks strength to fly further.

'Well, I'll be off now, then,' said the policeman. 'Good thing I was there to see to her.'

'Yes,' said my mother. 'It was lucky. Thank you.'

We tried to help grandmother off with her things. She wouldn't let us. She protested. She wanted to see my father. Talk to him.

'But he's gone to Copenhagen . . . He went to Copenhagen to fetch you. To meet you and help you . . .'

My mother shouted. She thought she would be understood if she shouted loud enough.

'Oh,' said my grandmother. 'Oh.'

She spoke as if she didn't believe a word of what we were telling her. But she allowed us to help her off with some of her things. Reluctantly she let herself be unpacked and revealed. An old woman. Frail. With a walnut face and close-set eyes.

'Oh,' she said, looking about her. Watchful. Suspicious. 'Copenhagen,' she said.

We wanted her to sit down. Very well; she would sit. She resigned herself to the inevitable and sat down on the very edge of a chair; she was transience itself. This was not her journey's end but a way-station, a junction. She had come to see her son and to talk to him. She had expected to meet him here. She had firmly believed that he was to be found here.

'But he's coming,' said my mother. 'He's only in Copenhagen,' she said, between tears and laughter; for what could she do?

'Oh! Copenhagen,' repeated my grandmother, but without altering her position.

She remained sitting on the edge of her chair, and not for a moment did she show any sign of settling down to stay.

She said plainly enough in her letter that she was coming here to die, I thought, and she may want to move on at once – to the churchyard, perhaps.

She folded her hands in her lap. They were narrow, with long seamstress-fingers. And they lay in shadow and seemed carved out of wood. Her clothes and person had a strange smell: a smell of woodsmoke and mustiness.

She looked here and there with her watchful little eyes, and paused at some photographs on the wall. My father as a soldier. A Dalecarlian woman with a pointed head-dress. A picture of my father and mother with me between them. She brightened up a little. She smiled.

'Ye-es,' she said. She rose and went over and pointed at the photographs one by one, saying, 'Yes.'

She went into the next room too, to look for her carpet-bag and the knotted bundle and the long thing in the grey wrapping-paper. To see if it was all there. And she came out again and sat a little further back in her chair.

My father came home. He was no longer so brisk and excited. No, he was willing to accept advice and guidance now if anybody felt like offering it. Things had turned out rather oddly in Copenhagen, though there was nothing strange in that; there was an almost natural explanation. He had been to meet the boat every single day, and stood on the quay to watch the vessels come in and sail out. He might have missed one, but he had asked. He had asked many people whether they had seen an elderly – perhaps old – Swedish woman come ashore.

And of course they had. There were so many elderly and old

Swedish women who came ashore and went aboard. The place was full of them, you might say. But nobody had told him that there was another place – a place they called Frihavn – and he could never have thought that out for himself. He just turned up to meet the boat every day and stood at his post and got to know people, and he might have gone on like that for a long time if my mother hadn't written him that letter.

Yes, he had plenty of explanations. And one couldn't really say that his journey had been in vain. He'd been able to look about him quite a bit, and had found changes – important ones. Whole new streets since the last time he'd been there. Neither my mother nor I had told him about them. As for grandmother . . . well, she had arrived quite safely without him. She wasn't as doddery as one might have feared, nor as bewildered and helpless. Besides, were not all things in the hand of God? Did a single sparrow fall to the ground without His will? We needn't have worried. When all was said and done, it hadn't been my father's idea to go and meet her. And here she was safe and sound on her chair, settling down and beginning to be understood and to understand what was going on around her.

All was well. My grandmother had a basket chair put up on the platform. She had her steel-rimmed spectacles and her hymn-book with the brass edges and brass clasp. She could sit and hear the bell ringing at the level-crossing. She could watch the trains going southward and northward, and the signals changing. There was no lack of amusement. She had never seen so much life and traffic in all her days. She could see the houses in Freden Street and note whether the mill was working or not. She had plenty to do. And she was nowhere near dying; just a little musty from the heat of the stove and so much sitting still, which was foreign to her nature and habits. Sometimes she went down to the gateway and stood looking out with her hands under her shawl. She watched the people passing. Then she would turn back into the yard again, take up her position over a drain and let her water go; then she

208

arranged her clothes, smoothed her skirt and smiled amiably at any strangers who happened to see her and were surprised.

'It's what she's used to,' said my father. 'She's done it all her life.'

'But there are other people all round us,' said my mother. '*We* don't live alone in the middle of miles and miles of forest.'

'Whether she goes to the drain or over to the corner,' said my father, 'I don't see there's all that difference.'

'And then she lies down and takes her nap on the bench,' said my mother. 'She goes out into the garden behind the stables, and brushes the snow off the bench and lies down . . .'

'Well, it'd be worse if she didn't brush the snow off, wouldn't it? She's used to sleeping out of doors when there's no frost in the air,' said my father. 'She's used to living in a different sort of country – a bigger country.'

'Try to explain to her that we live in a very small way here,' my mother told him. 'So small that I'd be glad if she'd wash herself now and then . . .'

My father shrugged his shoulders.

'She's come here to die,' he said. 'I think we might let her die in peace, without washing. Time enough for that afterwards.'

She sat reading her hymn-book. Usually she read the hymns that had to do with death and the grave. Most of these she knew by heart from childhood. But she always put on her steel-rimmed spectacles and opened her hymn-book and read or chanted them. She intoned her death-hymns to a monotonous and plaintive tune. And when she was alone and thought nobody could hear, her complaint rose and became more intense. She chanted in a trembling, old woman's voice about death and the transitoriness of all things. About the misery and wretchedness of earthly life.

She had her black days, when she said it would be all over with her soon. Now she was awaiting the summons. She had heard the sawfinch: that meant that spring was on the way. Old people died mostly at the winter's end. They died when spring was at the door. And they died at night, in the earliest light of dawn . . .

'Ay, ay,' she would say. 'Ay, ay – maybe the summons will come this very night.'

She made her calculations and divided her possessions. There were the plush cape and the spectacles, which my mother was to have. But if she'd been fetched in from the garden, or if my mother had asked her whether she wouldn't like some soap and hot water, she sometimes changed her mind and thought Kirstine should have the cape.

'Oh, yes,' my mother said. 'She'd be delighted with it – and with the spectacles too.'

Then there was the hymn-book with the brass edges and clasp, to which no one had a more natural right than my father. And for me there was the clock. That was the long thing in the grey wrapping-paper. It turned out to be an old Swedish clock which she had not wanted to part with. It had accompanied her through good times and bad and now hung on our wall there, ticking away and bringing a new sound to the room. You could watch the pendulum swinging quickly backwards and forwards behind a little window, and the clock struck so that one woke up at night; it could be heard all over the house.

Grandmother shared out her belongings and went to bed expecting the summons. But next morning to her surprise she woke up, still unfetched. She was every bit as much alive as she had been the day before, so she would really have to settle down and do something practical. There for instance was the sewing-machine, which my father had screwed together out of odd bits that he had found, or swopped something for, or even bought. It was like no sewing-machine my grandmother had ever seen; indeed, if the truth must be told, it was like no other sewing-machine in the whole world. But as long as one didn't demand fancy-sewing of it, or an unreasonable speed, and if one was careful not to break the needle, it worked beautifully. Grandmother would be able to sew anything she liked with it, once she had got used to its peculiarities.

'Everything has something,' said my father. 'Sewing-machines have their little ways just like people do, but it's all right so long as you know about 'em and make allowances.'

'Don't see why I couldn't make that organ the boy's always on at us about,' my father continued. 'It can't be so very difficult if you got all the tools.'

But I didn't want a harmonium built by my father. It would be bound to turn out a solid job, like my sled, which was never used, and was simply a waste of good firewood.

I went to Anton Berntsen in Ørsted Street, and had my own ideas about what ought to happen.

I went to Anton Berntsen and was allowed to play the harmonium with the built-in vox angelica; and I went to the organist and was asked peculiar questions about everything under the sun. Mostly I didn't know anything, but sometimes I answered in a way that caused surprise. It didn't seem anything out of the ordinary to me, and it made me extremely uncomfortable when he called his wife and exclaimed,

'You must hear what this young oracle's just said.'

He played to me and explained, and sometimes I listened. At other times I listened to the wind sweeping round the corner with its own noise. You could hear the sawfinches in Steensen's garden filing away the winter's rust, burnishing, and helping the sun to make the world shine.

The wind swept round the corner. And the sawfinches rasped their little snatch of a tune – two little notes – but there was spring in it. Wet, black trees. Pure air. Chilly air. The organist struck chords on the piano and I had to hear what was in them. Usually I did, but sometimes I couldn't.

'Do you hear them like colours?' he asked. 'Is E-major white and A-flat major red and D-major blue . . .?'

'Colours . . . No, they're notes. Just ordinary notes.'

'And isn't there a fanfare of trumpets in this C-major?' he asked. 'It's from the *Meistersingers*.'

It was all so new and unfamiliar – new names, new ideas, things you could only half understand or not grasp at all.

'Fanfare . . .' I said. '*Meistersingers . . .*'

Nothing in the world is so bottomless, so utterly boundless, as ignorance. I made out that I knew a lot and guessed at more, and I answered Yes and Perhaps and Well I think so too. And I heard him playing in a white E-major, and now it was blue, and later red or purple.

But at Anton Berntsen's I was allowed to be on my own. I could play on all the instruments that were there if I liked. I sat bicycling air into the instrument with stockinged feet so as not to scratch anything, and I played and used the built-in vox angelica. I practised and invented one or two things myself, and practised again. And Anton Berntsen came up from the workshop and stood listening for a bit. He stood there tall and pale, rather ill and tormented-looking, saying nothing or hardly anything. Sometimes he rattled a bunch of keys in his pocket, and when he breathed he sucked the air in through his teeth with a chilly noise. He seemed to be shivering with inward cold. At times he would go over and blow dust off a shining mahogany surface, or push in a stop or pull down a lid. Then he went upstairs. You could hear him walking thoughtfully up the stairs; you could hear him open a door and shut it again. You heard his steps across the floor and a chair pulled forward and him sitting down in it. A quiet man. A taciturn man. When he did say anything it sounded as if he were speaking out of a great affliction – wearily, and with some suffering. He didn't smile.

Outside in the street carts and carriages drove by, and now and then somebody would stop and look in through the window and see me bicycling, and listen and shake his head and walk on. Ørsted Street was out there and it looked sad. It looked tear-stained. Dreariness had Ørsted Street as its address.

But out towards the fjord lay the meadows, and the larks had come. They had come some time ago and they hung high up everywhere, singing. And the big trees in the churchyard had thick, swollen buds. The girls from L. Pode's Blind Home came from the woods or from the churchyard. I said good day to them and they knew my voice and said good day in return, and smiled their faded smiles. Late one afternoon the black-bird was there. The blackbird had come with its twilight flute – its soft twilight music – blue, the organist would have called it.

Grandmother sat and worked the sewing-machine.

18

THERE was no more bother over me at school. Nobody talked to my mother behind my back about one thing and another, or wanted explanations. During the dark months it wasn't easy to follow the morning lessons by the uncertain light of four gaslamps, but nobody said anything or scolded me.

'Just sit still and listen and follow as well as you can,' said the new master. We called him by his initials. We called him C. M. 'Follow if you can,' C. M. said, 'and if you can't, don't bother. It doesn't matter. Why do you try to write with an ordinary pencil? You ought to have a big thick blue one, like carpenters use.'

I didn't buy a big thick blue pencil.

'No need to unless we find it really is better,' said my mother. And it wasn't better. It was worse. Black was easier to see on white paper than blue. So I didn't buy a blue pencil.

But C. M. brought me one. I had to write blue whether I wanted to or not.

'Write with the blue one and make the figures big,' he said.

'No, it's no good . . .'

'Well, don't bother. Just listen; follow as well as you can, or go to sleep if you like. It doesn't matter so long as you keep quiet.'

But I didn't go to sleep. I worked out the problems in my head. I did mental arithmetic till my head buzzed and just wrote down the answers. I could do that with the big thick blue pencil, since he was so keen on it.

'Yes, that's right,' he said, 'though I can't think how you got it. Unless the boy next to you whispered it –'

'No, he didn't.'

'Well, perhaps not. Anyhow, it doesn't matter.'

He was a little round-headed man with a cement-coloured moustache and grey clothes. But there was something about his face – his teeth – which was like a rat I had once killed. I had once killed a rat and sold it for ten øre at the gasworks. I remembered its face. It was like C. M.

He was always sour or sulky or injured. We had the feeling that he disliked school. He disliked us, his work, society in general and life itself – he was sour and sulky and injured all the time. He had no favourites and no victims. Nothing mattered, and I mattered least of all. But there was no bother.

Lieutenant Christensen had got himself an alphabet, a frame and a stylus, and he sat at his desk writing braille. Rather ostentatiously, I thought. Rather shamelessly. He talked about it too, right and left, to anybody and everybody.

'We'll all be at it soon,' said Marentcius. 'Far better than a pen or a pencil. Marvellous, it seems to be.'

He didn't mean any harm by that. He just said it. He had decided to be a chemist and was going to another school soon and so he didn't care. We'd been more often together lately. For one thing he read German with me. Sometimes my mother did too, but that didn't work so well. She was more than willing. She spelt her way through the words and tried to say them and wanted to learn German herself. But it was better with Marentcius. I knew he wasn't doing it for my sake. I knew he wanted an excuse to be near Gertrud now and then, and I was a very good excuse. But Gertrud went about with so many people, and stood in the passage in the half-dark with so many. And disappeared into the woods and elsewhere.

Marentcius and I talked about Gertrud and about other girls; about girls in general and about stamps. But here the tiresome thing was that although I could see it was a stamp, I could never tell if a perforation was missing or if it had other peculiarities – and it was things like that that were important. For me it was just a stamp. Girls were more unlike each other. And perhaps one had a surer sense of their value.

'I'd rather touch a girl than a stamp,' I said.

A stamp really ought to have something wrong with it – some difference – and unless one could see the defects or differences one could never be a real stamp-collector. But girls should be faultless, if possible. In my eyes most of them were, and quite literally so. Everything had fewer faults than before. I saw no stains or scratches or disfigurements. I saw a nice house and a rare stamp and a pretty girl. But we talked about it a good deal, Marentcius and I.

He had become interested in other things too – flowers, for instance. He was interested in botany. And I pretended to take a great interest in botany, though here it was the same thing again. A flower might be very beautiful, but it gave me no pleasure to tear it to bits and see what was inside. I couldn't count stamens or find the stigma. I could only sit with a flower in my hand; often I knew the name of it, and at other times I didn't, but anyway that was unimportant. It was blue or yellow or red, and it had its scent, and it was a moving thing to hold in one's hand. And I was quite willing to talk to Marentcius about which family it belonged to, and watch him lay it in the press, and admire him for all the things he knew and for his deft fingers.

His mother was no longer so discouraging when I came to ask for him. Gone were the days when Marentcius had neither the time nor the inclination to be with me. No, for now we weren't so childish: we didn't play. We did serious things, both together and separately. It was interesting, for instance, that I should frequent the organist's house and have some standing there. And Marentcius, who was to be a chemist one day . . . We could carry on conversations that were almost incomprehensible to his mother. This commanded respect. When I talked about keys and colours – about the white E-major and the blue D – respect turned almost to awe.

But his father, who was iron-grey and sat at a little table by the window reading and reading because one day he wanted to keep a shop of some kind – his father might suddenly turn round to us and say Rubbish. He seldom said more than this one word, and he didn't really say it – he hissed it. 'Rubbish!' he hissed. 'Stop that highfalutin' rubbish.'

His voice was hoarse and dusty, as if he had weighed and sold flour all his life. But when he had said what he wanted to say he turned back to his table and his book, and went on studying with bent back and bowed head, trying to read himself into a shop.

But when we were alone, Marentcius and I – when we went to the sandpit and played at being geologists, or botanized in the woods – we talked mostly about girls. But I couldn't learn to make eyes, and I couldn't see whether anybody was making eyes at me.

'No, nobody,' said Marentcius. 'If they ever do I'll tell you. But they haven't so far.'

We wandered far and wide and were away sometimes for the whole day; we found queer stones and rare plants and were rather more grown-up, rather more weighed down with our gravity, than we could quite manage. But perhaps it was only I who felt like this, being so very superficial. Being content to hold a flower in my hand and call it a flower and marvel at its scent and its extraordinary blueness, and at the feeling of velvet or silk between my fingers. But as for what family it belonged to – how many petals and sepals it had, and how many stamens, and where they were placed – none of those things interested me. I had no intention of being a chemist, but I could show the same courtesy as Marentcius did when he asked about the colour of D-major, although he had no notion of what D-major was.

'You must admit,' said Marentcius, 'that it's queer to be able to see colours with your ears like that. It isn't normal,' he said.

We wandered about, engrossed in profoundly serious problems. But if we weren't careful we forgot our seriousness and talked about girls. And Marentcius had an intimate knowledge of Gertrud, and of Gertrud under her clothes, too.

'Yes, but when – ?' I asked. 'And how – ?'

'Oh, you know. You can hide in Klyver's landau – or take her into the woods. And she's as good as grown-up – under her clothes, I mean.'

But if we chanced to meet Gertrud – alone or with another girl – or if she was standing in the gateway when we came home, Marentcius simply went red in the face, and walked every bit as clumsily as I did. And he had nothing, absolutely nothing to say to her. He said good morning or good evening or silly ass. There was never any question of asking whether she could meet him, whether they should go into the woods together, or hide in Klyver's landau.

'You idiot,' he said. 'You only talk about that sort of thing when you're alone. If you don't know that much you'll never get hold of a girl.'

But I did know that much, very well. I just didn't talk about it.

One after another the rooms were emptied. Pictures were taken down from the walls and carried away. The chairs, the table, the couch. The beds were separated. We were moving.

If anybody asked, we were moving because grandmother couldn't get on with her dying. She went on living, in defiance of reason, and remained with us. We needed more room. But there were other causes too. There were too many smiles which suddenly faded when one of us went by, and revived when we had turned our backs. There were too many sideways looks at my father and grandmother. At my mother too. There was too much whispering and gossip, too many pointing fingers.

'Why is it we can't be like other people?' asked my mother. 'Why must people talk so?'

'Well, it's you they're so busy with,' said my father. 'You

and the boy and all that. They've smelt out more things about the past than *I* ever knew.'

There wasn't much talk when I was in the room. There was mostly silence. The same silence as ever. My mother did her paper bags. Grandmother sat reading her hymn-book, all about death and burial, and my father twiddled the matchbox between his fingers and looked in front of him seeing nothing and smoking his pipe.

'If only we could do what Alfrida did,' he said. 'Go right away somewhere – America . . .'

'Yes,' said my mother, looking up. 'That would just about suit us. America . . .'

I told Marentcius this one day.

'We may be going to America,' I said.

'Oh!'

A little time passed. Then I said again,

'It's quite likely we shall go to America.'

'We know lots of people who have done that,' said Marentcius.

He didn't care either way, but he told Gertrud. He cared enough to tell other people about it, anyway. My mother got to hear of it too. After that there was no more talk of America while I was there to hear and to gossip about the town and make things worse than they were already.

And yet one fine day something really came of it. One fine day it was suddenly decided that we should move. We moved five or six houses along the street.

'And if anybody asks you can say it's because grandmother's staying on and we need more room,' said my mother.

But nobody did ask. Marentcius came, though, and looked at the house, saying,

'So that's what America looks like.'

I made no answer to this. And Gertrud asked if we were going to live in a skyscraper when we got to New York. I said nothing to that, either.

We took things down off the walls and out of the cupboards

and emptied the rooms and carried everything away to the new place. At first it went quite quickly. There was a lot to take.

'More than you'd think,' said my mother.

'Yes, more than you'd ever remember we had,' said my father. 'What's the good of it all?'

'Oh, come – there's not as much as all that. There's nothing more than what we've honestly bought and paid for,' said my mother.

'And found,' said my father.

He was amazingly good at finding things. So much so that my mother said to me,

'If you wait long enough, your father will come home one day with a chamber-organ that somebody's thrown away.'

We moved, and carried our things to the new house where we were to live, and at first we were quick with it, but as the rooms were emptied we got slower. My father especially couldn't get his eye on what to take, or make up his mind.

He stood on the platform looking over at the houses in Freden Street and at a train that happened to go by.

'What train can that be at this hour. . .' he said. 'And I didn't hear the bell . . .'

He saw the signal made. He saw that the sails of the windmill on the hill were motionless, as if there weren't enough wind to turn them. He stood looking . . .

He walked with strangely empty hands from one room to another. And the wallpaper was faded except where the pictures had hung, and behind the back of the sofa. He walked about looking at the walls and reading the wallpaper—reading about all the time we had been here. Remembering . . . or perhaps not remembering. Was there something he had forgotten, and something else he said goodbye to and would rather forget, if he could manage it? That corner there, for instance; he had sometimes sat there in the night, rocking back and forth and cradling his head in his hands. Did he remember anything about that? Or did he remember, but forgot the reason? Perhaps there was no real reason – not one that would remain clearly in the memory. And across the floors paths had been worn. Paths from door to door and round the place where the beds had been, and where beds must always have been, since there was no other place for them. He walked about looking at it all. It was almost as if he were following a trail.

There was also the slanting window – the skylight, which I used to look up at in the evenings when I'd gone to bed and in the night when I woke. Sometimes there had come a star in one of the four squares. I'd seen a bright star there. But little by little the stars had grown pale. They had lost their outlines and become blurred and pale. Since a certain Christmas I hadn't been able to get my eye on any heavenly bodies except the sun and the moon. But once, in that skylight . . .

'Help me lift the green ottoman,' said my father.

And I helped him carry the green ottoman, which was so light that he could have carried several like it. But it was the last thing left.

We stood out in the street with the green ottoman between us, looking up at the house and the empty window-panes that stared back unseeingly. There was a smell of meat from the butcher's – smoked pork and smoked sausage and forcemeat and pigs' carcases. And a smell of new bread from the baker's. And the general store smelt of dried cod and paraffin.

We stood looking at the old house, my father and I, and it was as if one could see from the outside that we no longer lived there. Somehow or other there had been an expression in the windows, resembling my father and mother. It was no longer there. Now the windows looked like Sofie. They looked like Sofie at L. Pode's Home for Blind Women.

There was no more watching the trains come in and out, no more watching the signals change. No more looking at the mill on the hill to see whether the sails were turning or standing still. We could no longer hear the bell at the level-crossing. Not even in the evenings and at night when it was quite quiet. We looked down into a narrow yard with a house on the right and a tarred fence on the left. There was a little scrap of sour garden where nothing would grow, because it was shaded by two big pear-trees. But there were rooms overlooking the street – spacious rooms. Our belongings looked like nothing at all when they were arranged in them. The walls were almost bare. My mother wandered about with her thoughts . . . A new, bigger table, she was thinking – a proper dining-table with four chairs, such as decent people had. A linen-cupboard. And there . . . There one might have – what?

'Well, I was thinking of that organ you've been on at us about – the chamber-organ,' my mother said. 'And a mirror,' she said.

We had moved. But things weren't as simple as before. It was so easy to go into the old gateway, but here there was no gateway; only a green street-door and a passage. I went in at the old gateway and met the same people. Rudolf, who had become far too familiar with Lydia. And Gertrud, whose skirts were coming lower and lower down her beautiful legs, while something was beginning to bud beneath her thin summer blouse. They teased her about it, Rudolf and Lydia. It seemed to them ridiculous.

'You're children,' said Gertrud, and her neck went red. 'Babies,' she said.

Anders stood looking after her. He stared, altogether bemused, and followed her with his everlasting reins in his hand. He didn't ask her if she would play horses. He was just drawn after her, magnetically, almost like a sleep-walker, until she suddenly spun round on her heel and snapped at him – shooed him off as she would have shooed the butcher's dead dog.

'Why do you keep on coming here?' Else and Marie asked me sometimes. 'We'd been looking forward to seeing the last of you. Go to your own yard. You don't live here any more.'

They were right, of course. I didn't live there any more. But it wasn't easy to stay away. It wasn't much fun being alone in the narrow yard and the sour little garden. And Marentcius . . .

Marentcius was interested in what Gertrud hid under her blouse, and he had been given a bicycle. He could no longer be bothered to walk anywhere, and there was now no chance of his meeting the person he wanted to meet at my place – the only person for whom he would get off his bicycle.

Marentcius pedalled about and rang his bell and never put his feet to the ground if he could help it. If he could manage to exchange a few words with Gertrud he put one foot down, but no more. And for no longer than it took them to arrange something or other. A meeting, for instance. They met in the woods. Marentcius helped her up on to the cross-bar and rode away with her. They whizzed by me with a crunching of gravel, and without saying anything. They thought I didn't recognize them then. But the strange thing about me was that I often saw more than one would think. That was what they said. They didn't know that I had other clues. Marentcius's bicycle made a special little noise. And when I heard this special little noise I saw him too, and saw what he was carrying on the cross-bar.

But sometimes I met Marentcius alone. Late that summer he whizzed up and rang the bell and braked and jumped off. We stood just where the road came out of the woods, and talked together for a bit. We talked of this and that, and Marentcius was absent-minded; he looked here, there and everywhere, thinking I never noticed and thinking I didn't know why he was so uneasy and what he was looking for.

But Marentcius knew that Gertrud attracted lots of other people, from Anders to the new assistant in the general store, and that she wasn't stingy with her young self. She would go off with this one and that, and when it came to the point she looked upon Marentcius as a mere boy. Gertrud with her fourteen years was as good as grown up.

'I've begun to collect butterflies,' said Marentcius. 'If you had a bike you could come too.'

He looked up the steep path towards the allotment gardens. He looked along the road he had just travelled.

'Have a cigarette?' he asked. 'You smoke, don't you?'

And there we stood like little men, smoking. Inwardly we quaked with fear lest someone should catch us. But we stood there like little men, smoking and talking about butterflies and other trivial matters. Stamps . . . No, they weren't interesting any more. Arrow-heads and flint axes . . . No, to hell with archæology. Marentcius was good at swearing now, too. We talked in a common-sense manner about butterflies and the treatment of insects. And we talked about cigarettes – a great deal about cigarettes. We didn't talk about girls and said not one word of Gertrud.

There were bats in the air and darkness in among the trees and the sound of a football being kicked. It was a perfectly ordinary summer evening, and there was a concert at the 'Wood's Edge' café, and that was what I was listening to. I could easily have told Marentcius that Gertrud had gone there with the new shop-assistant and that she was probably sitting at one of the tables in the garden. But I didn't say anything. He stood there looking to left and right, and was absent-minded.

'Pity you haven't got a bike,' he said. 'We could have had a ride in the woods. It's such fun coming up behind the loving couples. They can't hear you until you're right on top of them.'

Marentcius rode home again. He rode to startle loving couples or catch butterflies. And Stougård came by on his way from the ice-ponds. He sagged a little at the knees, chewing his quid and a snatch of a hymn which sounded like English. And when Stougård sang English he had enough to do just to keep from stumbling.

'Got to watch where you put your feet,' he said.

Stougård took no notice of the world and no notice of me. He was being careful where he put his feet. But the organist stopped, put a hand on my shoulder and drew me with him.

'Don't listen to that bad music,' he said. 'But the evening, the summer evening,' he said. 'It's like Schubert . . . The Impromptu,' he said. 'The Impromptu in A-flat major.

Listen . . .' He hummed: 'Dadee-dee dadee-dee, dadee-dee-dee-dee . . .'

'Do you hear it? Do you feel it? the whole atmosphere . . . Come home with me and I'll play it to you.'

But one day I got my harmonium. My mother had had a talk with the organist. She had talked to him seriously and asked what he thought.

'I think he ought to have a piano,' he said.

'A piano? But he's already got a guitar and a violin, and so far as we can see he don't do much with either of them, though he's quick enough at learning the fingering and the tunes and all that . . .'

'I wish you'd give him a piano,' said the organist. 'Chamber-organs and black clothes and religion . . . all those things deaden the mind.'

To my mother this was quite baffling. In fact she couldn't make out what the organist wanted me to do at all. He just said I had something called talent.

'The boy has talent,' my mother would say. She said the word as if it was the name of some new defect in me – some illness. But he couldn't promise anything. He said,

'It's a curse to become a musician if one isn't one.'

What was one to make of that? How could one become something one already was?

And besides, my mother had never thought of my becoming a musician – playing at dances or in restaurants or perhaps travelling about to markets, as somebody or other had foretold. She had thought I might be an organist.

'Is that too much to hope for?' she asked. 'If it is you must excuse me. I don't know anything hardly about this sort of thing. None of us does,' she added.

But even that didn't make him say anything clearly, anything one could understand. Neither yes nor no. Only gestures with his hands, and queerness. My mother had to make up her own mind, and she did. I got my harmonium.

I was given my instrument, and everybody was amazed at what I could get out of it. My father and mother stood motionless listening to me, unable to speak and wondering where I could have learnt it all. They had heard cantor Petersen and Valborg talking about it, but only now were they seeing and hearing for themselves.

'What I can't make out is where he gets it from,' said my father. 'I tried an accordion once, but I couldn't do anything with it – and as for you . . .' he said.

'He must have learnt it,' said my mother. 'So far as I can make out he's been going about and playing a bit here and there, and gradually picked it up. And now the organist wants him to try the big organ in the church, too.'

'Yes,' my father said. 'But what I'm wondering is where he gets it from.'

I now had an instrument to play on, but it was infinitely more than that. It was a piece of mahogany furniture. It could be polished and it must be polished. And it had black and white keys to be polished. And there were candlesticks on both sides which could be adorned with candles and glass rings to catch the wax, and embroidered dingle-dangles. And you could stand china ornaments on it. It was a magnificent piece. A revelation.

There were no angels' voices in it, but there were people's voices for those who could hear them – vox humana. I couldn't. But I kept at it day in and day out. And grandmother chanted her death hymns to her own tune and was quite unconcerned. And my mother had her paper bags and was quite unconcerned. But my father sat in a corner and listened and wondered. He said nothing. He just sat there. He sat and grew melancholy and wondered.

I thought that my father was melancholy like King Saul, and that I could be a David for him. But it turned out that I was playing him further and further into his melancholy. Or perhaps not I but the notes in the new chamber-organ; perhaps they were too much for his nerves. Perhaps it was this vox humana . . .

226

I had better go about a bit as before and visit Valborg and the girls at L. Pode's Home for Blind Women, and Anton Berntsen and the organist, and do anything else that occurred to me. It was better to have quietness at home, and better if I wasn't there too often.

But at least the chamber-organ was there: a magnificent piece that could be shown to anybody who was interested. And a day would surely come when I could play on it again.

Times were as they had always been. Things seemed to happen – one's grandmother came to die, one moved or fled, one got new things – and yet everything was just as before. Nothing was different. The same silence. The same fear of something uncertain, which nobody talked about – nobody called by its name. Sunday school. Meetings in the Tønnes Street hall. Alleluias and guitar-twanging and long-drawn-out testimony by builder Laursen. The chemist and Sister Thora and Abeline and the Nielsens from Cross Street. And I who went only very reluctantly in the hope of meeting a girl called Nina. And she was hardly ever there. And I grew sulky and didn't want to sit there twanging with Abeline. And my mother spoke harshly to me and said was that my gratitude – gratitude to God and her and Wedell in Copenhagen and Valborg and everybody.

But Valborg was getting more and more grown-up and beginning to talk more and more like the others. She talked about nothing but God and Staff and about being the bride of Christ. It was exactly like her mother, who went about with arthritic joints and twisted hands and a rubber-tipped stick, and wore white and waited for Jesus and was going to be the bride of Christ. But my mother didn't like this. It was eccentricity. People were eccentric at times, and claimed indulgence. But I was awkward and ungrateful. And one day God would take me by the ears and teach me thankfulness. But it would be so very much better – better for both God and me – if this might come about in a more seemly way. If I of my own will could find the right road – like Valborg.

227

But I could do nothing of myself, and my mother had only to listen to what Laursen said, and Ullnes and Staff and Wedell: that God had ordained all things in His mind from everlasting to everlasting – alleluia.

But I thought that I might be better, or good, if I didn't always have to look in vain for the one I expected to find. Hoped to find. Longed for.

'You're ungrateful,' said my mother. 'And ingratitude carries its own punishment. He who receives a gift and doesn't return thanks never gets any more. You have much to be thankful for,' said my mother.

I didn't agree. But I said nothing. I was silent and sulky and went my own way.

'Someone told me you were seen in a gateway with Marentcius, smoking cigarettes,' said my mother.

'Oh.'

'If I thought that was true and if your father thought it was true, he'd take death over it – or his life,' said my mother. 'And so could I.'

I denied it, of course. I denied it, thinking that never again would I stand in a gateway. I could stop smoking cigarettes with Marentcius. I could go to the neighbouring house, where there was a big boy called Sophus. His place smelt of carbide and burnt gruel. Sophus and his mother cooked their food on a paraffin lamp, and it always smelt burnt. But he was a decent fellow. My mother thought he was rather stupid, but he was decent. And he had crime novels and stories of redskins, and he was willing to read aloud.

In one way or another I got everybody to read aloud to me, and my mother didn't think it was good for me. She thought all this reading aloud might do real harm.

At Sophus's place I smoked cigarettes and swore, and learned to play cards. But sometimes I thought I must be worse than other people, since I didn't mind risking my parents' lives.

And grandmother went down into the courtyard and took

up her position over the drain and arranged her clothes and smoothed her skirt and looked up at the window with a sly old smile. She may have seen me sitting in there with Sophus, but she said nothing about it. She never said a word to anybody. She just sat down on the bench under the bigger of the two pear-trees in the sour little garden, took a screw of newspaper out of her pocket, glanced up at the windows again and chewed pipe-scrapings. It made her black round the mouth. She looked slyly at the windows, and if nobody was there she quickly pulled out the crumpled bit of newspaper and took a pinch. Then she sat smiling with her black lips, rocking backwards and forwards; and she was happy. She didn't think anybody knew her secret.

They said I was growing up. But we were all growing. We had long wrists and gangling legs and thin necks and hollow backs to our necks. But I was growing too fast, and went pale and queer and had to have iron. And my father looked at me hard. He dragged me away and looked into my eyes for a long time and said he hoped I never touched myself.

'No,' I said, not knowing what he meant.

'They all run off and hide all over the place,' he said. 'And if you touch yourself, you might have spinal consumption and get paralysed.'

It dawned on me what my father meant. I was ashamed. But I was also filled with an icy fear. I was so frightened, that if one of my arms or legs went to sleep I thought the paralysis was coming. Sometimes my back hurt, and then I thought the consumption had begun. And I thought of a man who walked about on crutches because he was lame in both legs, and about a girl who was carried out into a garden every day and lay there in the sunshine with consumption. My fear was icy, and I looked at the man with the crutches and at the girl, who lay there pale and white among the bushes in a garden, and I thought that the same thing might happen to me.

We grew and became tall and pale. And Gertrud tried to

229

hide something under her blouse – something which grew bigger and more difficult to hide as the summer went on. And Lydia had begun to be different, and to go about with boys and giggle and be skittish. Anders was the only one who stayed the same. Anders who was now seventeen or eighteen or more, and couldn't learn it. He went about with his reins wanting to play horses, going into all the yards and getting shooed out again and looking like an elephant from behind. Anders had not changed.

'You might look after him a little,' said his mother. 'He's a good boy at heart, and he'd be ever so grateful.'

She wore a blue check apron and was bare-headed; she looked at us beseechingly – a whole bunch of us – and talked to us.

'If only you'd stop chasing him away as if he was an animal,' she said. 'He's such a good boy.'

'But he ought to be in an asylum,' said Rudolf.

The rest of us looked away or scraped the gravel with our toes in embarrassment. But Rudolf wasn't like that. He said right out,

'Anders ought to have been put in an asylum long ago. Everybody says so.'

'Oh, indeed!' said his mother. 'And why shouldn't Anders be allowed to live happily at home and be a joy to his parents, and give no trouble to anybody?'

She stood there in her blue check apron, angry and ready to cry. We became even more embarrassed; Else and Marie began talking about something else, and Lydia giggled.

'People say it's all wrong to keep him at home. And one day perhaps the police will come for him,' said Rudolf.

But suddenly she turned to me and said I ought to be ashamed of myself.

'You're not much better than Anders yourself, and one day the police may come and say *you* must go off to some place . . . Yes,' she said.

The others grinned. I didn't see anything to grin at. I might have been a horse now and again for Anders if she hadn't said anything. Now he could go on wandering about alone for all I cared.

She waited for a bit as if expecting me to say something. But I didn't, and she went away – slowly, with her hands under her apron.

Gertrud . . . Why was she never to be seen now? Why had she stopped going to school? Why should she sit behind a window and not be allowed to come out into the street, or even into the yard?

Gertrud wasn't quite well. She wasn't well enough to go to confirmation class and be confirmed next month. But she wasn't really ill either, because she wasn't in bed; she sat behind the curtains looking pale.

The doctor came. And people saw him coming and talked about what could be the matter. Before long he came out again, but nobody could get him to talk. He went straight from Gertrud to the shop, as if he were going to buy coffee or something. But nobody believed that. And it came out that he had only had a few words in private with the new assistant, behind the shop. A few words – he was only there a minute or so. It was enough. The new assistant's face was the colour of rye-flour when he came out.

Then the whispering began. Whispering on the stairs. Whispering in the kitchens, in the living-rooms, and between people who happened to meet in the street. They all whispered and looked up at the house where Gertrud lived. A slight turn of the head. A quick glance up at the window. Was she there now . . .? Was that her profile in the dimness behind the curtain?

When any children came near there was a quick hushing. The conversation stopped abruptly and everybody was silent. All the same we caught a word here and a remark there. And anyhow we had guessed. We probably discovered it before the grown-ups. We had discovered it and thought about it. Some of us had thought about nothing else for a long time. We talked about it too, especially Rudolf. He talked about it as if he'd been there himself all along, and seen and heard everything. Rudolf had listened. He had peeped through keyholes and hid behind a tree in the woods. In fact, he'd had a go with her himself. Often.

But Marentcius arrived on foot, with a small, worried face. My mother asked if he was ill. No, he wasn't.

'You don't look well,' she said.

No, he was all right. He just wanted to talk to me. He wanted to know something about music. He wanted me to go out with him. He had a plan for something we could do together. No, there was nothing the matter with him.

Marentcius looked at my new harmonium and allowed me to explain everything in detail. He wasn't entirely uninterested, but slightly absent-minded.

'We could go out into the woods and try to find something,' he said. 'Or go to my home and read.'

'But you said you had a plan.'

'Oh, the plan – I'd forgotten. Never mind about that now.'

So we went into the woods to look for a plant he hadn't got. Marentcius was getting more and more determined to be a chemist. Or perhaps it wasn't his own decision at all, but his mother's. He collected plants and pressed them and learned botany, so as to be a chemist all the sooner when the time came.

We went on our way. We went as if we were going to a set place at a set time. But we weren't. We were simply going past the place where Gertrud lived. We were both thinking about her. We were both thinking about the same thing and neither of us said anything. We talked about rare plants and chemical experiments. And Marentcius was a broken man. But he didn't say so. He talked about test-tubes and other apparatus he had been given, which he was going to show me. He talked and talked all the way until we had got well into the woods when all at once he stopped and began to cry.

'You're crying,' I said. 'What for?'

'I'm *not* crying,' he said. 'Why should I? I've got something in my eye, that's all, but of course you can't see that. No,' he said. 'Only idiots cry. How's that girl Lydia?' he asked. 'Is she all right?'

We walked. And the woods had begun rustling with autumn. Dead leaves lay all along the path. The grass on the hill-sides was withered and the crows were cawing.

Marentcius was a broken man, but a brave one. He didn't want anybody to notice it. He didn't even want them to notice that he had changed a little. But he looked careworn.

'I think you need iron,' my mother told him.

Grown-ups knew no other remedy. They thought iron put everything right. They never dreamed that anything could be the matter with us beyond what iron could cure.

But in the evenings when it was dark and few people were in the streets, Gertrud was to be seen. She stood looking out of the gateway, or stole to the postbox with a letter. If we were there she didn't speak to us, or even say good evening. And silence fell whenever she appeared. Even Rudolf held his tongue and had nothing to say. Gertrud stood looking out of the gateway with a shawl over her shoulders like a little, thin woman. Or she hurried to the postbox, never raising her eyes from the ground. One evening she ran right into Stougård's stomach. This was probably because he wasn't watching where he put his feet. Stougård was always ready to take the blame. And perhaps it was his fault, although he wasn't actually singing that evening.

'So it's you, is it?' he said. 'You don't look up to much. You ought to have come to me, you know. Fancy nobody having the sense to give you a good schnapps with some litharge of silver in it!' he said. 'What sort of people live in the world today, without heart enough to give a poor girl a bit of dry bread and soft soap? And now you've got to be sent away from home, I suppose . . .'

Yes, Gertrud had to leave home. One day she wasn't there.

233

You could see from the look of the house that she had gone. You noticed it. The gateway looked different, and the yard and the steps.

'I don't know what it is,' I said. 'A different sound, perhaps.'

'You and your sounds,' said Rudolf. 'But she's gone. She sneaked away last night. And the police have taken the shop-assistant. What are you doing here, anyway? You don't live here. Buzz off back to America.'

I wasn't the only one who'd hung about the gateway and the yard when I didn't live there. Lydia for instance had been coming there day in and day out as long as I could remember. But nowadays she walked straight past. Perhaps somebody had told her that she would find no fit company there. She crossed to the other pavement and went by as if the place had the plague. But because she walked along the wrong pavement I couldn't recognize her. I could see there was a girl coming, but not that it was Lydia. No, I wasn't good at recognizing people on the opposite pavement any more. Sometimes not even when they came straight towards me. One evening at dusk I went up to a strange man thinking he was my father, and I spoke to him as I spoke to my father. He only laughed and told me I'd made a mistake and that it didn't matter. But the shame of it, the humiliation, the feeling of impotence . . . I don't know why I felt ashamed or humiliated. I only know I did. I know it haunted me for a long time. It haunted me as a deep disgrace that I could no longer recognize my own father. As a sort of impotence.

I went more and more often to L. Pode's Home for Blind Women. I had learnt to read and write long ago. I'd learnt contractions, too, and didn't have to prick out the whole word, letter by letter; I could make just a simple little sign. And that was more than Lieutenant Christensen could do.

'You'll have to come and read your compositions aloud to me, that's all,' he said. 'Come on Sunday afternoons.'

I didn't mind that. It suited me very well to have something to do on Sunday afternoons, because then I could dodge the meetings in Tønnes Street.

But although I no longer needed to go to the Blind Home I went in and out of it as if I belonged there. I didn't stand outside looking at the girls in the windows, with their knitting-bags and the ovals of their faces – all the things that had once seemed so strange and intriguing to me. I went straight up and grasped the door-handle. As a rule the door was unlocked. I took hold of it and opened it slowly, so that I could hear every note of the stringed instrument, and called good day from the passage to tell them that it was I who was coming. If I forgot – if I went in without saying anything – they always asked,

'Who's that?'

They said,

'Why can't you get into the way of doing as we do when you come into a room, and say "It's me"? We all do that. Everybody does,' they said. 'We open the door and at the same time we say "It's me." That's all you need do.'

I went in and out of L. Pode's Home for Blind Women, and I thought it was a good place to come to. I didn't think the girls were odd. They were different from other people, of course, but they weren't as odd as they had seemed the first few times I saw them. They still sat knitting and brooding over their knitting. They resembled each other in certain things, but there were differences. At first they looked to me all alike, or nearly, and I didn't think I should ever learn to tell them apart. Now they seemed to me as different from one another as any other people were. It was only in superficial things that they were alike. They were alike in being blind. In sitting on their chairs and knitting long, grey knitting. Or in brooding over their empty hands. They were alike in that they hurried slowly and followed the wall and took care not to bump into anything. But their voices were as varied as other people's voices, only purer and more beautiful. Some of them had girls' voices. They might be as big as women, but they spoke like young girls and I could tell them apart by their voices alone. And this was a good thing, for I wasn't good at distinguishing faces. I could see hands and I could see faces, but I couldn't always see what the face and the hands were like. It depended on many things: on whether the room was dark, or the day. On whether I'd had drops in my eyes recently.

'What can you tell us today?' they always asked me when I came. 'Have you seen anything new – anything out of the ordinary?' they asked.

In the beginning I always told them that I hadn't seen anything either new or out of the ordinary. But this disappointed them and saddened them.

'Oh,' they said. 'Haven't you seen anything at all? What a shame!'

And I could hear from their voices how disappointed they were.

'Inger and Anna were in the woods and they didn't see anything either. If only we could find somebody who had seen something and could tell us about it . . .'

They were so disappointed that I felt I had to think of something – something to tell them.

I said, for instance,

'No, I haven't seen anything today. It was all quite ordinary. But when we were in Copenhagen last time, I was walking along and I came to a square –'

'Was your mother with you,' they asked, 'or did you go about quite alone?'

'I was alone,' I said. 'I always walk about alone in Copenhagen. Well, I came to a square where they were just going to cut off a man's head. And he was standing up on the scaffold with his collar turned down, so that his neck was bare. And all round there were lots of women all knitting, just like you're doing here . . .'

'Fancy! Did you really see that? Have you really seen a man being beheaded?'

'Yes,' I said. 'It wasn't here. And it wasn't today. It was in Copenhagen on another day.'

'If you say so,' said Sofie, 'when it's you telling us, of course it must be true. I wouldn't imagine anything else. But it's funny that Dickens talks about the same thing somewhere.'

'Yes,' said the others. 'It's in Dickens. It's in his *Tale of Two Cities*. But this is different. It sounds different when you tell us you've seen it. And it sounds different when it's in Copenhagen. Tell us where that square was . . .'

'I don't know anything about any Dickens,' I said.

So I learned to invent extraordinary things myself – things not in books. Queer people. Unusual animals. Animals they had never dreamt were to be found in this country.

'In this country!' I said. 'Just you come for a walk with me in Nørre Woods and I'll show you as many as you like.'

'But we couldn't see them,' they said.

'I'll catch them and bring them to you, and then you'll be able to feel them and know it's true.'

'Will you? Will you really do that one day?' they said. 'Oh, if you only would . . .'

I filled the Blind Home with lies up to the very chimney-pots.

I told them about Stougård and builder Laursen. They were both quite ordinary; yet each of them had extraordinary experiences. Laursen had the gift of seeing heavenly signs – great flaming crosses – mystical, fiery signs.

'But you didn't see them,' they said. 'You've never seen heavenly signs.'

'Not a fiery cross like that, reaching from earth to heaven and planted out in the sea outside Esbjerg.'

'Esbjerg,' they said. 'Oh, it was in Esbjerg, was it? It sounded like St John's Revelation. Was it really in Esbjerg?'

'But I've seen the stars in the sky,' I told them. 'I've seen the Milky Way hundreds of times.'

'Tell us what the Milky Way looks like.'

'It looks,' I said, 'it looks like a page of braille lit up, if you can imagine that.'

No, nobody could imagine that.

'Lit up,' they said. 'A page of braille, lit up . . .'

They asked me whether I had seen anything new and out of the ordinary, and to start with I said no, but afterwards I couldn't disappoint them, and I sat there conjuring and made them stop knitting or take their hands from their laps.

'What's it like when you play the organ in church all alone?' they asked. 'Aren't you ever afraid? And do you play with your feet too . . .?'

I told them I wasn't afraid, although the truth was that I had the feeling the whole time that somebody was slinking about behind my back and that the somebody hid in the pews or behind pillars or sank into the ground as soon as I stopped playing and turned round to look. I was terribly afraid to sit alone in that great church, where noises from outside sounded like scufflings in the corners or up in the choir behind the altar . . .

'No, of course I'm not afraid,' I said. 'I often sit there in the evenings when it's pitch dark.'

Sometimes I was so frightened that I just went there and stood inside the door for a moment, and then went away again without learning what I was supposed to know for my next lesson with the organist.

'I'm never afraid,' I said.

I came and sat here in the dark rooms with their dark tables and bare walls. The place didn't seem so dark and bare now. People went past outside and saw me, and probably thought, as I had once thought, that I was a photograph among other photographs. They were welcome to think that if they liked. They could think so as long as I was here. For everything was somehow different when one was inside. I myself was different. I was a person to be listened to. I was the one who never quaked with fear and who could tell them of unusual happenings. And I could see, too. I had eyes like a lynx. I struck them dumb with amazement by telling them just what I had seen from day to day – in the sky, on the earth and everywhere I went. Where else could I do this – where else was I not the least of the smallest, the most contemptible of all? Where except in L. Pode's Home for Blind Women could I go without being uninteresting or in the way – a person who must either make himself interesting – which was impossible – or have allowances made for him?

But sometimes it was the blind girls who had stories to tell. They told me about the Institute in Copenhagen. This was easy now that I had been there once. They talked about the long corridors and the stairs, and what the various rooms were called. The rooms had names, so that one could tell them apart. And they talked about the people who had been there or who were there still. People I should meet.

'For now it won't be so terribly long before you go,' they said. 'Six months or a little more. And it'll be a good thing if you know them all before you get there. You can say we asked to be remembered to them – all of us.'

They spoke of the Institute in Copenhagen and the people there as the souls of the dead in purgatory might speak of those yet alive and walking the earth.

'Do you remember,' they said to each other. 'Do you remember, Alma, when you forgot to make your bed? And do you remember, Anna, when you fell up the steps at the front door . . .?'

And both Alma and Anna could remember.

'Of course we remember,' they said. 'How could we ever forget?'

And at times I was there when they sang. But even that was no longer so strange to me: I had learnt many new songs. Only I didn't know anybody else who sang like that. I didn't know any who sang with that purity in their voices. I didn't know any who could sing so that the harmonies arose of themselves, as it were, one gliding out of the other and the echo of it hanging in the air. It hung there for a long time, and for even longer in oneself. One could hold it in oneself and call it forth again for the rest of the day.

They sang, and outside the chestnut-leaves were turning yellow and patchy brown. I couldn't see now that they were yellow or patchy brown, but I knew it. And because I knew it I seemed to see it. I seemed to see them falling in tilted flight through the air and settling on the road. I just thought I saw them, but I believed it so strongly that I could see them.

Sometimes I was told to go up and see L. Pode. He walked round a table, tall and broad, with big, soft hands. There was a carpet on the floor and other fine things in L. Pode's room, and it smelt of cigar-smoke.

'We like to see you up here, too,' he said. 'You can play the piano for a bit if you like.'

And Mrs Pode, whom the girls called 'little mother', sat with her white face and her white hands. And she walked over and stroked the keys and the mahogany with her white hand.

'Ugh, it's dusty,' she said, and she blew at it or took a cloth from behind the piano and dusted the place which her white hand had touched. But there wasn't much dust. Not anywhere.

'If they're not kind to you when you get to the Institute, just tell them you'll complain to me,' said L. Pode. 'They know that I know who's in charge there. But I'm sure they will be.'

I played some song or other for them. I did the best I could, for I'd never learnt to play on a piano.

'But you soon will,' said L. Pode. 'You've got a good chance of being one of the clever ones – one of the ones people take notice of.'

At the Blind Home they never said 'You can't do that', or 'If it can be managed', or 'You never know'. They said nothing that other people said. They believed I could do everything, and so I believed it too. In a way it seemed to make me see better. I saw amazingly well among all those blind people, and for a long time after I left them. It lasted until I met some of the others – Marentcius and Rudolf. It was worst with Rudolf. When I met him, I saw terribly badly.

For that reason I avoided him more and more. There was something about him that made me stupid and blind. Marentcius was different. At least he didn't do it on purpose.

I was studying with the pastor. I'd been doing this for a long time. He said I would have to come to him for a year before he could confirm me.

'For me, confirmation is no empty ceremony,' he told my mother.

'And not for me either,' she said.

'It ought not to be just an excuse for a family party.'

'But, pastor, who told you we were going to have a party?'

'Everybody does, and I've nothing against it,' said the pastor, 'so long as the occasion of it is not forgotten.'

'The boy's to be confirmed,' my mother said, 'but there's been no talk of any party. We shall have better use for the money later on.'

The pastor didn't think I could learn my catechism in less than a year, and in any case it didn't matter.

'If you must be confirmed,' said C. M., 'you might as well sit in the sacristy as here. Listen if you want to and go to sleep if you'd rather. It doesn't matter,' said C. M.

So I sat in the sacristy twice a week and listened to everything I already knew. And the pastor never asked me anything. One day when the others had gone he told me to stay behind. There's going to be bother over me, I thought. But there wasn't really any bother.

'You may have been wondering why I never ask you any questions,' he said.

'Oh,' I said. 'I don't know . . .'

'Or perhaps you never noticed it or thought about it?'

I didn't know what to say, for I noticed so much and thought about a good many things – when I was with the pastor, too.

'Well, so much the better, if it hadn't struck you. I was afraid it might worry you, and so I wanted to say that of course I'll ask you questions if you like. It was only for your own sake I didn't. I didn't want to make you feel awkward in front of the others. I know how cruel and merciless children can be to each other.'

'Yes,' I said.

'Would you like me to ask you?'

'No . . . Perhaps it's better not.'

'That's just what I thought,' said the pastor. 'But you needn't worry about your confirmation. I'll be able to help you when we get to that.'

So I sat and listened and was asked no questions. Or else I didn't listen, thinking that, as C. M. had said, it didn't matter. Or I thought about something quite different. I probably dozed, too. And the pastor talked about the Ten Commandments and explained parables. And I thought about other things or was half-asleep. I slept until I woke to hear him talking about the Good Samaritan and telling the other boys to be kind to me. I didn't sleep any more after that. I could have sunk through the floor for shame – shame and humiliation and the feeling of impotence.

It so happened that I met the pastor when I was going to play the organ.

'Don't go fiddling with anything you shouldn't,' he said.

'No,' I answered.

'Has the organist shown you how to work everything? The electricity and so on?'

'Yes, everything.'

But one day the girls were to see the church and learn about it before they were confirmed. I was up there practising when the pastor brought them.

'Will you play something for us?' he called up to me.

Of course I could play for them. It was just a question of what.

'A hymn,' he shouted. 'We were just going to sing . . .'

So I played the hymn they were just going to sing. And I used as many stops as I could find. I thought I would stun the lot of them – stun them with organ-noise and hatred and despair.

'That was rather loud,' shouted the pastor when I'd finished. The girls tittered. I could hear them tittering; it sounded as if they were stroking silk or rustling taffeta.

'That was rather loud,' shouted the pastor. 'But take care now when you come down. Mind you don't fall down the stairs. Shall I come up and help you?'

242

I didn't answer. How could he help me? He had never helped me with the slightest thing. Nobody had helped me. I didn't want them to. I just felt . . . well, I didn't really know what I felt. I was powerless. I was humiliated and impotent.

'I can't quite make him out,' the pastor told my mother. 'But he has a difficult nature – I can see that. I can definitely see it. He's very reserved. One can't get anything out of him . . .'

My mother thought about this a good deal. It hurt her and made her anxious.

'If you've got a difficult nature on top of everything else –' she said.

I thought about it too, I thought about it in my shame and my humiliation and my impotence. I thought about it with hatred, but I said nothing.

'You must try to be good,' said my mother.

'Yes,' I said.

'If you have a difficult nature it'll make trouble.'

'Yes.'

'Trouble for yourself and everybody else.'

'Yes.'

There was nothing to say but yes. But I saw then that my mother was no different from the rest – from the pastor. I would be reserved and go on saying yes, until one day I . . . until what? I didn't know. I went about in humiliation and impotence and would probably never say anything but yes.

Grandmother sat in her basket-chair by the window, reading her hymn-book and waiting for death. She waited for death and peered out of the window for it as other people looked out for the postman. But death wouldn't come. Her face and hands were rather grimy because of her strong distaste for water, and she smelt even mustier than when she first came. But she sat with her steel-rimmed spectacles on, reading her hymn-book and chanting from it. Every day the same hymns about death and burial. And she was expecting the summons. She expected to be called away every hour of the day and night.

'Ay, ay,' she said. 'Something tells me that it'll be tonight,' she said.

But it wasn't that night or any other night. She woke up in her camp-bed every morning and coughed a little, discovering whether she was alive; then she came to the conclusion that strangely enough she wasn't yet dead, and marvelled at it, and got up. She stuck her thin legs in their woollen stockings out of bed, stepped on to the floor and stretched a little. Her joints creaked and her old bones cracked. But she was alive. Then she put on what few clothes she had been persuaded to take off the night before. She would rather have kept everything on.

'Ay-ay-ay . . . still in this world, then,' she said.

She was given her hot coffee and she brought out bits of dry bread from under the cushions of her wicker chair and anywhere else she had contrived to hide them, and she found sweets in her skirt pocket, and so a new day began. Steel-rimmed spectacles. Hymn-book. First she read, moving her lips noiselessly, but little by little her voice emerged. Little by little she forgot time and place, and before very long she was chanting in her cracked, quavering, old woman's voice.

My mother had her own chores to see to. She went to and fro tidying up, and then began her work. Grandmother chanted her regular number of death hymns. And when that was done she settled down to watch for the postman or to wait for death. And nothing happened.

She thought about doing some sewing. She wondered how Britta Johansson in Växjö was getting on. Whether she was still alive or had been called away.

'We could write to her,' said my mother.

'Write . . . no,' said grandmother, waving the idea away with a hand carved out of wood. 'No,' she said. 'And the pastor,' she said. 'And the schoolmaster.'

'It's a dismal life for her,' said my mother, 'and lonely.'

'Dismal? Lonely?' My father looked up from the book in the red cloth cover. 'She's tired, maybe, because there's too much going on here, but . . . She's never seen so many people in her whole life as come in and out of here in a week. No, the trouble is she can't seem to die. The trouble is she gets tired, waiting so long.'

And my father was right, for although we didn't think grandmother ever concerned herself with anything but hymns and death – although we never dreamed she was doing anything but wait – yet she had worked out a kind of plan. She went for a walk in the garden and lay down on the bench and let the leaves of the pear-tree shower down upon her while she closed her eyes and went far away, or perhaps dozed a little. And she stood over the drain. And she came in again and said,

'If I started tomorrow I could stay a few days with Britta Johansson at the Sandströms' place in Växjö. I could go to church there on Sunday and go on home afterwards.'

'What!' said my father. 'Are you going away?'

'I was so sure I was going to die,' said my grandmother. 'That's why I came. I never thought I should be just sitting about and waiting.'

I think my father was startled. But he was never one to jump up and talk about difficulties. He paused in his reading, rather surprised – politely surprised, no more. *He* wasn't startled; no, he thought it was a sensible idea.

'But we must write first,' my mother thought. 'We must write to the pastor, or whoever it is.'

'No,' said my grandmother, putting down her hymn-book. 'No,' she said, 'certainly not.'

She had written before coming to us because this was a foreign country – a place she had never been to before. People she had never seen. But now – now she was simply going home. Home, see? Not a strange place, but home. So what was there to write for? And she smiled patronizingly.

'Certainly not,' she said.

'Well, what about money?' said my mother. 'People can't wander about from country to country for nothing.'

'No,' said my grandmother, 'you can't do it for nothing.'

But she said it in a way that showed she had given the matter some thought.

'And now we've gone and moved,' said my mother, 'and bought the camp-bed . . .'

My father thought it would have happened anyhow.

'It was meant to be. You couldn't have stayed in the old place any longer,' he said.

Grandmother hunted about for scissors, and found them, and set about doing something to an old petticoat she always wore. A seam had to be unpicked – quite a broad seam, yes, but only a little bit of it – just from here to there . . .

She was going to unpick it, but thought it would be better to do this in the other room. By the other window. There was more light there – a better light. And she went into the other room and stayed there for a little and came back with some bank-notes in her hand – some quite ordinary ten-crown notes. Crumpled. Grubby. They had been crumpled together for a long time and lain in their place. But you could see it was money. Not unusual money: ordinary ten-crown notes – couldn't they be used? Wasn't that enough? Should she unpick more of the seam?

No, my father thought; that was more than enough.

'That'll take you further than you have to go,' he said. 'Yes,' he said. 'That's good money.'

That was exactly what my grandmother had thought. She had been thinking about it for a long time. Or for some time, anyhow. She had thought about it ever since she realized that she was not to be called away just yet. And she didn't intend to travel round the world. Not a step further than her own home.

'But why tomorrow?' said my mother. 'I can't think why you should want to go all of a sudden like that.'

'One day's as good as another,' said my father.

'I could go to church with Britta Johansson on Sunday then.'

'Yes, if she's alive. But you don't know whether she is or not,' said my mother.

'Well, if she's not alive of course I can't go to church with her. I shall go alone,' said my grandmother.

She had become excited and talkative, just as my father became excited and mysterious when he decided to go on a journey. We hadn't forgotten.

'I'll go home for a bit,' said grandmother. 'And when the earth reminds me again I'll come back.'

This is what she had thought, and this is what she did. She went home and stayed there for seven or eight years. Then the earth reminded her. And she came back and sat waiting in the same wicker chair, with the same steel-rimmed spectacles and the same hymn-book. She sat waiting for the summons, for death, for ten long years. And still no one came to call her away. But by then her patience was exhausted. She was being made a fool of; it was sheer mockery of a person of advanced age – a person so aged as to have every claim to reverence and respect.

When grandmother was ninety-two she went home again to Sweden. She was more than offended; she was angry. She went home to join Britta Johansson in an old people's home and live a pleasant life; and there she stayed.

She was ninety-seven when the gates were opened to her and she was called away at last. But that has nothing to do with this story.

Grandmother didn't leave the next day. My mother had something to say about that. She wanted us to travel together as far as Copenhagen, and then I could go to the professor for a final examination.

And that was what happened. We went to Copenhagen. We saw my grandmother to the boat and got her on board.

Wouldn't she like us to cross over with her and see her on to the train on the other side?

What nonsense! The other side was Sweden – didn't we know that? On the other side she could understand everybody and talk to everybody: policemen and clergymen and school-masters – everybody.

She stood by the rail with her old plush cape on, and shawls, and handkerchiefs on her head. A little grimy in the face – as much of it as could be seen – and about the hands. And she went on standing there as the ship moved away from the quay.

'Goodbye,' we shouted to her across the narrow strip of water that was rapidly widening. We stood on the wharf and shouted 'Goodbye, grandmother.'

'I'll come back,' she said. 'I'll come back when the earth reminds me.'

She stood by the rail like a grey bundle. Soon I couldn't see her any longer. My mother waved once, twice, but either my grandmother didn't see or she ignored it. She stood in her place and sailed away, sailed home to Sweden, and disappeared.

There was a tramp walking in front of us. We kept a long way behind him. We came from a little town where if we didn't know everybody at least we felt we did. There was a man there called Jacob Hedehus. He had once been punished for assault. He had been in prison for years. Now he lived by tarring things for people. One shuddered to see his bearded face over the top of a roof-ridge or a board fence – shadowy from the dimness of a damp cell and old misdeeds. Yet Jacob Hedehus was someone we knew. There was no need for him to dress up in Salvation Army uniform, even on Sundays; everybody recognized him. We knew him. We knew all there was to know about him, and more. He brought no sense of horror. Very different were the shady characters to be met with in the streets of Copenhagen. Here was this tramp, for instance, whom we were not bold enough to overtake and leave behind us. He dragged his foot slightly. His shoes were full of holes and so were his trousers. His shirt grinned out from a place where no shirt should be seen. And his jacket . . .

'There, now we'll get past him,' said my mother.

She had chosen her spot. Other people were about; we could call for help if necessary, and have a good chance of getting it.

'Now we'll hurry past him,' said my mother.

We did pass him, too, but hardly more than that. He just had time to grab my collar and hang on.

'What the hell,' he said. 'If it isn't sister Lisbeth – and the mole,' he said. 'Are you in town again?'

So things had come to this pass with Uncle Anton. Unrecognizable – anyhow from the back – his mere appearance frightened his nearest relations.

'Yes,' he said, and he dragged both leg and shoulder. 'Yes. You weren't always so easily frightened,' he said.

'I don't know what you mean by that,' said my mother. 'But you're enough to frighten anybody the way you are now.'

'Even in broad daylight –'

'Yes,' said my mother.

'You look just the same as ever,' said Uncle Anton. 'And I've always been afraid of you. I was afraid of you when I was small and when I first went out to work and you were big and had to take care of me.'

'You've had a bad time.'

'Yes.'

'But you've been your own worst enemy.'

'Yes,' he said. He said it without reservation. 'Yes.'

My mother asked him whether he had work. But he hadn't.

'Just now I'm on holiday,' he said.

'Is it overwork?'

No, it wasn't exactly overwork. He was just gathering strength. Strength to start all over again.

'Brother Ole's been here and he's enrolled me in the Temperance Society.'

'Would you like a meal?' asked my mother.

'A meal . . . How dreary that sounds,' he said. 'It sounds as if you were going to sit down and eat just to fill your stomach. No,' he said. 'The kind of meal I want you'd never give me.'

'But if Ole's enrolled you in the Temperance Society –'

'Yes, but luckily that doesn't take effect until next week.'

'Where do you live?'

'A place where they don't like you to bring strangers in. But you couldn't do that at sister Jane's either.'

'You're hard on your sisters.'

'Yes.'

'And how would you have got along without – without Jane?'

'Do you think I could have done any worse?'

'No. But I don't think it's anybody's fault but your own.'

I thought of Staff and Ullnes and the eternal mind of God, and all the things they preached about every Sunday in the Tønnes Street hall.

'I live at St Peter's Guesthouse,' said Uncle Anton, 'and it's not nearly such a hospitable sort of place as it sounds. But it has one advantage: the doors can be opened from inside.'

'I don't know what you mean,' said my mother.

'Nothing special. It's just a convenience you get to appreciate. Especially when you've had to do without it – even for a short time. A very short time. But I promise you, sister Lisbeth, that from now on things will go onward and upward. Onward and upward in your sense. I shall get just as smug and phari-saical and censorious as the rest of you. I'll be just as narrow and just as respectable. But you must give me a month or two to do it, and you must allow me one last week before I begin in earnest.'

We were just by Kongens Nytorv, and we needn't have been afraid, for lots of people came past and most of them turned to look at Uncle Anton. To me he didn't look so extraordinary. I couldn't see that he was any different from what he had always been.

'And you, little mole,' he said. 'You get handsomer every time I see you. You take after your mother in that – give her her due. But you'll be wiser . . .'

'I shall be satisfied so long as he doesn't get like you,' my mother said.

'You may be right, sister Lisbeth. But there's no chance of

that. My days are over – my good days,' he said. 'Over in another week.'

We were going to see the professor, and Uncle Anton came with us part of the way, but not far. He was going to meet somebody, he said. It didn't sound true. He just made it up so that we could be rid of him; he didn't want to embarrass my mother. She mustn't walk the streets with a tramp.

'But we'll meet again when you come to Copenhagen,' he said to me. 'By that time I shall be quite proper, even in your mother's eyes. Goodbye then, the two of you.'

He didn't take our hands. He just crossed the street and disappeared.

Then we were at the professor's again. Measuring the field of vision and reading cards and trying lenses . . .

'No foggy vision? No coloured rings round the lights?'

All the usual questions in the usual order. And he seemed to know the answers beforehand.

'Good,' he said. 'That's all right. The disease has been arrested. Perhaps his sight is just a little weaker. It's not important, and in one way it's a good thing. Now they'll have to admit him to the Institute. I think you've got a chance,' he said, taking me by the back of the neck. 'If we manage to preserve . . .'

I didn't understand what it was we were going to manage to preserve.

'If we do,' he said, 'you've got a chance you wouldn't have had if . . .' I understood that much. 'Now I'll make you out a certificate.'

I'd expected all along to enter the Institute. I'd never dreamt of anything else. So for me it was no relief, and for my mother a blow. She had still hoped . . . In spite of everything she had clung to a remnant of her miracle-hope and had not been able to let it go. But a long, long time had passed since I had wondered about such things. I never wasted a thought on them now.

I would gladly have gone in then and there. If it had been

left to me we would have gone straight to the Institute. I knew it well, from all the blind girls had told me.

I knew many of the people who lived there. What was there to go home for, now?

19

So we had the old silence again. Little more had been said while my grandmother was there, but she had sat in her wicker chair talking half-aloud to herself, complaining a little and chanting a little. It hadn't been quite so quiet. Father and she might sit opposite one another for a whole evening without saying a word. Or a Sunday morning. He read his Bible or the red book that he kept going back to. He looked into other books that happened to come within reach, but he never settled down to reading them. The things that happened in them were all made up. His own book was different: a man had once assured him that it was true.

Grandmother had gone now, and the old silence returned. We were sparing of everything, including words. Nobody spoke. Only in the afternoons, when my mother and I were alone, was there any talking.

The season was dark, with rainy weather and half-light. She had to help me with my lessons and spell her way through German, which she didn't understand and never quite grasped that I or anyone else understood. Could there really be people – thousands of people – who never spoke anything else, and were quite content to do so? Did one really only have to go a few miles south to find them? But all at once she would say,

'Oh well, I suppose it's as good a language as any other for holding your tongue in.'

She smiled then. She smiled, so that it became a sort of little secret between us.

I was not the only one who noticed the silence.

But she gave up her time to help me with more than lessons. There were the books that I borrowed from the organist and from Valborg. We spent hours with these, and afterwards she had to work all the faster. And she had to stay up later at night. But for her this was no sacrifice: she had come to enjoy reading and learning, so long as she didn't feel she was stealing time from something more important. From her work. So long as she could overcome the idea that it was really a vice.

'But it's not for my own pleasure I'm doing this,' she said. 'I do it so that time won't seem so long to you.'

And it had become strangely long. Everything seemed to be provisional. I had to get through the next few months. I had to get through a winter. Be confirmed. It was a wheel that creaked round and turned the days forward, one by one. And the wheel turned so slowly that it sometimes seemed to have stopped. Once I had had a school time-table on which each day had its own colour. Now every day was grey and endless. If it hadn't been for grandmother's clock which ticked and struck I should have been like the blind girls who were always asking what the time was. I didn't have to do that. I could see the hands, and it struck so loudly that you couldn't fail to hear it. But often the hands seemed not to have moved between the times I looked at them. Often an eternity passed from one strike to the next.

'Go for a sharp walk,' said my mother. 'Or you might go and see Marentcius ... Aren't you going to practise for the organist? It seems a long time since you saw Valborg ...'

The wheel creaked and never moved on. Time stood still.

Marentcius's father had at last read himself into a shop. So much, at any rate, could come of reading books. Bowed and iron-grey he had studied book-keeping and accountancy and many other things in his free time, when he came home from work in the evenings and on those long Sundays. Now he had read himself into a shop – a modest little place in a basement. But Marentcius was full of it. He had that to look after now, as well as his own future as a chemist, which seemed to be approaching with giant strides. In reality a long time must pass before Marentcius could get off his bike and step behind some counter or other as an apprentice. So far he had merely gone to another school and would take his exam in due course. But he talked as if it were all going to happen next day. Whereas to me, who had been told I could leave in a few months, the future seemed infinitely far away.

Naturally we talked about it at home.

'They've got a shop now,' said my mother. 'But then Marentcius's father doesn't sit down with the paper as soon as he gets home. He's read other books beside the Bible and an old red novel. He's done more useful things than smoking and twiddling a matchbox in his fingers.'

Silence.

My father read his Bible and twiddled his matchbox. He did it as if he hadn't heard a word, or at least as if the remark couldn't have been aimed at him.

Silence for a long time.

He put the Bible away; there was something he had to see to in the kitchen. He had to fill his pipe and go into the yard. When he came upstairs again he said,

'There was a time when there was no steady work to be had. When a man had to go to a new place every day looking for work and never knowing if he'd get it. I remember we thought then: if only there could be a change for the better we'd ask for nothing more.'

That is what he said. It wasn't addressed to anybody. He had thought it as he put away the Bible and went into the kitchen and filled his pipe and went down into the yard. He had thought this, and now he said it. Nothing else. He said it with many words – unusually many. Perhaps needlessly many. At any rate there was every reason to be silent for a good long time afterwards.

But the organist . . . Yes, he went on treating me as one treats a sensible grown-up person. He talked and told me things and asked me things as if one could attach some importance to what I thought. We went to the church and played, and he was pleased with me. I even had to sit down below while he played and tell him what I thought of it. Whether it was all right . . . Whether it was better on this register than on the other.

'Like this . . . or like that?' he asked. It was like the professor trying lenses. 'This . . . or perhaps this one's better. How about a mixture . . .?'

I had to decide. He left it to me.

I sat by myself in one of the pews of the empty church, and beyond the big windows in the chancel and the little ones in the aisles there was grey daylight, though inside the church it was half dark. Up on the organ-bench in the gallery sat the organist, with light shining down on his music, and he turned and asked out into the emptiness and half-darkness,

'Did that sound better?'

If only somebody could have heard this. A certain person who had no eyes for me at all. Nina. If only I could bring her here some time. If only she could somehow get to know that I wasn't quite as uninteresting as she thought. That I was worth glancing at, at least . . . But no. These were fancies – childishness. Sheer childishness, which one must be careful never to betray. In the organist's world they probably didn't waste thoughts and dreams on that sort of thing.

'Don't you think it sounds a bit harsh with the two-foot pipe?' he asked from up in his place. 'I think the blend makes it richer. What does it sound like from down there?'

No, in his world they'd never think about girls. That was all dreams and childishness and fantasy.

'But you must practise imagining,' the organist said. 'Improvise. What do you think about when you play . . .? What do you see . . .? What do you dream about . . .?'

'Nothing . . . nothing to speak of.'

'Don't you think about the spring – the murmuring spring . . . Don't you see green trees and flowers? Tell me what's in your mind – what you imagine.'

'Nothing. Nothing at all.'

'Empty,' he said. 'Completely empty. Pity. But practise. Think about something you like and play about it.'

I thought about Nina and played about her. I didn't say anything, but I played as well as I could.

'No, that wasn't good,' said the organist. 'You're probably right when you say you're empty. But it may come. It'll come when you're older. Just a little older. It'll come when . . . oh well, it won't help to explain it yet.'

But once I did tell Nina about it. I did it cautiously. I was too restrained for her to think I was swanking. All the same, it was true that the organist took me with him to the church and used me to play to.

'He uses you to pump air or whatever it's called,' she said. 'You work the bellows for him.'

'No I don't, because it's electric.'

'Then he makes you look after the electricity,' she said.

And I didn't really mind her thinking that, for that too was a responsible job. If one did that one couldn't be completely useless – even in her eyes. If only she wouldn't express it in that way alone, and in no other.

But the organist was thinking of the future too: what would I see and hear when I got to Copenhagen? Concerts, operas . . . 'You must go to the Gallery too – you must hurry up and go there while you can still see . . .'

I had no idea what the Gallery was, and I didn't ask. But it did seem to me that the organist was rather hazy about why I was going to Copenhagen. I had never been to the theatre. I had only once been given a ticket for a concert. He probably thought I always sat in the front row, after seeing me there that one time.

I was going to Copenhagen to be in an Institute. And I expected a great deal from that – only I wasn't quite sure what I did expect. But nothing like theatres and galleries and other places which cost money to get into. My mother had told me that I might perhaps have twenty-five øre a week – twenty-five øre to spend on everything I wanted. Would that be enough, or ought I to speak out at once and say No to concerts and operas and galleries, so that the organist wouldn't go on telling me about things that could never come true?

It was better to go to L. Pode's Home for Blind Women. Nobody there dangled things before me that would never be real. There everybody knew exactly what future awaited me.

'Now and then you'll go to the theatre,' they said, 'but not very often.'

'No, not very often,' someone repeated.

'And if they let you be a musician you'll go to concerts too.'

'Yes, if they let him,' said some of the others.

'But there are lots of other things that are fun. Quoits and skittles. And it's fun just to walk round the garden with the others. And on the 'Tute's birthday there's a dance.'

'Yes, a dance,' said the rest. 'You can be sure of that.'

I tried to imagine Sofie and the other girls dancing, but I couldn't quite do it. I knew what they looked like when they walked together two by two, or three – one in the middle to lead the two others. I knew what they looked like when they came back from the woods or the churchyard. But dancing . . .?

I went to see the girls at the Blind Home and talked to them about the Institute. And when I went home I sometimes took the path across the meadows. It was so damp there now in the autumn and early winter that as soon as one's foot left the ground the footprint filled with water. One could hear the water seeping into it. Fog might drift across the fjord, but it was real fog and not just something that started inside one's head and spread out from it and hid the whole world.

I followed the little path, hearing the water seep into my tracks, and came to the ice-ponds and went into Stougård's place. Even now one might sometimes find him fairly sober. Find him sitting by his charcoal fire baking potatoes and having time to talk. But often he would be lying and snoring on the floor, with an old jacket rolled up under his head. And if you woke him he sometimes shooed you off – confusedly – thinking he had been visited by some queer animal, until he realized his mistake.

'I thought –' he said. 'Well, I don't know what I did think. I thought at first you was a rat,' he said. 'That's how silly you can get, when you been lying here a bit cold and slept a bit too sound and too long . . . Well, so you've come,' he said. 'That's rare these days. But it's how it should be. Birds of a feather . . . We've had our time together, you and me. In those days we were about as old and wise as each other. Now you're the wisest, at any rate. That's how it goes, and it's nothing to cry about . . . Have a spud and a dram . . .'

Stougård got to his feet, blew life into the embers, brought out the potatoes and the bucket of salt, and began to sing.

> *'With Thee, O Lord, a thousand years*
> *Are reckoned as a day,'*

he sang.

It was a new hymn and it sounded half-English. But I had grown so used to his foreign-sounding speech that I understood.

> *'Our earthly life is but a span*
> *Of three score years and ten –'*

'Hell, how it smokes!' said Stougård, coughing. 'But now we'll have a spud and a dram. How does it go – "Do you like it, and can you take it – ?" '

'With Thee, O Lord, a thousand years . . .' he sang, and blew the embers and coughed, almost suffocated by smoke and hymn-singing.

In the rainy mist over the fjord a steamer hooted, and behind the house the woods stood motionless and unmurmuring. The wheel creaked even here with Stougård. The hours were no shorter here than at home. They were simply long in a different way. Fog and rainy mist and seeping water.

'Now it'll soon be real winter,' said Stougård. 'Then you'll have other things to think about. You'll all have other things to think about. Do you remember when you came here to

259

skate? The ice-ponds were big enough in those days. Now they're too small – far too small. That's as it should be.'

And the woods were unmurmuring. The trees stood and let the fog settle on their black boughs, and condense, and turn into drops – drops that fell upon the dead leaves or into one's face as one walked along the path; now and then a drop hit one on the back of the neck and ran like a bead of ice down one's back. And there were only the crows screeching and the sparrows chirping in chorus like the girls in L. Pode's Blind Home. And there was a training-college and a margarine-factory if one went that far. And the Steensens' garden and Pilke Hill. And there were dreary grey houses and behind a fence a garden which we called Heide's garden because the name of the man who owned it was Heide. There was no other reason. And there was a chance of meeting Lydia, who chose to walk on the opposite pavement, or perhaps others chose for her; anyhow she did it and went on doing it. And Anders was there with his red knitted reins, still just as silly in the head and wanting to play horses; or else he followed Lydia as once he had followed someone else.

'Lydia,' said Anders. 'Lydia . . .'

He didn't ask her to play horses. He just walked along calling her. He sounded as if he wanted to tell her something. Confide something important to her.

But if at last Lydia turned and asked what he wanted – and she was quite likely to do this, for Lydia wasn't like certain other people – if she did turn and ask 'What do you want, Anders?' Anders just stood there with his mouth open, looking feeble-minded and unable to say a word.

'You're not to follow me,' said Lydia. 'And you're not to call after me if you don't want anything.'

'No,' said Anders, standing stock-still with a dropped jaw.

'Anders,' called his mother. 'Anders, come along home; you'll get wet.'

'Yes,' said Anders, and he began to walk home; but he turned round again to look after Lydia, and stopped.

'Anders dear,' said his mother, coming up and taking hold of him. 'Be a good boy now and come along home. You're getting cold out here. We don't want you ill, do we?'

'No,' said Anders. 'Not ill,' he said, and he went with his mother.

Lydia came and went on the opposite pavement; and it might seem a trifling thing – a thing that hardly mattered. But it wasn't. It meant something. People walked on a certain pavement. They had their own side of the street, whether they were children or grown-ups. Lydia walked on the other side. Her father walked on the other side. It was more than just keeping their distance from people with whom they had formerly shared the pavement. Something had happened, and they wanted to have nothing to do with it. They would not be associated with it or involved in it. But it made Lydia more friendly. She didn't mind stopping to chat when one met her, and it seemed natural. She was even friendlier than before. We had once been sweethearts, she and I. In great innocence. On a certain occasion she had kissed my cheek, but that was to make up for another big wet kiss I'd been given. It was to hide that she didn't like me any more. I had seen her mother. I had learnt something about her mother – something I knew already. In spite of that little kiss – that faint touch on my cheek – Lydia had never liked me since that day. She hadn't been able to conceal it, or forgive me. She had envied me my sister. At times she sank as low as Rudolf, and glanced out of the corner of her eye or over her shoulder to see if I'd noticed it. But now she was just friendly. I could meet Lydia by chance and talk to her, although I wasn't fit company, and she was friendly without reservations or ulterior motives. Now I knew that she didn't care about me – that I was indifferent to her. Now she could afford to be friendly.

Christmas again. I had been wondering what my father would say, or what he might be thinking. Last year he had bought things – bought like a rich man, because he thought it was to be the last Christmas that I should have the light of my eyes. But I wasn't much blinder this year. And we still had all the decorations, of course. And yet I felt something like pangs of conscience. My father had allowed himself to be overpowered. Would he now feel regretful, or perhaps a little ashamed?

I wondered about it and felt something like pangs of conscience. I needn't have, for my father took it quite differently. I should be enjoying it all over again. In a way, therefore, the expense was halved. And if I were to have a third and a fourth Christmas, still possessing the light of my eyes, it would work out cheaper still. If he'd had a bit more schooling and learnt division properly, he might have been able to calculate that we'd had the whole lot for nothing. He had acted honestly and paid for everything. And it had given him great joy. Now God was blessing his action – and making it cheaper. To him it was simple and self-evident. He would remember to tell builder Laursen about it; he might make use of it one Sunday when speaking in the Tønnes Street Hall.

No, I needn't have worried. Except that Kirstine didn't come, as I'd hoped and expected. But she was becoming incredibly grown-up – and anyhow she was coming to my confirmation.

'She can't travel backwards and forwards every three months,' said my mother. 'Ninety miles,' she said.

Christmas was Christmas again, as it had always been until last year. Except that the organist made me play in church on the day after Christmas Day, in the afternoon.

'Well, that's no more than right,' said my father.

He wasn't surprised. There was nothing unexpected in it. What else had I been running to the organist for, every other day?

My mother didn't take it quite like that; she thought it was a bit too soon. She wouldn't come. But she stood at the first corner on the way home. She hid and waited, bareheaded, with two forgotten knitting-needles stuck through her bun.

'In Jesus' name,' she said. 'How did it go?'

I didn't say much about it myself. I didn't spend many words on it, either at home or to Valborg, who had heard about it and was proud, feeling she had some share in it. I didn't mind the thing being talked about, but nobody was going to get anything out of me, so as to go about repeating it. I just went my way, inwardly shining.

New Year's Day passed, and the month of January. Winter began, and the days were no longer quite so long or so impossible to get through.

Perhaps my sight was worse than it had been a year ago. It must have been, for the professor said so, and he had measuring apparatus. And yet for some reason I managed better. I didn't run into things so often; I didn't always have bumps on my forehead and a grazed nose. I had learnt to be careful. I had learnt from the blind girls how to hurry slowly. But I managed very well, and could go everywhere with everybody. I tobogganed down the long slope with Marentcius and helped him drag the sled to the top again, as long as he held the string. He didn't have to pull. I could do that, and was glad to do it. And when Marentcius was beside me I walked as confidently as anybody. I worked out lots of little dodges. I found that feet could be used for more than walking with, and that I could feel the tracks of the runners through my boots if I paid attention. This helped a great deal, especially when it got dark; and we often stayed out late. And we weren't always quite alone together. Marentcius had developed a knack of drawing girls out of the darkness. He found them where there had been nothing to be seen but dark tree-trunks and the darkness between.

'There they are making eyes,' he said. 'Making eyes to come with us.'

Even Lydia was there, and once or twice she didn't find us unfit company. Afterwards she went with others.

'God guide her!' said Marentcius. This is what Madsen from the gasworks said to us every Sunday in Sunday-school: 'God guide you, children!' 'God guide her,' said Marentcius. 'Look what idiots she's tobogganing with.'

Anders was there too. We took pity on him and let him ride with us. His mother was standing at the bottom of the hill.

'What good boys you are,' she said. 'I'll never forget how nicely you've played with little Anders. I can go home with an easy mind now,' she said.

Anders had one more turn; after that we let him look on. Partly because somebody shouted to ask whether this was the loony-wagon coming.

'You can stand here and watch the others,' we told Anders. 'You can watch them upset and see the girls showing their knickers.'

'Yes,' said Anders, and he stood. He had his reins with him.

We stayed there a long time that evening – so long that many of us had to be fetched home. We saw Lydia's father and heard him calling her.

'Have any of you seen Lydia?' he asked a chance group of us. Neither Marentcius nor I said anything. I think we both decided not to tell tales. The others didn't answer either. So he went further, still calling.

'Lydia!' he shouted. 'Ly-di-a.'

'I expect she's only gone into the trees to pee,' said somebody. The others giggled.

'Lydia!' her father went on calling, first up the hill and then down. We pretended not to notice and went on tobogganing.

But next time we came down there was a crowd. There was a crowd round the place where Anders was standing. We could hear Lydia's father. We could hear his voice but not what he was saying. We could hear that he was angry and bawling at somebody.

'What's the matter?' we asked some of those who were standing in front of us.

'Nothing. Some girl went in among the trees and that dotty chap went after her and showed her something her father don't like her seeing.'

264

'Be off home with you,' we heard Lydia's father say. We could hear he was angry. We could hear that he was biting his cigar. 'Be off home at once.'

'Yes, home to your drunken mother,' said somebody.

Lydia cried.

'And you,' her father said. 'I'll deal with you.'

The ring opened and made room. Lydia's father was dragging Anders away. Anders was whimpering.

'We've had you about the place long enough, you half-witted beast. If we don't look out there'll be a murder here before you're locked up where you belong. No, no, my fine friend. I'll deal with you right away. You're for the asylum, and tomorrow.'

He dragged Anders away and we heard him scolding him all the way, while Anders whimpered and pleaded.

'Why couldn't he just slosh him?' said somebody. And another:

'She didn't see anything she didn't know about already.'

But nobody laughed. We heard Lydia crying a little and her father scolding and Anders whimpering and saying 'No – oh no . . .!'

'No!' said Anders; but the voices died away round a corner.

Down the slope came a single long, slender sled, and a toboggan. And somebody asked what had happened and people mumbled something. But the group broke up and we went home.

Next day was Shrove-Monday and a school holiday. Most of us were going to dress up. Some had Indian suits, others had sewn bells on their clothes. And they wore masks. I had never been allowed to wear a mask.

'Do you think you should disgrace the face God gave you?' my mother said. 'Do you think you should try to look like the devil himself?'

I could turn my big jacket and wear it inside out if I liked.

'But you won't take money, I hope,' said my father.

'You got too much sense for all that now, anyhow,' said my mother. 'In another two months you'll be grown up.'

'Besides,' said my father, 'do you think it's fitting for you to play the organ in church one day and run about the streets like a clown the next?'

But it had been like this every year, so it was no great loss to me. I hadn't expected permission, and I didn't really want it anyhow. We were too big in my class. But I could stand at the street door and watch the others – the ones who didn't think themselves above it – or I could go wherever I liked.

I went down and looked at the masks – as much of them as I could see nowadays. I stood at the street door, and I went a little way towards the old gateway. I saw Lydia pass, and recognized her. And I met Rudolf, who was dressed up although he was the same age as I was. I was glad I wasn't dressed up.

Anders' mother came out with nothing on her head and her hands hidden under the blue check apron, and asked whether any of us had seen Anders. She asked in a thin, anxious little voice.

'You haven't seen Anders, have you?' she asked. 'He went out early and we haven't been able to find him since.'

No, we hadn't seen Anders.

'I expect he's gone off to be half-witted somewhere else,' said Rudolf. 'But if we see him we'll tell him to hurry home.'

'Somebody was angry with him last night,' his mother said in her thin little voice. 'I'm so afraid they've frightened him.'

'Oh,' said Rudolf. Nothing else.

She went on. We saw her stopping other people and asking them. We saw her going into street doors and yards. A little later she came back. She looked at us and opened her mouth as if to ask, but she didn't ask. She walked on bareheaded with her hands under the check apron and turned the corner into Langelinje. After a time she came back from there too. Rudolf went away; he had to go off and collect money. And I went my own way. I wanted to see Stougård, or go to some other

266

place. But Stougård wasn't there, so I went on further into the woods. It was so fresh and fine again in there, with new snow over the slopes – snow without footmarks. And the sun came out and shone on the branches, where there was snow too. Some of it I could see and the rest of it I probably only remembered. But I wasn't quite sure how much I was seeing and how much remembering.

The trees, the big trees, were on the way down or up. They had halted and were lingering there with their feet deep in the earth beneath the snow. They stood on their feet waiting for it to be spring, so that they could make up their minds whether to climb up the slopes or down. The sun was shining, striking a glitter from the hard frozen snow that clung to one side of the trunks. On the other side the stems were grey or black. But all of them had been bound by the frost to the place where they were standing. Winter had bound them. They were not allowed to go either up or down, forwards or backwards. They weren't allowed to walk two by two or in threes, or form a quadrille. They had to stand patient and still, each on its own spot, and wait until spring came to release them and set free the dancing in the woods – the green dance.

My head was full of that kind of childishness as I walked. And I thought if anybody knew – the organist, or C. M. the schoolmaster, or Marentcius or anybody else – if they knew that my head was full of all this childishness as I walked here, they would lose any feeling they might ever have had for me. They would think me a silly Joseph, and sell me to the Egyptians as a dreamer. But nobody would ever know. I would never give myself away, either awake or asleep. I would show that I was craftier than any Samson.

There were lots of people out on the fjord already. I couldn't see them. Everything was just a golden shimmer of snow and sunshine before my eyes. But I could hear them. There was an unbroken yelling of boys' voices, as in the playground, from the part of Skyttehus Bay where they were skating. I didn't mind. I was really well content to walk here and be myself.

Alone. I was getting more and more inclined to do this now.

'Inclined to be odd,' said my mother. 'We shouldn't be different from other people,' she said. 'We should try to be like everybody else.'

'I wonder if it isn't something Nature arranges,' my father said; he stopped turning the matchbox in his fingers and brought his eyes back from somewhere or other. 'I wonder whether Nature arranges it so that people who find it difficult to be among other people get a hankering to be on their own.'

But I didn't think I did so badly among other people. I was only walking here being childish, and nobody knew that. Nobody should ever know. I walked along the paths in the woods and others had walked there before me. But off the paths – in among the tree-trunks and up and down the slopes – the snow lay fine and white and untouched. There may have been the tracks of birds and beasts; if so, I didn't see them. But I had seen them at one time, so I could always see them again. I could see them whenever I liked. I had only to think of it.

I wandered about and wasted most of the morning there. But I heard the trains come and go, so I could keep some check on the time, and at last I knew I should have to be getting home again.

I came out of the woods, where it was very still because the trees were holding their breath to listen for the sawfinches. It was quiet, but the sawfinches were sawing, and now and then a drop fell from a branch in the sunshine – a sunshine tear. It was from this stillness I came – a living stillness.

In the street at home another kind of stillness was waiting. It was not a living stillness. No masks. No jackets inside out or suits with bells on them. There were people in front of the baker's, and another group further on. People at the doors. A muffled stillness.

Something was wrong. You could feel that something was wrong – you could have felt it even without seeing the people standing in groups and talking among themselves. You could feel it in the air. It was written on the buildings, across the house-fronts and windows. And I realized that it could really have been felt when I left that morning. It had been written there even then for all to read.

'They've found Anders,' said my mother when I came in.

'Yes,' I said.

'They found him in the privy. He's hanged himself.'

'Yes,' I said.

'He hanged himself in the red reins he always carried about with him.'

'Yes.'

People whispered or talked in subdued voices for an hour or two. Then gradually the voices found their normal level. We still talked about Anders, but we talked about other things as well. We talked about all the money Rudolf had collected and what he was going to buy with it. Anders' mother came by on her way to the butcher, still bareheaded and wearing the blue check apron. But she was red under her eyes and her nose was red.

'Well, so you found Anders, then,' said Rudolf.

She stopped for a moment and sniffed and was near crying.

'Yes, we found him at last,' she said. 'Somebody had frightened him. He was so frightened of going to the asylum. He was such a good boy – so gentle,' she said.

'He ought to have been sent away long ago,' said Rudolf, when she had gone.

I went to see Stougård. He was singing by his charcoal fire. He was singing about our mortal span.

'There'll be no standing this place soon, with all these creepy-crawlies,' he said. 'Nothing shifts 'em, neither *braendevin* nor hymn-singing.'

There was a sour smell of yeast and stale beer as usual. And of baked potatoes and something sweet – spirits or *braendevin*. Stougård was his usual self. He was never surprised to see one.

He said something or he didn't, according to his mood. And he didn't seem surprised when one went.

'Well, well,' he said. 'So Anders came to his senses at last. He came properly to his senses. He wasn't so potty as some folks thought. He wouldn't let 'em lock him up. Ah, well,' said Stougård. 'If only I could get rid of all these creepy-crawlies,' he said.

I stayed with Stougård for a bit and ate a charred potato, which tasted better than most other things, and I pretended to have a drink, and enjoyed myself. We didn't talk about Anders any more. The window-panes were curtained with ice-flowers, which never thawed as long as the frost lasted. And outside were the ponds with ice on them. Later in the afternoon the dry rushes began rustling, and from further away one could hear the yelling voices of boys on the fjord where they were skating.

'If only you could drive these blasted vermin back into the ground,' said Stougård. 'But you can't, neither with *braendevin* nor hymn-singing.'

20

It wasn't confirmation that did it. That was nothing. The important thing was getting jacket, waistcoat, collar and tie and cuffs, with the likelihood of wearing this impressive outfit day in and day out for the rest of one's life. The exciting thing was waiting to see whether from now on people would say 'you' to me instead of 'thou' and take their hats off when they passed me in the street, instead of just nodding or putting a finger to the brim.

'When we get to the catechism, I thought I'd ask you questions on mercy,' said the pastor. 'I'm telling you this now, so that you can be prepared.'

'Yes,' I said. I had been prepared for a whole year. I said yes and felt that he expected me to say thank you.

'I shall talk to you about the Samaritan,' he said. 'The Good Samaritan.'

'Oh,' I said.

I had brought five crowns for him. He looked at the crumpled note lying on his flat hand, where everybody could see it. He looked at it and stood with his hand out – he stood for a moment too long with his hand out, looking at the note.

'You've been coming to me for a year,' he said. 'A whole year.'

'Yes,' I said, and went.

All that was unimportant. It didn't mean anything. But my sister came . . . I thought of that and of all that was to happen afterwards.

A blue letter had come from Copenhagen with a list of what

I must take with me to the Institute: two suits, an overcoat, two pairs of boots, three shirts, six handkerchiefs . . . A long list, and the statement that I was expected there at the beginning of May. Another eternity. Six or seven weeks, or about forty-five days. The wheel creaked and would not turn more than one day forward at a time.

But there lay the letter in its blue envelope, and it said that I was expected.

We had got going with our preparations. Shirts, socks and handkerchiefs were piling up in a drawer cleared for the purpose, and my journey was talked about openly. Even my mother no longer brushed it aside as something we'd been thinking about but couldn't be sure of.

'We've been thinking it might be best,' she used to say. 'The professor in Copenhagen thinks so, but so many things can happen. We keep hoping,' she said.

Now, thank goodness, she was hoping no longer. No longer could so many things happen. Now I was just going, I was leaving some time in May.

'At the beginning of May,' I corrected her.

'Well, the beginning of May, then.'

It was an eternity to wait. The days came one by one and had to be endured singly.

But at last we reached the day itself. My sister had come. Uncle Anton had come. He wore fine new clothes, with a cigar in a holder, and a hat. Unrecognizable but acceptable.

'Yes,' he said. 'You've got me where you want me at last. But I'm no better company for that, as you'll find out.'

We went to the church and my sister came to my place with me.

'You've got a pair of handsome children,' said Uncle Anton. We weren't supposed to hear that, but we did.

I sat on my chair in the centre aisle. I couldn't control my thoughts. I thought about the hymn-numbers that I'd helped the verger to put up the day before. I thought of the pastor in his room behind the pulpit; of his hand-basin and his pot.

And I thought of the organist warming his hands up there, and the ladies of the choir doing their embroidery under cover of the gallery rail. But now and again my sister put out her hand and touched me. She was sitting just behind. And when my sister touched me I could control my thoughts and listen to the music and attend to what the pastor said, and follow it all. Sometimes she tried to whisper to me; but I couldn't hear what she said, and I dared not turn my head. And my mother hushed her. Kirstine sat there, infinitely grown-up – and infinitely young.

She was so full of gravity and so full of nonsense. And she had a way of being serious, deeply serious – almost melancholy – when others were playing the fool. And she couldn't help playing the fool when other people became too serious. I suffered from the same weakness; and that's why I didn't dare hear what she was whispering, or turn my head.

And now we came to the catechizing. The pastor began to question us, to find out whether we knew enough for him to confirm us. And when he came to me he told me that he was going to speak to me about mercy.

'Yes,' I said.

'I want to speak to you about the parable of the man who came down from Jerusalem on his way to Jericho.'

'Yes,' I said, remembering as I had always remembered. Remembering a particular day when the pastor had talked about this particular parable. 'Yes,' I said, with no intention of saying more than that.

And he went through the parable with me point by point about the priest and Levite. I let him tell it, and said no more than yes. I wasn't quite without ideas about the Good Samaritan, all the same. I was just remembering and being obstinate in my own way. I felt my mother shrinking together behind me in disappointment. I felt her thinking that the pastor had been right about me and that I ought really to have studied with him for more than a year. And I felt that my sister was full of nonsense, and that Uncle Anton was thinking how utterly unimportant it all was. And my father, who attached little weight to such things. Perhaps he couldn't quite understand how I had so completely lost my memory. But there might be many reasons. He himself wouldn't care to stand up there and be cross-examined. Besides, if one were ever doubtful as to who one's neighbour was, one could always look it up in the Bible.

I never knew if this was quite what he thought. But I was right about the others.

'I didn't think it would be like that,' said my mother. 'But I shall try to forget it. And I hope everybody else will forget it too, especially the pastor. Now, if only that chicken isn't tough . . .'

So we went home, and there were presents and guests, and luckily my sister was as much the centre of it all as I was. It was almost as if she had just been confirmed, in spite of her being so tremendously grown-up. But we never had a chance to talk to each other. We couldn't run away and hide together. Confirmed people couldn't do that sort of thing; they had to control themselves and be sensible. We never managed to talk to each other until the evening, when the time of her going was already near.

'I was sure I should be able to come to Copenhagen too,' she said, holding my wrist as she had always held it, in a way that made one strangely weak. 'I was so sure of it. And now they won't let me. They won't let me be in such a big town alone. I told them I wouldn't be alone, because I should have you, but they won't let me . . .'

She said even more than this. Much more. But I wasn't listening. I felt only a great grief and a great hopelessness stealing upon me, washing over me and engulfing me.

'But when you've learnt all you have to learn,' she said, 'when those years have gone by . . . One day we'll be so grown-up that nobody will be able to stop us doing anything,' she said.

But I wasn't listening. I only felt her hold on my wrist

and a wave of black despair swamping me. And from the next room came many voices. Strange voices, all talking at once.

'When you've finished with it all,' said my sister, and she kissed my forehead. 'We'll have such a lovely time,' she said.

School was ending. I was glad. For some of it I had no feeling: handicrafts, for instance, and drawing. But there was no getting out of it on that account. I just went on and on, working myself further and further into dense stupidity. Other things I could do only too well, because I had stayed still and trodden water for over two years. My work with Lieutenant Christensen had become, for other reasons, a sort of private tutoring which bordered on literature. Apart from that it was a matter of waiting for the others. Going no further than the others. School went no higher than the ceiling, and I'd had my head against that for a long time. There had been talk of another school: one that led as far as the counter of a chemist's shop, or even further. But what good was that to me? One single voice suggested this mad idea, and the speaker risked drawing ridicule upon himself. What did I want with school?

'Follow if you can,' said C. M., 'or sleep if you'd rather. It doesn't matter.'

Now there was a sort of exam. In his subject too; in mathematics. It wasn't worth mentioning. I mention it only because it isn't worth it. We were each asked questions in turn. And C. M., who had never wanted me to do anything but sleep, or write with a thick blue pencil which I couldn't see – C. M. hit on the tremendous joke of passing on to me all the questions that the others couldn't answer. I didn't mind. He was welcome to ask me anything he liked.

'There, you see how stupidly things are ordered in this world,' he said. 'The rest of you will need this knowledge and you haven't got it. And this boy, who won't ever need anything, can do it all.'

275

That is what he said, and he bared his rat's teeth in a sour, silent little rat's smile.

'Goodbye to you all,' he said. 'I know you won't miss me. Well, it's mutual.'

Goodbye to us. Yes. We rushed out of the door, down the stairs, through the gate. We rushed away into life – away into life to the best of our knowledge.

Finished with us – goodbye to us.

One or two of us halted, hesitated and turned to look back.

There was the school – a perfectly ordinary house, built by human hands. We had once believed it to be a mountain reaching to the stars – a mountain of knowledge of good and evil, mostly good. Some of us in our attempt to climb up and find a foothold had acquired broken heads and legs. Not all had been helped by those who should have been ready with help. A number fell and, maimed, went their way alone.

There we stood back and reflected for a moment before going on. But it was goodbye to us. We wouldn't be missed. We wouldn't even be remembered. This had to be said to us explicitly, that nothing might be left unspoken.

The April wind – the east wind – came soughing in from the fjord. A stiff wind, whose chill bit to the bone. We came out of the warmth of the classroom, and freedom and life came to meet us with sharp teeth. We were cold inside, we shivered, and went each to his own place.

Goodbye to you – and goodbye to me.

One went the way one had gone every day, year out and year in, thinking it would never come to an end. The chestnut trees. L. Pode's Home for Blind Women. The churchyard.

Should I go in and say goodbye to Sofie and the others? No, it was a few days too early.

Anton Berntsen, then . . . Yes, I could do that.

'I just wanted to say goodbye.'

'Oh,' he said. 'I didn't know you were going anywhere.'

But I was, and I'd thought I had a lot to talk about to Anton Berntsen. Now we both stood with nothing to say.

'Well, so you're going away,' he said, without curiosity.

He rattled a bunch of keys in his trouser-pocket, walked over and whisked dust off a mahogany surface that was perfectly shiny already, and sucked air in through his teeth so that it sounded as if he were cold.

'But we'll meet again,' he said; he reached out and took up a book that was lying on one of the harmoniums. 'This is a book by a man called Gustaf Fröding,' he said. 'Gustaf Fröding.' [1]

'Oh,' I said, not seeing what this had to do with me.

'Remember that name.'

'That's easy.'

'You must read this book one day.'

'Is it about organ-building?' I asked.

Anton Berntsen didn't smile; his face just brightened a little.

'Organ-building . . . No,' he said. 'Except in so far as it's about everything,' he said; and again it sounded as if he were speaking out of a great affliction.

We stood once more, not knowing what to say.

'Would you like to stay here for a bit and play?'

'No,' I said. 'I'm going home, and then away.'

'Well, goodbye, then,' he said. 'And when you come back don't pass without looking in . . .'

Goodbye. Yes, but this farewell was a bond.

The wheel creaked and turned one day forward at a time. A lot of people had to be seen. Marentcius and his father and mother in their new basement shop. All three of them were standing behind the counter, although there were no customers. No doubt Marentcius was dreaming that he was already in his chemist's shop and that instead of flour and soft soap there were powders and precious ointments under the counter and on the shelves. And his father stood there, iron-grey and

---

[1] Gustaf Fröding (1860–1911), Swedish poet; the greatest poet of the late nineteenth-century romantic revival in Sweden.

taciturn, weary-eyed from reading and wearing a collar and tie. But where were the customers . . .?

And there was Valborg, who had helped me like a sister with everything to do with upbringing and music.

Above all there was my own childishness. I had now to take leave of that for ever. And I had the silly idea that my childishness lived in the woods. I would be able to meet it at the bend of a path, at this place or that. Places hidden in the summer, but not now.

Goodbye to that tree, and to that. And here was where the cooper hanged himself. The wind caught hold of the bare branches and there was a rattling as of bones up there. But sunshine came between. Goodbye to that path. And here was where I once met a girl called Nina, and she told me I needn't touch her. Goodbye, Nina – as much of you as there is in the wind and in the light between the trees. Goodbye until we meet again.

And there was the bench where my father liked to sit. And the path leading into the place where a shady character called Jacob Hedehus had once assaulted a young girl and went to prison for it . . . I followed the path and came to a place where some young beeches gave shelter – a little round glade. The grass there had begun to turn green and the sun was shining.

I sat down and heard the chaffinches and titmice and bluetits and I don't know what else . . . I heard the stillness too. But in the stillness and the sunshine – that good, early sunshine – there came suddenly another, delicate sound. A sound of crackling silk. A sound as of tiny sparks jumping from branch to branch. It was the sun splitting the husks of the young beech-buds.

Goodbye, my childishness. Goodbye, my childhood.

I thought I would go and see Stougård too. This time I wouldn't cheat: I'd take a proper gulp from his bottle. We might have some wise thing to talk about. In some people's company one became stupider than one really was; in others', cleverer. Stougård belonged to this last kind. I went to say goodbye to him, but I never got there. They were dragging him along – two men. He was shouting and yelling and hitting out. Stougård had become violent. They were getting him to the hospital, so that he could be shut up in a cell where he belonged.

Goodbye then, Stougård, I thought. Goodbye, and thank you.

The chestnut trees were standing waiting, waving their pale green leaf-hands and wanting to go with me to the steamer as they had gone with me every day. They stood with their lighted candles and green crowns, and a play of shadows in amongst the green. And one took over from another.

'In Jesus' name,' said my mother. 'We'll start now, in Jesus' name.'

My father carried the suitcases, one in each hand. They were heavy with all the things I had to take with me.

It was a Saturday afternoon, with bustle everywhere. Nobody had time to notice people going to catch the boat. They'd be back, or they wouldn't. What of it?

'Ah, well,' said my father. 'If we'd had to take you to the churchyard . . . But we'll be seeing you again before very long.'

'There are the holidays,' said my mother. 'In a couple of months they'll be having their summer holidays, like the school.'

Holidays, I thought. Holidays . . . I'm leaving. I'm going my way, and I haven't the least thought of holidays in the whole of my head.

The chestnuts came with me. They followed steadfastly, as they had always done.

'And there's L. Pode's Home for the Blind,' said my father.

As if that was anything new.

'Did you say goodbye to Sofie and thank her?' he asked. 'It was good of her to teach you.'

Yes. I had done my duty.

'At one time I wondered whether Sofie wouldn't have been

enough for you,' my father said. 'I thought she'd taught you enough for us to keep you at home.'

That's what my father said as he carried my suitcases.

'And here's the school,' he said.

'The school,' my mother repeated. 'As if he didn't know the school and the Blind Home and . . .'

'That wasn't why I said it. I didn't mean anything by it. I just said it.'

But I only heard about half; I was far ahead. I was already aboard the steamer. I had cast off. I was away. I was in Copenhagen. I was far into the future. I raced ahead, and my father thought he could hold me back, hold back time, with little words – trivial little words about all too familiar things. He thought he could grasp the intangible – the past, which perhaps he had been a little slow in catching hold of when it was still the present. Was that what he thought . . .?

He walked and carried. He was carrying all my luggage, all my past and my present, and he wanted to help me into the the future as best he could. But sometimes, when he thought I was racing ahead too fast, he believed he could hold me back by saying here's this and there's that. Things known of old. Trivial things. Today he saw them in another light. I didn't. For me they were just familiar and trivial. On, on . . .

'Well, here's the boat and there's the gang-plank,' he said. 'You go first – or shall I . . .?'

Obvious things, but with a shadow that gave them quite a different tone, a deeper significance.

'I'll put the cases here,' he said.

People coming and going – lots of people. And suddenly Lydia – she who had been brought up to be so particular about the company she kept. Lydia was there wanting to say goodbye, and had come on purpose for that. I hadn't expected it. Never imagined it. But there had been a time in a distant past, when we were children among other children . . . a pair of round arms . . . violet eyes – eyes that darkened when she was angry . . . how could one forget?

Then I shook hands with my father. When had I ever done that before? We never touched each other as a rule. We said something or we were silent. But here we were shaking hands and not knowing what to say. Except:

'Well, so long, then. Have a good journey . . . and . . .'

Lydia had disappeared as suddenly as she had come. Now my father was going down the gang-plank. Now they were taking it away. Suddenly the wharf was empty. My father was going away . . . I felt a little stab. He'd done with me, then. Goodbye to me.

It took some time to manœuvre away from the quay, and turn, and come out of the harbour. Big hulls – grey and black. Masts and yards. Coal and cattle-cake, lime and corn. There stood 'The Cabin', a square white house with a red-tiled roof: a restaurant, where they were just setting out the tables.

'There's father,' said my mother. 'No, not there – the other side.'

And there he stood on the outermost mole. He looked rather small; not thin and spindly – just small. But I saw his face with the sun on it. I saw his hands with the sun on them – heavy hands that lay on the table before him, grey as clay, when he read by the light of the kitchen lamp with its shiny brass shade.

'Goodbye, father,' I shouted. And I heard that it sounded like a cry of distress.

His hand was lifted; he must have been waving . . .

The sun was astern of us – the golden sunshine of late afternoon, which dazzled one to look into. But I wasn't going to look back. I refused to weep the weeping that was in my breast. I would look forward.

The woods to the south and the woods to the north were pale brown with the husks of buds that would split tomorrow or the day after. Within a week every tree would be green. Sun-gold on the water ahead and sun-gold over the brown, budding woods. The shores were still so near that now and then I could see houses. And new woods – woods I had never walked in and perhaps never would walk in.

But they drew back, these shores. First one and then the other. They opened out at last like a pair of arms that had held me fast, held me prisoner. They opened out and freed me.

'Well, in Jesus' name, then,' said my mother. 'I believe it's getting chilly already . . .'

The gulls were following us on our way – and the terns. The white terns.